Thy Father's Will

A historical novel based on the true story
of a family forever altered
by the damaging consequences
of decisions made for all the right reasons

KIRSTEN JACOBSON STASNEY

Kirk House Publishers
Minneapolis, Minnesota

Thy Father's Will
by Kirsten Jacobson Stasney

Book design by Karen Walhof.

ISBN 13: 978-1-933794-15-0
ISBN 10: 1-933794-15-1

Library of Congress Control Number: 2008943609

Kirk House Publishers, PO Box 390759, Minneapolis, MN 55439
Manufactured in the United States of America

For my father
Philip Andrew Jacobson

Joseph Marvick

Joseph Marvick children, 1910
Anna, Charlotte, Ida, Severt, Lula, Olive

PROLOGUE

January 1958

"Happy are those whose hearts do not condemn them,
and who have not given up their hope."

SIRACH 14:2

Obituary
Anna

*O*n a deep blue day of bitter cold and blinding sunlight, Anna turned her head from the chilling wind, pressing her scarf over her mouth and nose to retain the warmth of her breath. She had spent most of the morning at church practicing the organ, her fingers stiff and uncooperative in the drafty sanctuary. Although not particularly difficult, the music she selected for the Sunday service had taken time to perfect, and she left the church with a headache.

Once home, Anna carried the mail into the kitchen, heated some leftover chicken soup on the stove for a late noon lunch, and sat down to eat and read the mail. She slit open the thick ivory envelope from her dear cousin Lydia first. She had not heard from her for some time.

A folded, yellowed newspaper clipping fell from the stationary. Anna froze when she saw the *Story City Herald* dated Thursday, May 16, 1918, with her father's photograph beneath the headline, "Banker Marvick Takes Own Life."

The searing pain of the buried past surged through her veins and filled her throat, obliterating time and place.

She was nineteen when he died, preparing for final examinations in her junior year at St. Olaf College. The message that she must return home at once due to a family emergency came from her oldest brother-in-law, Peter. As the train traveled from Northfield, Minnesota, to Story City, Iowa, she stared through the window into the starless night, fearing what she imagined to be the worst—that her beloved brother Severt had taken a turn for the worse and succumbed to his illness.

Peter met her at the station. "Anna." The weight of grief lined his face and hung his shoulders. He did not attempt to smile.

"It's Severt, isn't it?" She pressed her fingers to the corners of her eyes and swallowed to catch the tears.

Peter placed his hand on her shoulder and guided her from the depot where the ticket agent stood staring from the doorway. "We'll talk at home."

Anna nodded, thinking how lost her sister-in-law must feel. "Poor Cosette."

Her brother-in-law did not respond, his expression odd.

They drove in silence to Peter and Olive's home, which was dark except for a light in the parlor.

"Charlotte and Jack are here with Olive," Peter said.

"I thought Charlotte would be home in bed." Seven months pregnant with her first child, Anna's sister had not been feeling well. "How is she?"

"She's having a difficult time of it."

Seated on the brocaded divan beside her husband, Charlotte began to weep when she saw her younger sister. The unchecked emotion alarmed and embarrassed Anna, but she attributed it to pregnancy. Jack put his arm around his wife and pulled her close.

Olive seemed unsteady when she stood. "I'm sorry I wasn't at the door to greet you." Anna's oldest sister appeared dazed, her hair falling from its pins. "My dear girl. Come sit beside me."

Anna kissed Olive's cheek and sat down on the parlor chair beside her. "Is Papa in Arizona with Cosette?"

A small strangled cry came from Olive. Across the room, Charlotte choked on her tears.

Peter cleared his throat. "It is not what you think. We have not lost Severt."

Danger compressed Anna's chest, and fear pricked her arms and legs. She did not want to hear what Peter had to say.

"Anna, I don't know how to tell you this." Peter's voice was hoarse.

Olive reached out and stroked Anna's hand in strict measure.

"There has been a tragedy." Peter took a deep breath. "Your father has passed away."

"No." Anna shook her head and closed her eyes. It wasn't possible. There must be some mistake. "No."

"We are all in a state of shock."

Olive continued to stroke Anna's hand.

"I don't understand. Papa wasn't ill."

"Your father was shot."

Anna's eyes burned and her ears throbbed. "Shot?" Someone had murdered her father?

"He was unconscious when they found him. They rushed him to the hospital, but it was too late. The doctor couldn't save him."

Anna had the urge to push her sister's hand away, to run from the room, to deny what had happened and wake from the dreadful nightmare. Tears blurred her eyes and coursed down her cheeks.

Peter began to pace. "There is something else."

The hard bones of Olive's fingers clenched Anna's hand.

"I would not have believed it and wish I could spare you." Peter coughed. "There is no easy way to say this. But it seems your father took his own life."

Charlotte wailed and pressed her face into Jack's shoulder.

"No." It wasn't possible. Shaking her head, she pulled her hand from Olive's and stood. The room blurred.

"Anna." Olive reached for her.

Anna ran from the parlor.

"Anna." Exhaustion and desperation edged Olive's voice.

"Let her go."

Anna stumbled up the dark stairs to the guest room. Closing the door behind her, she threw herself face down onto the bed and covered her head with the pillow.

In the days that followed, Peter's family brought meals they did not eat. He answered the telephone and the door, accepting condolences but explaining the family was unable to visit. Anna listlessly wandered the house, light-headed from lack of sleep. Charlotte and Jack stayed home, and Anna's sister Ida, the last to see their father alive, remained at her farm in the country. The pastor came to visit, but Olive did not have the energy to leave her bed to meet with him, and Peter took care of the funeral arrangements.

They did not speak of what had happened.

At the funeral service, Anna sat in the front pew with her four older sisters, three of them pregnant with children who would never know their grandfather. She remembered little about the service other than the church overflowed with staring friends, extended family, and townspeople. Pastor Vangsnes prayed that

God would remember the great good the deceased had done, have mercy on him for his great sin, and give comfort to the family in their time of mourning.

Anna never returned to St. Olaf, where her father had been a benefactor, but instead transferred to Northwestern where no one knew her or her family.

Remembering, the pain and shame surged within her, and the wool dress that never seemed warm enough suddenly felt stifling.

Lydia wrote that she found the article while going through her things and thought Anna might want another copy. Her cousin could not know that Anna had never seen the *Herald* article or read any report of her father's death. Lydia could not know that, after the funeral, the family never again spoke about what had happened and did not mention his name. Anna had never discussed her father with family or friends. She did not speak of him to Alfred, the childhood friend she married the following year. She did not talk to her children about their grandfather. She had buried the memories with him and had no desire to unearth them.

The detailed newspaper report of her father's last days and of the community's reaction disturbed her. The report revealed a "farewell letter." Anna stiffened. She had never seen or heard of this letter, and yet the entire town learned of its contents in the newspaper. Had her sisters seen the letter? Had Peter?

"In this letter, which was written in a steady hand, Mr. Marvick bid good-bye to all his children, thanked them for their tender care of him, and said he had sinned greatly, and that sin must be punished." The newspaper concluded that the letter "showed he was laboring under a great mental strain of some kind and that his mind had become deranged." Deranged. It was the last thing anyone would say about her father, the man described as "our well-known and honored townsman . . . always a liberal supporter of church activities as well as the civic interests of the community generally," whose "principal joy in life seemed to be his family."

The old paper soft against her fingertip, Anna slowly traced the outline of her father's face. Carefully, she refolded the article and letter and slid them back into the ivory envelope which she set on the table beside her unfinished lunch.

Standing, she pressed her hand against the wall to steady herself for a moment, then walked to the winding staircase at the front of the house, climbed to the second floor, continued down the hallway to the attic door, and ascended the narrow stairs.

Iced light filtered through the small frosted panes of the attic dormer window. Anna crossed her thin arms across her chest and held herself tightly against the chill. Sighing deeply, her breath floated, fragile in the freezing air.

The heavy painting rested against the north wall of the attic, shrouded within the faded curtain. Forty years had passed since his portrait had been removed from the wall, wrapped, and stored away.

Yellow and orange threads adhered to the larger-than-life image of her father, but the damaged condition of the portrait painted shortly before his death did not concern her. He sat on his favorite chair with the high back and curved arms, wearing a grey Hart Schaffner and Marx three-piece suit, lavender tie, white shirt, and pocket handkerchief. His hands rested on his thighs, and he wore his gold wedding band.

Her throat swelled as her father stared at her in solemn silence—the face of the father she had loved and lost blurred in the blinding tears.

"Papa," she whispered, then bowed her head in her hands, and sobbed.

Spent, she lifted the cloth over her father's image, wrapped it around the frame, and laid the shrouded portrait to rest against the far wall. Turning her back, she left the attic.

After she lit the match, she stepped back. The day the shovels covered his casket with the black earth, she had turned from the grave to forget.

The small flame reflected on the polished brass of the fireplace screen. In moments, all that remained were ashes.

Her father would not have taken his own life. The foundation of their family, he loved his children and always looked after their best interests.

Outside, a crow called in the cold.

I

1907

"Two are better than one,
because they have a good reward for their toil.
For if they fall, one will lift up his fellow;
but woe to him who is alone when he falls
and has not another to lift him up."

ECCLESIASTES 4: 9-10

In the Beginning
Joseph

On an unseasonably cool Sunday in April 1907, the warm smell of roasted beef wafted from the kitchen through the spacious home on the north end of Grand Avenue in Story City, Iowa. The family had been called for dinner, and Joseph rose from his sitting chair in the living room, pausing to habitually straighten the brown Hart Schaffner & Marx suit vest and jacket. Continuing their debate about the morning's sermon, his only son Severt and future son-in-law Peter crossed the hall ahead of him to the dining room.

As he passed the grand piano, Joseph picked a small piece of lint from the sleeve of his jacket. Arranged on a white Hardanger cloth from Norway, framed family photographs covered the closed lid of the piano. Joseph's grey eyes focused on his wedding portrait. He had not looked at the photograph closely for some time, and the younger, thinner version of himself seemed a stranger. In the portrait, he sat in a chair, his new bride Annie standing beside him in her elaborate, fitted wedding gown, her hand gloved in white lace resting on his shoulder. Her beauty seized his soul, as it had on that day. Unbidden, the old, unwelcome ache of loss burst from the cellar of his heart. Irritated by his weakness, he frowned. Nearly eight years had passed since her death, and he and the children had moved on and were doing well. There was no sense dwelling on it. He willed the pain of loss away, and the heavy wooden door of his heart slammed shut. Lifting his chin, he turned toward the animated voices of his children, and his brow cleared.

Joseph took his chair at the head of the walnut table which comfortably seated twelve. This Sunday, his sister and future son-in-law were joining the family for dinner, and his daughters had set the table with nine place settings of the Haviland Limoges china, crystal, and silver their mother had chosen years before.

A cool gust of wind lifted the curtains at the open dining room window, the billowing white lace reflecting in the mirror of the walnut hutch against the opposite wall.

"Severt, please close the window." Joseph nodded at his son.

Severt groaned as he pushed his chair back. "I told Ida it was too cold in here." Slight of build, the handsome high school junior often joked that his only disappointment in life was that he hadn't inherited his father's height and sturdy stature. Of greater importance to his father, Severt consistently ranked at the top of his class. Joseph expected him to continue to excel, first in college and later in banking or real estate.

"I'm sorry, Severt. I should have let you close it before you sat down." Ida, two years younger than her brother, set a bowl of creamed corn on the table. The likeness of her mother, Ida's almond eyes graced a perfectly formed oval face. Soft tendrils fell from thick waves of rich chocolate hair loosely braided and wrapped around her head. "I suppose it is a bit cold, isn't it? I just thought it would be nice to let in some fresh spring air and hear the birds sing."

"Good intention, Ida, but it's forty degrees out." Severt shoved the window closed with both hands.

"Thank the Lord! I was beginning to freeze!" Eleven-year-old Charlotte rubbed her hands and pretended to shiver.

"Charlotte." Joseph's youngest sister Margretha took a seat opposite him at the other end of the table. "You know better than to take the name of the Lord in vain."

Joseph considered his younger sister, who had cared for the children and kept house for him for three years following his wife's death. She could be excessively harsh at times, which made her seem older than her years. Unfortunately, her stern demeanor detracted from her otherwise pleasant physical appearance. Unmarried in her early thirties, she now kept house for her elderly parents in their home across the street.

Breathless, eight-year-old Anna ran to the table. Last to be seated, Joseph's youngest child slid into her chair beside Charlotte, lifted herself off the seat to adjust the full navy skirt beneath her, and faced her father.

"Let us pray." Joseph paused as the others bowed their heads in prayer.

Satisfied with the silence, he bent his head. "Heavenly Father, we give thee thanks for the many gifts thou hast bestowed upon us: good health, earthly possessions, and the food we have before us. Thy will be done. Now let us say grace. . . ."

The voices around the table joined together in the familiar Norwegian table grace, "I Jesu Navn gaar vi til bords; At spise, drikke paa dit ord. Dig Gud til aere os til gavn, Saa faar vi mat, I Jesu Navn."

"Amen," Joseph finished.

"Amen," his family echoed.

With the exception of the table prayer, Joseph did not permit his children to speak Norwegian at home. He regretted his own second-generation immigrant accent and believed English should be the only language spoken in the community. Others disagreed. Like many in their generation, his own parents refused to speak English, despite having lived in America for over fifty years, and Norwegian remained the language of the church.

"Papa, would you kindly carve the roast?" Joseph's eldest daughter Olive nodded to the platter on the table before him. Flushed from getting Sunday dinner ready in the heat of the kitchen, she patted an embroidered handkerchief on her moist forehead. She wore her straight, light brown hair pulled up and rolled high above her forehead.

"It smells delicious, Olive." Beside her, Peter Donhowe smiled at the woman he would soon marry. Tall with a prematurely receding hairline, Peter worked in the men's clothing store Joseph had founded and sold at a handsome profit years ago to Peter's older brothers, John and Henry. Respected leaders in the community, the Donhowe brothers also sold sewing machines and tombstones, and owned the dry goods and shoe store in town. Their father Ole held the most important lay position as klokker at St. Petri Lutheran Church. Joseph could not have chosen a better family for Olive to marry into.

Joseph carved another slice from the roast. "Clothing business still strong, Peter?"

"Doing well. Helps to have a thriving business community," Peter said. "Received a shipment of new Hart Schaffner suits last week. I'd like to show them to you."

"Always interested in the new merchandise. I should buy a new suit for this wedding of yours." Joseph glanced across the table at Olive. "I want to look my best as father of the bride."

"Severt should get one as well." Olive poured from the pewter pitcher into her crystal water goblet. "He could use a nice new suit." She smiled at her brother. "We don't want you looking tattered."

"Severt never looks tattered," Charlotte said. "He wants to look impressive."

"He certainly impresses the girls in school." Ida tilted her head toward her brother with a teasing smile. "Especially Cosette Henderson."

Severt reached for the bowl of potatoes. "She's too young for me," he said of his younger sister's close friend.

"You think so?" Nineteen-year-old Lula winked at her brother. Joseph's second eldest would assume responsibility for managing the house after Olive married. He hoped Lula would be as efficient as her sister in planning and preparing meals, supervising the maids and dressmakers, assigning tasks to the three youngest daughters, and managing the household finances.

Severt heaped mashed potatoes on his plate, taking all the yellow butter melting on top of the creamy mounds before passing the dish to Anna. "Be careful, the bowl is hot."

"Peter," Margretha took a dinner roll from the basket and set it on her plate. "I imagine you heard the news about Jake before the service this morning?"

"Actually not," Peter said of his brother-in-law. "But we all knew it was just a matter of time."

In church, hushed whispers had rustled the reverent silence when Reverend Vangsnes announced Jake Jacobson had "passed into the great beyond, a month over the age of thirty-five, in the prime of manhood."

"You could say it's a blessing," Lula said. "He was so ill for so long."

"I wouldn't say it was a blessing," Margretha said. "But I must say it didn't come as any surprise."

"His heart seemed to just get worse every year," Peter said, "and at the end, he wasn't anything like the old Jake."

"Quite a shame." Margretha raised an eyebrow. "He wasn't much of a father to his son."

Anna reached over and clutched Charlotte's arm. "I feel so, so sorry for Alfred." Releasing her sister, she leaned back in her chair with a loud sigh and closed her eyes. "His mama died when he was two, and now his papa is dead too." Opening her eyes, she gazed at the ceiling. "Now he's entirely alone."

"He is not alone, Anna," Olive said. "He has his grandparents to take care of him."

"And the Donhowes." Peter smiled at Anna. "We will look after him."

"His grandparents are so, so old." Anna rolled her eyes. "Ancient, like Bestemor Laurense and Bestefar Syvert. I could not imagine living with them."

Severt laughed.

"You are so dramatic, Anna." Ida shook her head with a smile.

Margretha glared first at her nephew and then her niece. "Anna. Speak of your grandparents with respect."

Charlotte shrugged. "Actually, I don't see how it will be much different. Alfred has lived with his grandparents ever since his mama died. And his father was always so sick and weak. He was never like Papa."

"You're too young to remember him before he took ill," Severt said. "Before his accident, he was strong as an ox. I remember cheering him on in competitions. He always seemed to take first place, whether it was running or wrestling or husking."

Peter nodded. "He certainly was quite the athlete."

"They say Jake died of a broken heart." Ida's silken voice was soft with sympathy.

"That is total nonsense." Margretha dabbed the corners of her mouth with her napkin.

Joseph agreed. "People do not die of broken hearts, Ida. His heart failed from overwork on the farm."

"Jake never was the same after Mattie died." Olive glanced at Peter, who had adored his vivacious older sister Mattie. "I do believe he threw himself into his work to forget his heartbreak."

Lula nodded. "Everyone knew they were such a devoted couple. And she was so young when he lost her."

"And Alfred, poor child," Olive said. "I remember him at the funeral, asking when his mama was going to wake up. It was heartbreaking."

Anna hung her head and pushed out her bottom lip. "Poor, poor Alfred."

Joseph frowned. A year old when her mother died, Anna would not remember how she had wailed and cried out, "Mama," in the dark days that followed. When Mattie died the following month, Joseph had been shutting away his own loss, and her funeral had been difficult for him to attend. He remembered Jake pacing at the church and house without speaking or recognizing anyone. It was a shame Jake had not found the strength to put his grief aside for his son's sake and had given up his will to live.

Peter held his napkin over his mouth and coughed.

Joseph avoided looking at his future son-in-law. He remembered Peter at Mattie's funeral, hunched and heaving in a chair by the casket in the parlor. His older brothers should have led the sobbing young man to a bedroom. Peter had been fifteen at the time, beyond the age for such an emotional demonstration.

"Well!" Ida's bright voice broke the silence. "Enough of this talk!"

"I agree," Lula said. "Papa, did Ida mention that Cosette's father scheduled the Ladies Quartet at the Ames Chautauqua this year and has given her a solo?"

"Did he, now?" Joseph smiled at Ida, pleased both by the shift in the conversation and Ida's opportunity. The cultural highlight of the summer season, Chautauqua provided the finest entertainment and enlightenment.

"My!" Margretha nodded at her niece. "That is quite an honor, to sing at Chautauqua. Very good."

"You girls have established a fine reputation throughout the region," Olive said.

"People love hearing Norwegian folk songs performed," Ida said.

Margretha nodded. "They certainly do. I must say, Michas Henderson should be commended for the time he has spent managing your schedule and escorting you to different towns to sing."

"Not to mention coaching you on your Norwegian," Severt laughed.

"John will be disappointed Jennie didn't get that solo," Peter said, referring to his brother's daughter.

"I expect he will." Disappointed, perhaps, Joseph thought, but not surprised. Audiences praised Ida's beauty, charm, and pure soprano voice. Many of Joseph's business associates attended the Ames Chautauqua, and they would be impressed to see his daughter's name as a soloist on the program. They would be more impressed when they heard her sing.

"Jennie has a lovely voice," Ida said.

"True. But you have the greater talent." Joseph could praise his daughter, knowing she performed with a radiant confidence not shadowed by conceit.

"Thank you, Papa. Naturally you favor my voice because I am your daughter." Ida leaned toward him, reached out, and rested her hand on his arm. "I will gladly sing for you any time. You are my greatest fan."

Anna shook her head. "It isn't only Papa, Ida. Everyone I know says your voice is the most beautiful they have ever heard. Like a songbird."

"Each of us has God-given talents," Margretha said.

"Some more than others," Severt laughed. "I can think of some people who seem to lack any talents."

Charlotte and Anna looked at each other and laughed with their brother.

"That merely places more responsibility on you to use yours wisely," Margretha responded.

"Oh, my." Olive wiped her brow with her handkerchief. "Papa, I'm so sorry, but I neglected to mention that Pastor spoke to me last week. He quite insists the younger girls attend Norsk Skole this summer. I told him it was your decision, and he needed to speak with you about it."

Anna made a face at Charlotte.

Joseph frowned. "He mentioned it to me this morning."

"Is that why Pastor pulled you aside after the service? He seemed to be discussing a matter of grave importance." Severt imitated the long, staid face of the pastor and laughed.

"Severt." Margretha fixed her eyes on her nephew. "We do not laugh at the pastor."

"Be respectful," Joseph said to his son.

Margretha rested her fork on her plate and sat back. "Surely the girls will attend."

Joseph met her critical stare. "I believe I've made my decision."

"The little girls won't attend Norwegian school? How do you expect them to prepare for confirmation?" Her eyes narrowed.

Joseph's neck and shoulders clenched at his sister's inappropriate challenge of his authority in front of the children. He measured his words deliberately. "My opinion has been well known. As I have discussed on more than one occasion with you and our mother, I believe in the importance of a church education. I am, however, strongly opposed to having my children taught in Norwegian. The girls will attend summer school when it is taught in English, and not before."

"Well!" Margretha raised her eyebrows and exhaled loudly through her nose.

"Marvelous!" Anna hugged Charlotte.

"I hope you girls know how lucky you are," Severt said. "I had to sit in school for weeks each summer, sweating and reciting in Norwegian all day long."

"You're always complaining about working, Severt," Charlotte said.

"Hard work never hurt anyone." Margretha stabbed a piece of meat with her fork.

Joseph wiped the sides of his thick mustache with his napkin. "Girls."

Immediately serious, Charlotte and Anna both sat up straight, hands in their laps, and attentively faced their father.

"I want it to be clearly understood that I expect both of you to learn your catechism. I expect you to memorize it word for word."

Anna beamed. "Oh, yes, Papa!"

Charlotte nodded, smirking at her brother.

Joseph turned to Lula. "I trust you will ensure they have the materials they need."

Lula nodded.

"I also expect you to set sufficient time aside each day this summer for them to study."

Lula smiled. "Certainly, Papa."

Margretha sawed her knife through her meat. "I believe I will come and test them periodically myself."

Anna grimaced at Charlotte.

"I'll speak with the pastor tomorrow." Joseph focused his attention on his food. "I'm ready for some coffee, Olive."

A Father's Will

Joseph

The following day, Joseph stopped by the church on his way to his office.

"God dag, Joseph." Reverend O.P. Vangsnes nodded, rubbing the pointed white goatee on his chin.

Joseph returned the nod. "Good day."

"Vaer sa god." The clergyman nodded to the chair across from his desk. "Sitte."

"Thank you, but I won't be long." Joseph sat on the carved wooden chair, resting his hands lightly on his thighs.

"Business is good?" The clergyman emigrated from Norway as a boy, and he spoke with a thick accent.

Joseph nodded. "No complaints."

Reverend Vangsnes nodded. "Good. You shall have more to give to the church." His eyes flickered with amusement.

"I give a share of what I have been given."

"You have always been a generous supporter."

Joseph had not come to converse about his giving. "There is a matter we must discuss."

"You've come to speak to me about Norsk Skole, ja?"

"I have."

"I trust you have reconsidered." The thick white eyebrows lifted.

"My position has not changed."

O.P. Vangsnes' pale blue eyes steeled. "You are a stubborn man, Joseph Marvick."

Joseph returned the pastor's hard stare. "I could say the same of you."

The churchman leaned forward. "I find it unfortunate indeed that you consider me stubborn when I am merely urging you to fulfill your duty as a Christian parent. As a minister of the church of God, I am heartily devoted to inculcating the Katekismus upon the young people. My office requires me to urge parents to send their children to school to train them to the honor and praise of God, and I shall not waver from my charge to do so." The pastor leaned back and folded his arms across his chest. "It is not my will, but God's be done. If that be stubbornness in your eyes, so be it."

"Reverend Vangsnes, as I have expressed to you in our many previous conversations, my objection is not to what is taught, but rather the language it is taught in. Surely you do not argue it is God's will that our children speak Norwegian."

"Young people must be taught by uniform, settled texts, otherwise they easily become confused. Martin Luther wrote this himself in the Book of Concord." The pastor paused for effect. "Our texts are in Norsk, and our children are confirmed in Norsk. They must be prepared to repeat the Katekismus word for word in Norsk. That is precisely what they learn in Norsk Skole."

"It is long past time that our young people be confirmed in English. I have been urging such a change for years. What good is it for our young people to memorize words they do not understand? I considered it great progress when you arrived and began holding the evening services and Sunday school in English. It has been seven years, Reverend. It is time to continue making progress."

"Ah. English services." O.P. Vangsnes rested his chin in his hand and shook his head. "Many of the congregants complain that it has been the ruination of our church. Our venerable klokker, Ole Donhowe, for one. Your fine parents, for another." His eyes narrowed. "Some left, you know, and have not returned. Can you imagine what they would say if we held confirmation in English?"

"We no longer live in Norway. If some choose to speak the old language in their homes, that is their choice. But English is the language of this country, and our children should be taught in English. I believe that is as true for the church as the public schools. As such, I see no reason for Norwegian school in the summer. My children will not recite in a language they do not understand for eight hours a day for six weeks in the summer."

"Are you ashamed of your worthy ancestry?"

"You know better than to ask that question of me. My leadership in the Norwegian Pioneer Association is sufficient proof that I am proud of my heritage."

"You are a stubborn man, Joseph. Your children shall suffer as a result. If they do not attend Norsk Skole, they shall not learn their Katekismus and they shall not be confirmed. I deeply regret that you neglect your Christian duty as their father, which, I remind you, is a damnable sin."

Clenching his jaw, Joseph took a deep breath. "You presume my decision to withhold my children from summer school is a decision to keep them from learning their catechism. Your presumption is false. I have every intention of performing my duty as a Christian father and will ensure the girls learn their catechism word for word. Even if it means to be confirmed they must memorize the necessary words in Norwegian."

"And who will teach them?" The pastor raised his eyebrows. "You? I do not believe you have either the time or the inclination."

"Lula will teach them at home."

The preacher sat back. "Surely you jest."

Joseph pulled his watch from the inside pocket of his gray wool jacket. He had other more pressing business matters that required his attention. After glancing at the time, he snapped the watch shut. "I believe we are finished." He stood. "I have heard your arguments, but you cannot persuade me to change my decision. I ask that we agree to respectfully disagree."

"I remind you. You are a leader in the church and the community. Others will watch what you do. You could influence whether others send their children to Norsk Skole."

"Each man makes his own decision for what is best for his children."

Shaking his head, O.P. Vangsnes slowly rose to his feet. "You are making a mistake, Joseph Marvick."

"I have instructed Lula to obtain the necessary materials. I trust you will make them available to her." Joseph shook the pastor's hand. "I must be on my way."

His decision final and irrefutable, Joseph left the church.

Wedding Feast

Anna

Anna and Charlotte did not begin catechism studies at the beginning of the summer. Final preparations for Olive's June 12th wedding absorbed the family, and their father conceded Lula did not have adequate time to devote to their instruction. He emphasized that the girls would have to study all the harder the remainder of the summer.

Anna's excitement grew as the eventful day approached. The dressmaker came for the final fittings of Olive's wedding dress. A carpenter measured the first floor of the house Papa bought for Olive and Peter as a wedding gift, rented wood, and built tables for the reception. The cook hired several girls to help serve the four-course dinner, and Olive and Lula borrowed extra sets of china, silver, crystal, and linens from relatives. Charlotte and Anna helped make menu cards for each place setting. Three days before the wedding, the cook arrived, and sweet yeasty aromas permeated the house as she baked white and dark bread, dinner rolls, the wedding cake, and several other kinds of cakes. The day before the wedding, the blacksmith shod and groomed the family's team of black horses, and a hired man washed and shined the fringed surrey.

Finally, the wedding day arrived. At quarter past two in the afternoon, Papa led the hitched team of gleaming horses to the house.

"You can help carry the train," Lula said to Anna and Charlotte. "We don't want Olive's lovely dress to get dirty, do we?"

Anna thought Olive looked like a princess in her dress of white chiffon over taffeta, trimmed with lace and satin. Anna and Charlotte each carefully lifted one end of the train which trailed several feet behind Olive.

Anna wondered what her father was thinking as he watched his oldest daughter approach the surrey in her wedding dress. He had told Olive he wanted the day to be perfect and didn't want her counting pennies when she planned the wedding. If anything went wrong, he would not be happy.

Anna tripped. Horrified, she gripped the train and focused on keeping it off the ground while she regained her balance.

"Pay attention, Anna," Charlotte hissed.

"No harm done," Olive said.

Anna hoped her father hadn't noticed her carelessness and watched her feet.

"Well," Papa said. "Ready to go?"

"She'd better be!" Lula laughed. "The service starts in forty-five minutes."

"Your dress is very fine, Olive."

"Thank you, Papa."

Papa awkwardly patted Olive's hand. "Before we go, I would like to wish you the greatest happiness with Peter, from this day forward, in what I hope is a long and fruitful marriage."

"Thank you, Papa." Olive's smile glittered with tears, and she dabbed her eyes with a handkerchief.

Papa looked away. "Well. We'd best get going."

Anna wished she could ride with them, knowing the neighbors would be standing on their porches and along the street, waiting to gain the first glimpse of the beautiful bride.

Her father assisted Olive and Lula into the surrey, climbed in himself, and, with a nod, drove down the street.

The wedding began at three o'clock. With Mendelssohn's grand "Wedding March" vibrating from the new pipe organ and reverberating throughout the sanctuary, Anna's father escorted Olive down the aisle. She carried a bouquet of white roses, and lily of the valley adorned the headdress of her veil which floated behind her above the train of her dress. Lula stood at the left front of the church, wearing her white cotton graduation dress, which the dressmaker had trimmed with tucks, lace, and insertion. Peter, dressed in a new black suit of fine broadcloth, white vest, and white tie, stood tall and proud on the right, beaming as his bride approached. His best man stood beside him.

Seated down the pew from her father, Anna observed her family during the long sermon about the responsibilities and duties of the husband and wife in their relationship to God and each other and in their future as parents. Olive seemed quite focused on Reverend Vangsnes, but occasionally exchanged glances and smiles with Peter and once with Lula. Anna thought their feet must be getting tired standing at the altar for such a long time. Beside her, Charlotte shifted slightly to peer at friends and relatives in the pews behind them. Next to Charlotte, Severt looked rather bored. Beside him, Ida smiled radiantly toward the couple at the altar. Anna did not look much at Margretha and her grandparents, but felt certain they did not relax their stern expressions or move a muscle throughout the sermon. At the far end of the pew, her father seemed intent and serious and, surely, Anna thought, very proud as the father of the bride.

God granted Olive's wish for sunshine, and a pleasant breeze kept the family and wedding guests comfortable as they were ushered out of the church. The Marvick family greeted family and friends, and Charlotte and Anna ran around the churchyard with their cousins, feeling self-important as sisters of the bride.

Gradually, people began walking to Peter and Olive's house for the reception, and Papa brought the fringed surrey to the front of the church. Olive gathered up her train and veil, and Peter put his hands around her waist and lifted her into the surrey. He jumped in beside her, and Papa clicked to the horses.

When the surrey was out of earshot, Lula waved to those remaining. "Everyone! It's time to get to the house, and we'd best hurry. We have a surprise waiting for the bride and groom."

The younger girls skipped along behind Lula. Turning the corner toward the house, Charlotte pointed. "Anna, look."

In front of Olive's new home, the St. Petri choir lined up, facing the choir director.

Ida and Lula ran across the lawn to join the choir. Cosette Henderson and Jennie Donhowe made room for Ida in the front row between them. Lula took a place at the end of the middle row beside Clara Olson.

Scanning the crowd, Anna spotted her mother's sisters. "Let's go stand with Aunt Maggie and Aunt Linnie!" Maggie lived on a farm about twelve miles from Story City near Radcliffe. Anna wondered if she had always been called Maggie. She thought the name suited her. Her mother's sister certainly was not a Margretha. Maggie stood laughing with her younger sister Linnie, who had come on the train from Chicago with her two young children to attend the wedding and visit family.

"My darling girls, how beautiful you look on this special day." Their aunt Maggie beamed at them and in turn wrapped each girl in her arms, pulling them close. Anna felt stiff in her aunt's loving, lingering embrace. The Marvicks did not hug.

Anna was curious about her aunt Linnie. After Anna's mother died, Papa felt it would be too much for Margretha to care for a baby along with the other five children, and he left Anna in Illinois with her mother's family until she was three. Linnie had helped care for her, although Anna had no memory of her. She did remember crawling into her Grandmother Rasmussen's large lap and listening to her sing in Norwegian to the rhythm of the old oak rocker. Like her fathers' parents, her other grandparents did not speak English, and Anna believed her father brought her home when he did so she wouldn't have a strong accent like her mother's sisters.

"Here they come!" a voice in the crowd yelled.

"Whoa." Papa pulled the team to a stop in front of the house. Stomping their hooves and snorting, the horses shook their heads.

Selma Vangsnes, the pastor's daughter who directed the choir, lifted her right arm and nodded to the porch where the piano had been moved for the reception. Her hand sliced the air, in time to the opening bars of "'Tis Thy Wedding Morning."

Anna tapped Charlotte's arm. "Look how surprised Olive is." Their oldest sister's mouth gaped, and her hands flew to her face as the choir serenaded them. Turning to Peter with a wide smile, she dropped her hands into his. Peter wrapped his arm around his new wife and held her close, his gold wedding band reflecting the afternoon sun.

After the choir finished singing, Anna heard sniffling and turned to see Maggie wiping her eyes with her embroidered handkerchief.

"Wasn't that just lovely?" Her aunt wiped her nose with her handkerchief. "Annie would have loved it."

Linnie bounced her baby on her hip. "I've never heard that song before. How perfect for a wedding!" She looked down at Anna with tears in her eyes. "Don't you agree, little Anna?"

The tears embarrassed Anna. "It's from the operetta, "The Rose Maiden." I'm going to have it at my wedding when I grow up."

"What a wonderful idea!" Linnie reached down and cupped the back of Anna's head in her hand. She held it for a moment and then straightened.

"The choir performed it last month in a hall downtown," Charlotte added. "It was composed by R.E. Francillon."

Linnie smiled. "Is that right?"

"Yes. Papa says St. Petri has the finest music of all the churches in town." Anna wanted to impress her aunts.

"Does he, now?" Linnie exchanged smiles with her sister and shifted her little boy from one hip to the other.

"At Christmas and Easter the choir performs sacred cantatas and choral numbers like the 'Hallelujah Chorus' by Handel." Charlotte caught the loose hair blowing across her face and impatiently pulled it back.

"The choir director and her sister studied at the Chicago Music Conservatory," Anna said. "Papa said we can begin piano lessons with them when summer is over." She did not mention that her father had emphasized that there would be no lessons unless the girls had memorized their catechism.

"What lucky girls you are!"

The breeze carried the flavors of fried halibut and roasted veal from the summer kitchen in the back of the house. Hungry, Anna knew she would have to wait until the third seating to eat. The adults would be served first.

Anna thought of the food her Aunt Maggie served when they visited. "When we come this summer, will you make your special lefse and fried chicken and new peas smothered in cream?"

Her aunt smiled. "Of course, dear."

"Cream puffs, too?"

"Anything for Annie's sweet little girl."

Anna grinned at her aunt, thinking of the sweet cherries they bought for lunch in Ellsworth every year on their way to the farm. Ellsworth was such a little place compared to Story City. Charlotte and Anna felt quite superior when Lula drove them through the small town last year, and they sang "There are no flies on us; Great big horse flies on you," to the tune of *America*. They laughed about it at home, but did not share the story with their father, knowing he would disapprove of their behavior.

"Let's go look at the tables before they start eating." Charlotte tugged on her sister's arm.

Hair streaming behind them, the young girls raced across the yard and bounded up the front porch steps of Olive's new house.

Inside, bouquets of fresh flowers adorned each of the linen-covered tables set with china and silver, and celery cut to look like flowers garnished the plates.

Several girls who had been hired to help serve were setting plates of strawberries dipped in sugar on the tables. Pointing to a celery garnish, one of the hired girls asked another, "What kind of flowers do you think these are?"

Charlotte rolled her eyes, and Anna snickered as they ran to the next room.

Two of the women from the choir stood beside one of the tables with their backs to the door. One held a menu card. "Did you see this?"

The other woman nodded. "Can you believe it?"

Anna admired one of the cards.

Menu

Strawberries
Vegetable Soup
Wafers   Celery

———

Fried Halibut
Creamed Potatoes   Bread

———

Veal Roast
Brown Gravy   Mashed Potatoes
Corn   Rolls   Jelly
Pickles   Olives
Coffee

———

Chilled Fruit   Marguerites

———

Ice Cream   Cake

"My, my," one of the women clucked. "Joseph didn't spare any expense for Olive's wedding, did he?"

"And her dress! It must have cost a fortune!"

The women turned from the table and noticed Charlotte and Anna in the room.

"Well! Here we have the little Marvick girls! An exciting day for you. Yes?" Both of the older women's faces were very red. Anna wondered if it was the heat, but didn't feel that warm herself.

"Very exciting," Charlotte replied flatly. "Come, Anna. Let's go find Lydia." When they stepped out the door, she whispered, "They're certainly jealous."

Anna giggled. Flying out the front door, they nearly ran into Margretha, who was assisting their grandmother Laurense up the porch steps.

"Watch where you are going!" Margretha said sternly as Charlotte nearly collided with her.

"Excuse us!" Charlotte and Anna said in unison. The girls stopped and stood to the side of the porch, allowing their grandmother and aunt to walk to the door. Respect for elders was one of the three R's their father taught his children: Respect, Responsibility, and Resourcefulness.

Anna thought Grandma Laurense looked like Papa except very short and dressed like a woman. The old woman tripped along with short, fast steps. She wore her usual black dress with a fitted waist and plaited silk vest, a small silk standing collar with a white rushing pinned with a gold brooch, small turned-up silk cuffs, a silk belt, and a full gathered skirt that nearly reached the floor. Parted in the middle, her brown hair was twisted at the sides and pulled tightly into a bun at her neck, and she wore her black satin, shirred bonnet, the long ribbons tied neatly under her chin.

"Did you have time to read your Bible today, Bestemor?" Anna asked. Each morning, the old woman read the well-worn Bible in the carved walnut rocker she had brought from Norway. Anna wondered why she kept reading it, because it seemed she had already memorized it cover to cover.

Her grandmother stopped on the stairs, gripping the railing to frown at her granddaughter. "Ja." Grandmother Laurense never spoke English. She understood English, though. Anna could tell by her eyes. The old woman never had to ask what they were saying and was quick to pass judgment with Bible passages quoted in Norwegian.

Margretha took the old woman's arm. "Let me help you."

Grandmother Laurense pushed her daughter's arm away and marched up the rest of the stairs.

Grandfather Syvert followed behind his wife and daughter. Anna's brother Severt was named after this grandfather, but spelled it differently to avoid confusion. Grandfather Syvert stood nearly as tall as her father. He did not bend down to talk to his grandchildren, but extended his arm to pat them stiffly on the head. His eyes were a pale, nearly transparent blue and his hair completely white. A long white beard pulled his thin face down to his collarbone.

Anna's uncle followed her grandfather.

"Uncle Andrew, do you know where Lydia is?"

Her uncle shook his head. "Can't say I do."

Though they didn't see each other often, Anna felt particularly close to her favorite cousin, Lydia. Their fathers were in business together, and Papa traveled to meet with Andrew in South Dakota every month. Anna's father was president of the bank he and Andrew founded in Sisseton, and they also owned a land and loan company together. Anna did not understand why they called buying and selling farm land a real estate business, but she was not about to ask and have her father think she was dull-witted.

Charlotte pointed and waved. "There she is!"

Lydia waved back, and the girls raced toward each other.

"Isn't Olive beautiful?" Lydia's blond curls cascaded down her back.

"Oh, yes!"

"Mama said this wedding sets the standard—everything is just perfect, and so extravagant!"

"Wait until you see the wedding cake!" Anna licked her lips and closed her eyes in ecstasy.

"Papa wanted Olive's wedding to be special." Charlotte reached back to adjust the large silk bow that tied her hair at the back of her neck. "He said it was her special day, and she should have whatever she wanted."

"Isn't that grand!" Lydia tossed long strands of curls behind her shoulder. "You are the luckiest girls I know."

"We couldn't have a better Papa." Anna smiled proudly.

Farewells
Joseph

*L*ate that evening, Joseph escorted Peter and Olive to the train station. Olive reflected on how perfect the day had been, and Peter murmured in agreement.

Joseph found the rhythm of the horses' hooves on the gravel a welcome contrast to the voices of the day, as was the relative cool of the evening after the heat of the warm sunny day. Crickets serenaded while fireflies flashed in the calm of night.

His firstborn had married well.

Joseph recalled the day of Olive's birth. How lovely Annie had looked, despite her exhaustion. Smiling, she had held their baby out to him as she lay back on the pillows, her unbound damp hair curling around her face and neck and trailing her breast. He loved her more that day than their wedding day, although he had never thought that possible. Intimidated by the infant's fragility, he declined to hold Olive, and Annie laughed at his hesitation. "Joseph, my dear! She's more hearty than you think!" And with that, Olive began to cry, and Annie pulled her hair aside, unbuttoned her nightdress and put the baby to her breast.

Shifting the reins to one hand, Joseph pulled his pocket watch from his vest. The gold cover clicked open when he pressed the clasp. "Half past ten." Snapping the cover shut, he returned the watch to his pocket. "You'll have time to settle into your sleeping compartment before the Flyer departs." He nodded. "Good." He did not like rushing to catch a train.

At the station, Joseph wrapped the reins around a post while Peter lifted Olive out of the buggy. The couple would spend the first days of their honeymoon in Chicago. Joseph waited with Olive while Peter first went to the ticket window and then settled with the drayman, who had already delivered their baggage to the station. Olive had several bags and a trunk, and Peter had several bags of his own. It had been years since Joseph had traveled with his wife, and he had forgotten how much a woman could pack for a trip.

Joseph remembered his wife boarding the train to Chicago with baby Anna in her arms, her cheek red and swollen where she had picked a pimple with a brooch. When the infection set in a few days before their departure, he suggested they delay or cancel their travel plans. "But Joseph," she pleaded. "You know how I've looked forward to this trip. I haven't seen my family in years. I've looked forward to this for months, and you know how I've missed my sisters so." She had reached over, placed her hand over his and smiled up at him. "The doctor bled me to get rid of the bad blood and gave me salve. I'll be just fine." But she had not been fine. The further the train traveled from home, the worse the swelling became. He took her to a good doctor he knew in Morris, Illinois, where his parents lived, but by the time they arrived, it was too late. The poison had progressed too far for hot packs to do any good. The doctor shook his head when he examined her, and Joseph read the death sentence in his eyes. Annie died within a few days. Too ill to travel any further, she never saw her sisters or parents again. He should not have been swayed by the desires of the woman he loved, however difficult it would have been to disappoint her. He should have trusted his better judgment.

Olive's voice broke through the memories. "It seems strange to be leaving for so long." Reaching up, she adjusted her hat. "Three weeks!"

"You should enjoy Chicago," Joseph said.

"It's a good thing I am with Peter." Olive smoothed her skirt. "I would fear getting lost otherwise."

"I won't let go of your arm, my dear." Peter smiled down at his new wife, resting his hand lightly on her shoulder.

"Fine hotel, the Brevort." The couple had a room reserved at Joseph's hotel of choice in Chicago.

"It sounds quite elegant." Olive's eyes shone with a soft light. "Anna made me promise to send her a postcard from there."

"I believe I heard Anna request a postcard of every place we are going," Peter said.

"She was quite excited about the trip. But when it came time for goodbyes, you would have thought I was leaving forever, never to return." The light in Olive's eyes dimmed.

"Quite the drama." Peter shook his head.

Joseph had found Anna's sudden tears quite unexpected. Normally such a lively and joyful child, she must have been overtired and overcome by the excitement of the wedding.

"You must understand, Peter." Olive turned toward her new husband. "This is the first I've ever left her."

"She's too old for such a tearful display. And three weeks is not such a long absence."

"She's just turning ten at the end of July." Olive adjusted her hat once more. "Not so old, Peter."

"She will be just fine with Lula, Olive." Peter turned to the porter who had stepped onto the platform.

"These yours, sir?" The porter pointed to the bags and trunk the drayman had piled on the platform.

Peter nodded. "Yes." He opened his jacket, removed the tickets from the inner pocket, and held them out to the porter.

"I'll take them for you." The porter lifted the trunk and, bowed by the weight, hauled it up the stairs into the train car.

Peter held out his hand to Joseph. "Well, we had better get on board now. Thank you again for such a splendid reception. People will be talking about it for months."

"Perhaps years!" Olive's eyes glistened as she kissed him lightly on the cheek. "Papa, thank you for everything."

Discomfited by the visible sentiment in his restrained daughter, Joseph nodded and stepped back. "It gave me great pleasure to see you so happy today. I wanted it to be a day you would remember." He smiled. "Enjoy your honeymoon, and give my best regards to the family in Illinois."

Joseph watched the newly married couple board and waited for Olive to wave from the window of their private compartment.

It was nearly midnight by the time he arrived home, where he found Charlotte and Anna in the kitchen.

Remembering Anna's earlier tears, he noted the black circles beneath his youngest daughter's eyes. "It is long past your bedtime, girls."

"We needed a glass of water." Anna took a sip. "It is unbearably hot up there in the attic." The girls had given up their room to their uncle Andrew and his wife.

"I'm certain it is." Their father had heard this excuse before. "Finish your water, then, and off to bed with you." Taking into account that it had been a big day for the girls, Joseph softened his tone. It was understandable the girls would have difficulty settling down for the night.

Joseph left the kitchen and found his youngest brother in the living room, leaning back on the divan with his legs stretched out before him, smoking a cigar.

"Did Olive and Peter get off all right?"

Joseph nodded.

"Good." Andrew sat forward and pulled his legs up.

Joseph remained standing in the doorway. He could hear the whispers and giggles of the two girls and was about to return to the kitchen when Anna and Charlotte appeared. Their unpinned and unbraided hair hung in thick waves to their waists. Bare feet stuck out beneath their white cotton nightclothes.

"To bed." Joseph pointed to the stairs.

Andrew blew smoke at the ceiling. "Nice wedding. Must have cost you."

"Not every day your daughter gets married."

"True."

Joseph considered the expense of the wedding as he listened for his daughters' feet on the stairs. He did not believe in indulging his children in general. A daughter's wedding was a time to feast and celebrate, however, and he had been generous. "I believe the girls have finally gone to bed."

"When will you be in Sisseton next?"

"I plan to be there in a couple of weeks." The Citizens National Bank of Sisseton had grown into one of the leading institutions in northeastern South Dakota and required an increasing amount of his time.

"When do you plan on looking at that land in North Dakota you mentioned?"

"I'm going to Bismarck first thing next week. If the land in Burleigh County is any good, it would be a bargain at $12.50 an acre. I wouldn't want to lose it to another agent."

"Why such a low price?"

"That is the question, isn't it? From there, I'll go on to see if we can pick up some of that wheat land in the southwest. They're asking $18 an acre, but we should be able to negotiate something lower with a cash offer."

"Sounds good." Andrew stood and stretched. "I'd best be off to bed. I'm not accustomed to being up so late, and my dear wife will wonder what has happened to me."

"Yes." Joseph glanced at the swinging pendulum of the grandfather clock and stood. "It is quite late."

At the hallway, the brothers separated. Andrew climbed the stairs to the bedroom where his wife waited. Joseph continued down the hall to his room where the bed sheets were cold and empty. After he extinguished the light, memories evoked by the wedding filled the darkness with loss, and sleep eluded him.

Farewells

Anna

The girls climbed the stairs to the hot attic and found Lydia fast asleep on the end of the mattress. Charlotte pulled back the sheet and pushed their cousin over to make room for the two of them. Anna slipped her legs under the sheet, propped herself up on her elbow, and whispered, "Do you think it will be very different with Olive married?"

"Hardly," Charlotte fluffed her pillow beneath her head. "I imagine we'll see her nearly every day." She yawned, her eyes closing.

"I suppose so," Anna said.

Charlotte opened her eyes and smiled kindly at her sister. "Don't worry, Anna," she said. "Olive won't be gone for long. She'll be back before you know."

Anna considered her sister's words. She would miss living in the same house with Olive, and it concerned her to think of her older sister traveling far away on the train. Especially after what had happened to her mother. On the other hand, Anna didn't want to appear like a small child. Charlotte was right. Three weeks was not such a long time.

Charlotte's breathing slowed to a rhythmic rasp.

Anna observed her sister who lay on her back with her mouth open. Through the attic window, the black silhouettes of the mature elm trees swayed in the breeze and crickets rubbed their legs together on the earth below. Pressing her arm across her nose, she lay back and tried not to smell the mothballs.

Anna did not remember her mother. Olive had filled that role since the day she brought three-year-old Anna home from Illinois. Papa sent Olive in advance to get acquainted. Anna remembered thinking the strange woman seemed very nice but did not understand when the woman told her their Papa was coming soon to take Anna home with them. Olive helped Aunt Linnie pack a new suitcase with all of Anna's clothes, and then her grandfather drove them in the buggy to the train station while her grandmother held her close.

On the platform at the station, Anna felt the tremor beneath her feet as the train approached, appearing like a big, black monster. She clapped her hands over her ears to shut out the terrifying noise of the engine thundering to a stop and the deafening throbbing of the bells. The tall, strange man they called Papa reached for her, and she turned from him and buried her face in her grandmother's soft, safe bosom. Her grandmother cried and hugged her and told her she was a lucky girl to be going home with her father to her brother and sisters, and said she loved her very much and always would. Then the man they called Papa picked her up and carried her onto the train. She wiped her eyes and sat silently between Papa and Olive, and tried to be a good girl like her grandmother told her. On the trip, Olive smiled and fed her sweets and read her books and played little games with her.

Charlotte had often told Anna the story. "The family was very excited to have you come home to live with us again. Papa announced that we needed to do everything possible to make you happy. He bought you a new swing set and let you call everything you wanted yours. I never said anything, but I didn't like it when Olive made me give you all my toys."

Now, Anna had difficulty imagining how they all had seemed like such frightening strangers to her. She thought of Alfred, an only child left without parents. At the wedding, Alfred had laughed and teased like he usually did. Anna felt comfort in Peter's assurance that the Donhowes would look after him. Yes, certainly her friend would be fine.

It had been fun to be the sister of the bride. Someday she would walk down the aisle in a beautiful wedding dress on her father's arm and be serenaded by the choir afterward, and she decided she, too, would visit Chicago on her wedding trip.

Nothing had changed. Olive would be living nearby, and Papa would always be there to take care of her. Anna closed her eyes and slept.

II

1911 – 1913

"Children, obey your parents in the Lord, for this is right.
'Honor your father and mother'
(this is the first commandment with a promise),
'that it may be well with you and
that you may live long on the earth.'"

EPHESIANS 6:1

Fourth of July

Anna

The crackling burst of Fourth of July fireworks woke twelve-year-old Anna before the sun rose. She jumped from the bed she shared with Charlotte, ran to the window, pulled aside the white curtains, and peered into the darkness.

Charlotte moaned and turned over. "What a racket," she mumbled. She buried her head beneath her pillow.

Pressing her face against the window screen, Anna scanned the street in both directions. "I don't see anything. I was hoping to catch Alfred in the act. He's always bragging about being the first to celebrate." She squinted into the shadows of the old pasture across the street. "Actually, I dared him to set one off nearby so I could see it this year. And I missed it."

"Some of us would rather sleep." The pillow muffled Charlotte's voice.

Lula sat up and swung her legs over the side of the bed. "I'm glad he woke us. We have quite a bit of work to do before the parade." Arching her back, she stretched her arms.

Eyes closed, Ida yawned and rolled from her side to her back, her body unfolding across the bed.

When the older girls were at college, Charlotte and Anna shared the large bedroom, and each slept in their own double bed. Home for the summer after completing their first year of music studies at St. Olaf College in Northfield, Minnesota, Ida and Lula now shared Charlotte's bed. Olive had agreed to keep house for Papa so Lula could attend college, and she and Peter and their little girl had moved into the older girls' bedroom. Anna thought the more the merrier, but Charlotte complained it was too hot with four bodies in the same room. Despite her grumbling, Anna knew Charlotte enjoyed listening to the college girls talk at night when they thought their younger sisters were asleep.

Peering into the early morning dusk, Anna recalled her sisters' conversation from the night before.

"What did Ed have to say in his letter today?" Ida whispered. Edwin Roe, Lula's beau at St. Olaf, wrote nearly every day.

"He sent you greetings. He said to remind you he expects you to keep me out of trouble."

"Did you tell him about the party at the Haerem's?"

"I did."

"You told him about the wine at dinner, and then the rum pudding and the other drinks they served after we played whist? What was that last drink called?"

"I don't remember. Something they brought from Norway. I told Ed I've never heard such clinking of glasses before. He said it sounded like I had become a drinker and had best watch out!"

"Lula! Perhaps you shouldn't have told him. It sounds so scandalous."

"Don't worry. You know Ed. He found the story amusing."

"He's in love with you."

Charlotte nudged Anna while they waited for Lula to respond.

"I miss him. Wisconsin is so far away."

"It's too bad you fell for someone who isn't from around here."

"I never met anyone like Ed here at home." Lula yawned. "Speaking of local boys, Walter Henderson certainly has been coming around this summer."

"He has."

"He's always had an eye for you."

The box springs groaned and the sheets rustled in the other bed. "He's certainly persistent."

"He isn't the one for you, is he?"

"Well, I wouldn't mind if he turned his attention to someone else."

Anna was certain Ida had many admirers at St. Olaf. College. College life sounded so exciting. She and Charlotte agreed that they too would study music and share grand times together at St. Olaf.

Suddenly, a flash of light and sound burst from the north corner of the old pasture. A dark shadow raced toward the fence. "It's Alfred! I see him!"

Across the street, another dark form loomed in the light of the kitchen window of her grandparents' house. "Bestemor is up." Their grandmother did not like fireworks.

Anna skipped away from the window to shake her sister. "Get up, Charlotte! I can't wait to decorate the car!"

Charlotte did not move.

This would be the third year the Joseph Marvick family drove an automobile in the Fourth of July parade. The few cars in town were the highlight of the parade.

Charlotte and Anna had cried when their father sold the horses and bought a car in 1909, the same year he became president of the Story City National Bank. The horses had seemed like members of the family, but the girls could not contain their excitement when they saw the bright red, six-passenger Ford with brass trimmings. Everyone in the family was proud to own the third car in town except their grandmother, who thought it an unnecessary sign of wealth. "What need is there for an automobile when a good pair of horses or the train would do just fine?"

"Charlotte!" Anna pulled the pillow from her sister's head.

Without opening her eyes, Charlotte reached for the pillow. "Give it back."

Ida slid from bed, brushing the hair from her face with her hands. "Be patient, Anna," she said softly. "You know it takes Charlotte longer to wake up than the rest of us."

"I hope the black-eyed Susans didn't wilt too much overnight." Lula stepped out of her cotton nightdress.

"I'm certain they'll be fine, Lula." Ida sat down on the bench of the dressing table, picked up the large ivory-backed, round brush, and pulled it in long slow strokes through her waist-length waves of hair. "It stays cool down in the cellar."

"Don't worry. We just picked them yesterday." Anna opened the top drawer of her dresser and lifted out a pair of stockings.

Ida set the brush on the table and began winding her hair into a soft roll at the back of her head. She smiled slyly. "Cosette certainly enjoyed helping Severt fill his tub."

Lula dipped a cloth in the washbowl, wrung it out, and lifted it to her face. "She does have a liking for him, doesn't she?"

"She always has. Another romance, I believe." Ida caught Lula's eye and smiled.

"Lula, your idea to cover the car with flowers is brilliant!" Anna pulled a stocking up her leg. "You are the most creative! Artistic like Aunt Margretha."

"I don't claim to have her talent." Lula lifted her hair and sponged the back of her neck. "But it certainly will be more interesting than last year, when our car looked just like the others."

"Papa was proud of the car last year." Ida stuck another pin in her hair. "He said it looked sharp and patriotic, wrapped with wide red, white, and blue ribbons and the American flags."

"Best looking car in the county," their father had said.

By the time the girls reached the kitchen, Olive had fed two-year-old Laurentia, made a pot of coffee, and started boiling eggs. "If you girls set the table, we'll be ready to eat soon." She lifted her daughter out of the high chair and set her on the floor.

Anna squatted and put her arms out. "Come, my darling girl!" Her short blond curls bouncing, Laurentia ran laughing into her young aunt's arms, and Anna scooped her up.

Anxious to decorate the car for the ten o'clock parade, the family quickly ate their breakfast, and the men finished their coffee in the kitchen while the women and girls cleaned up. Papa talked about his recent trip to Mexico and the good profit he expected to make on the 1,500 acres of land he had invested in there. Anna wished her father would describe what Mexico was like, but he always said time was money and he didn't waste it sight-seeing. She was wondering how her father could have his mind on business on the Fourth of July when she heard three firm taps on the kitchen door.

Their grandmother marched into the kitchen, followed by Aunt Margretha.

"We've come for the automobile decoration." The screen door rattled as Margretha pushed it shut.

Grandmother Laurense nodded without smiling.

"Would you like some coffee, Bestemor?" Ida asked.

Their grandmother shook her head tightly, her black eyes darting from one girl to the next.

"We've had breakfast." Margretha turned to Lula. "I'm surprised you haven't finished cleaning up yet. It will take some time to pin all those flowers on the car."

"Yes, I know. I've been fretting about it."

"We should get first prize this year, don't you agree, Papa?" Anna wiped a plate with her dishtowel. "I'm so excited!"

Papa studied her. "You always have enjoyed a parade."

Olive smiled. "Remember when Anna was four and won the grand prize riding on one of John Donhowe's Shetland ponies?"

Severt rolled his eyes. "Must we relive the memory every year?"

"Must have been her hair." Their father said the same thing every year, and every time Anna felt special.

Lula smiled at her youngest sister. "Olive was so proud. She washed your hair and brushed it until it shone and then let it fall free to your waist for the parade."

"I was jealous." Charlotte wrung out the dishcloth.

Grandmother Laurense shook her head and clucked, "Charity suffereth long, and is kind; charity envieth not; charity vaunteth not itself, is not puffed up." She quoted the verse from the Bible often, and if Anna did not understand each Norwegian word, she knew what it meant.

Charlotte wiped off the table. "Don't be concerned, Bestemor. I'm not jealous of my little sister anymore."

Anna did not remember either Charlotte's jealousy or winning the grand prize. Her favorite Fourth of July was the year she and twelve other girls representing the original states rode John Donhowe's ponies in the parade, following a float with little girls in white representing the forty-six states of the union. "Remember when I was a rider in the Living Union float?"

"I must say," Margretha said. "I do believe that was one of the most clever entries in the parade I've ever seen."

Anna respected her sophisticated, fashionable aunt's opinion. Margretha had lived for a year in Minneapolis studying art at the Institute, and she had many expensive books with photographs of important fine art by famous painters like Renoir. Anna often visited her grandparents and aunt across the street, hoping to find Margretha at her easel. Her aunt painted scenes of soft green landscapes and clouds of purples and pinks drifting across blue skies. She also painted delicate flowers on fine china. Though she appreciated her aunt's artistic talent, Anna privately preferred the strong vivid colors in Renoir's paintings to Margretha's watercolors.

While Severt, Peter, Lula, and Ida carried the tubs of flowers from the cellar, Papa took a chair from the kitchen and placed it outside in the shade for his mother.

Grandmother Laurense set her sewing basket on the lawn beside her and immediately began stitching needlework on a piece for a quilt. "Idleness is a source of evil," she said loudly in Norwegian. She peered at the car. "I liked the horse and buggy better than this loud machine."

"Progress, mother," Papa replied in English. He stood beside her with his hand on the back of her chair.

The old woman pursed her lips together tightly and narrowed her eyes, firmly piercing the bright red material with the needle and pulling it through the other side.

Severt helped secure a black lining as a foundation around the automobile and then watched his sisters and aunt pin on flowers as fast as they could.

"No American flags?" Peter asked.

"Not this year," Lula said. "The red, white, and blue would clash with the flowers."

Margretha shook her head. "It would not look right."

"It seems to me red, white, and blue are better suited for the Fourth of July than these flowers," Papa said.

"But Papa, this idea of Lula's is so original!" Ida took a handkerchief from her sleeve and wiped her brow.

"Do as you please." Peter shrugged. "I hope the judges agree."

"You are always talking about being progressive, father." Severt laughed. "Perhaps you should have stressed the importance of being patriotic as well."

"Who is to say we aren't patriotic?" Charlotte threw a flower at her brother. "We're riding in the parade, aren't we?"

"Don't waste any flowers!" Lula's cheeks were flushed from the heat.

Severt picked the flower from the ground and threw it back.

Lula sighed as she stretched her back. "Oh, I so wish Ed could be here to see this!"

"Why don't you send him a photograph?" Margretha stood back and examined their work. She pointed to the front end of the car. "That spot looks a little bare."

Lula reached into the tub beside her. "It would be nice to have a picture to go along with my description."

"Perhaps you'll have a clipping from the newspaper," Ida said. "I would think either Gustav Amlund would photograph our car for the *Visergutten* or A.P. Olson would publish it in the *Story City Herald*."

"I wouldn't count on it." Severt tossed the hair back from his forehead. "They're more likely to choose a patriotic picture for the paper." He grinned at Peter, who smiled with a shrug.

"My, it's warm." Olive fanned her face with both hands.

"A glass of the lemonade from one of the park stands would be so refreshing about now," Anna said.

"The flowers look like they need refreshment of their own." Severt grimaced at the car adorned with drooping black and yellow flowers.

Lula stood back, shading her eyes with her hand to look up at the sky. "Heavens. We have to wait in line an hour before the parade even begins."

Charlotte winced. "Hopefully the judges focus on our unique idea and don't pay attention to the state of the flowers."

Lula, the designated driver for the family, drove the car in the parade. Charlotte and Anna sat in the back as they had the prior two years, proudly waving to the large crowds who still traveled by horse and buggy. As a member of the Ladies Quartet, Ida rode in the Donhowe and Charlson car with Jennie Donhowe, Nellie Charlson, and Cosette Henderson. The young women were dressed in white, and the automobile was decorated in the traditional red, white and blue, with a huge white sign advertising the men's clothing store above the back seat. The rest of the family joined the spectators that spilled from Story City's large shady park.

When the parade came to a halt at the west end of Main Street, the judges slowly walked down the street past each of the automobiles and then back again for a second look. The judges were all members of the Reception Committee of the Norwegian Pioneer Association. One owned the Butter Tub & Tank Factory, a second the butcher shop, and the third was a carpenter. The three men finally stopped and stood together away from the crowd. The owner of the factory did most of the talking, wiping his red sweat-streaked forehead with his handkerchief while the others nodded.

In the driver's seat, Lula alternately held her handkerchief against her moist forehead and dabbed it around her neck. Despite the wilted condition of the flowers, Anna and Charlotte assured her they would be awarded the seven dollar first prize in recognition of their originality.

"What's taking them so long?" Charlotte twisted to look down the street. "Look, there's Jack." She waved across the street at Melburne Donhowe, who preferred being called Jack. John Donhowe's son and Peter's nephew, Jack had recently begun walking Charlotte home from church on Sunday evenings after the service. He returned her wave with a warm smile.

"I hope they decide soon, or I will be as wilted as the flowers!" Anna let out an exaggerated sigh.

Finally, the judges walked to the Donhowe and Charlson automobile. When they handed May Charlson the blue ribbon, Lula's smile disappeared and her shoulders drooped.

"Papa expected first prize this year." Charlotte wrinkled her nose.

Anna nodded. His expression staid, their father stood nearby conversing with a group of city leaders, including his brother Martin, the mayor. Anna had heard her father explain once to Severt that it was never good to let your emotions show on your face, especially in business.

She watched her brother, leaning against the Donhowe and Charlson automobile, talking to Cosette and Ida. He clearly had not learned the lesson his father had tried to teach him. Anna wondered if Severt knew how apparent his feelings for Cosette were. The same could be said about Cosette's cousin, Walter Henderson, who stood beside Severt. Walter certainly did not hide his interest in Ida. He took every opportunity to walk her home from the Sunday evening church service and watched her at every social gathering. Ida acted graciously, as she did with everyone. If Anna hadn't eavesdropped at night, she would never imagine Walter did not particularly interest her sister.

"The heat was just too much for these flowers." Lula lifted her chin and smiled brightly as the judges turned and walked toward their car.

Handing the second prize ribbon and three dollars to Lula, the butcher said, "Clever idea, flowers. Would have had first prize if you'd added an American flag." He put his thumbs under his suspenders and lifted them off his belly.

"We should have listened to Papa," Lula said as the judges walked away.

"Why?" Charlotte asked. "We had the best and most original car." She reached forward to pat her older sister on the shoulder. "This is only proof that the judges have no appreciation for art."

"That's right! What do you expect from men who sell metal tubs and wood houses and butchered meat?" Anna thought her remark particularly clever.

Charlotte laughed.

"Shush, Anna. They could hear you." Lula turned and smiled at her younger sisters. "I wish you two had been the judges, but then again you would have been biased, wouldn't you?" Her smile fell as she looked at her father. "I just wish I had not disappointed Papa."

Charlotte waved at Jack. "Don't be sad, Lula. He will forget all about it when Ida sings her solo with the Ladies Quartet this afternoon."

Fieldwork

Joseph

*T*he tinkle of the bell on the barbershop door interrupted the talk about the Canadian reciprocity bill passed by the Senate.

Seated in the barber's chair, with a view of the door through the mirror, Joseph watched Martin Henderson step inside the shop.

Martin nodded. "You talking about that bill the Senate just passed?"

"We were." The barber continued snipping Joseph's hair.

"Crop prices are going to fall, that's for sure." Martin dropped into one of the chairs by the front window. The wood of the chair legs scraped across the floorboards as he leaned back and stretched out his legs.

"You're right about that," the barber said.

"I don't think we need to worry about prices," Joseph said. "The way I read it, the bill is limited. Given the fact it doesn't include coal and logs and lumber, I think it's highly likely the Canadians will reject the agreement."

"You have a point there," Martin said. "Hope you're right. I don't know how a farmer like me can make a living if we let the Canadians come in here with cheap prices."

"It's just not right," the barber said.

"Those politicians in Washington just don't care about the farmer." Martin shook his head.

"Cummins does." The barber pointed his scissor at the newspaper stand.

"I agree," Joseph said. "We have a good man with Senator Cummins. The trouble is, he and the other insurgents can't win. The real problem is the rift in the Republican Party. Half the Republicans voted with the Democrats. I wasn't surprised to see every Republican from the east voted for the bill. Ever since Taft was elected, he's been pushing legislation through Congress to please the conservatives in the east. By turning his back on the progressives, the president has given rise to the insurgency. The country is divided, and Taft is to blame."

"I don't like the man myself," Martin said. "Don't trust him, neither. All he seems to do is travel around getting entertained. Seems like he's just out for his own pleasure instead of looking out for what's good for the rest of us."

"I thought he was a Roosevelt man, but he sure didn't keep his promises." The barber shook his head.

"Got the vote and then changed his color," Martin said. "If I would've known what he was going to do, I never would've voted for him. I'm sure not voting for him next election, I'll tell you that. We need Roosevelt back, that's what I think."

In the mirror, Joseph watched Martin cleaning his fingernails with a pocket knife. He suspected the man rarely used a nail scissors, if he owned one at all. "In the next election, there's a good chance the country will fall into the hands of the Democrats."

"I hope you're wrong," the barber said.

"So do I, but I'm afraid that's where we're heading. And if that's the case, the Democrats will push through the income tax they've been endorsing." The hair rose on the back of Joseph's neck as the barber combed it up for the sharply snapping steel blades of the shears. He did not like the sensation.

"Better to have an income tax than a federal tax on land," Martin said. He sheathed his knife and returned it to his back pocket. "By the way," he caught Joseph's eye in the mirror, "I saw your son yesterday in Ames."

"Don't mean to argue with you, Martin, but it could not have been Severt. He's out working in the fields this week." The fans in the room did no more than circulate the hot, humid August air. Constrained beneath the black fabric wrapped around him, Joseph could not reach up to wipe the sweat sliding down his face.

The barber set the shears down and wiped Joseph's neck with a cloth. "Must have mistaken him with someone else."

Shrugging, Martin said, "No mistake about it. It was Severt, all right."

"Nothing wrong with your eyesight, is there?" The barber laughed. "Got dust in your eyes from working in the fields?"

"No doubt about it. Saw him plain as day, walking down the street with some other young man round about his age. Had my son Walter with me, and he called hello to the two of them. Said he knew the other young man." Shrugging, Martin added with a smirk, "If Severt was supposed to be working, it might explain why he seemed in such a hurry to move on."

The barber inspected Joseph's well-trimmed mustache, snipping selectively. "Severt must have had some business in Ames. He's a fine young man, no doubt about it. Not the kind to shirk his responsibilities."

Joseph knew Severt had no business in Ames this week. One of Joseph's tenants was threshing wheat and counted on Severt as an extra hand. Complaining about the heat and hard labor, Severt had tried to persuade his father that he would get better experience working in the bank, but Joseph insisted he help out on the farm.

Martin leaned forward, rested his elbow on his knee, and rubbed his chin. "Maybe that college education is putting ideas into his head. Just a couple of years there, and my Walter's more headstrong than he ever was. Thinks he knows it all and doesn't have to listen to nobody. Makes me wonder what they're teaching in them schools. Disrespect, seems to me."

"Taft's got plenty of schooling, him being a lawyer," the barber said. "Doesn't think like the rest of us, that's for sure."

Joseph took advantage of the turn in conversation from Severt. "I don't believe education is the problem with the Republican Party."

Angry and disappointed, Joseph wanted to confront his son at once. He wanted to believe there was some explanation to justify why Severt would have gone to Ames during the week, but suspected his son more likely had not lived up to his responsibilities.

***

That evening while the girls cleaned up after supper, Joseph waited in the living room. Eventually he heard the motor of the car.

The kitchen screen door banged shut, and the girls greeted their brother.

"I hope you left enough for me. I'm famished!"

"Go clean up now, and we'll get some supper ready for you."

Joseph called out as his son passed by the living room door, "Evening, Severt."

Severt paused. "Evening, Papa." He continued toward the stairs.

Standing, Joseph said, "I would like a word with you."

Severt stopped and turned, hesitating as his eyes met his father's. "I need to clean up. I'll be down shortly."

"There is a matter I have been waiting to discuss with you." Stepping forward, Joseph clenched his teeth and motioned to the parlor. "I do not wish to wait any longer."

Severt forced a lighthearted smile and looked away. "In the parlor? My clothes are filthy."

Joseph breathed deeply to control the anger that twisted in his chest. "Do not argue with me, Severt."

Severt dropped his hand from the stairway railing and followed his father.

Joseph slid the parlor door shut. He watched his son walk across the room and pause before the divan. Severt slowly turned but did not take a seat. Joseph strode toward the center of the room and faced his son.

"Threshing get done this week?"

"Not quite. They should finish up tomorrow." Severt shifted his weight from one leg to the other as he brushed at a stain on his sleeve.

"Think you should go back and help them finish?

Severt glanced up. "They said they could manage fine without me."

"Work hard this week, Severt?"

Severt wiped his brow. "It certainly was hot. Hottest week of the year. They say it got over 100 degrees nearly every day."

"Too hot for threshing?"

Severt looked down as he itched his nose. "Never sweat so much in my life."

He should be sweating, Joseph thought. "Is there something you would like to tell me?"

Severt bit his lip. Frowning, he shook his head. "No." He scanned the room, as though searching for an escape or an excuse.

"There is nothing I should know about this week?" Joseph's eyes narrowed. He prided himself on his own honesty and the honesty of his children. His son's evasion was no better than an outright lie.

Severt looked up. "This week?"

Across the room, the pendulum of the grandfather clock swung, sounding each passing second while Joseph stared at his son.

"I saw Martin Henderson at the barbershop today."

The blood rose in Severt's face, and he looked away.

"Seems he saw you in Ames Wednesday." Joseph paused. "Did the renter send you to Ames on an errand, Severt?"

Severt did not look up as he shook his head.

"Didn't think so. They were counting on you as an extra hand. You had a responsibility. In this family, you should understand what responsibility means."

Severt remained silent, his head down.

"Look me in the eye, Severt." Joseph's teeth ground together between his jaws.

Severt looked up. "I apologize, Papa. It will not happen again."

"No, it will not." Joseph's voice was controlled but hard. "Your actions are inexcusable."

Severt hung his head.

"What is your explanation?"

"The heat was unbearable."

"Too hot for the others?"

"No, but they're farmers." Severt winced as he shrugged. "They're accustomed to working in the heat."

"Severt." Joseph's eyes narrowed. "You think farmers like the heat any more than you do? They have work to do, and they do it. Without complaint. Your grandfather had no time for complaining, not from his sons or his hired hands. He expected us to get the job done. I expected as much from my son. I would not have believed you could act so irresponsibly."

The corners of Severt's mouth twitched as he stared at the floor.

"How many days were you gone?"

Severt looked up quickly. "Just the one. I worked hard the rest of the week."

"What reason did you give them for leaving?"

Severt cleared his throat and rubbed the outside corner of his eye. "Said you had some business that needed to be taken care of."

"A lie." Taut with tension, the muscles in Joseph's neck resisted as he shook his head. "I assured them you would be there to help. They relied upon us, and you let them down. You have disgraced me. Is this the way a son of mine behaves?"

Severt's eyes briefly met his father's as he shook his head.

"I could not be more disappointed in you, Severt."

"I'm sorry, Papa." Severt looked up. "It won't happen again."

"No, it will not. And tomorrow you will return to the field to fulfill your responsibility."

"But Papa."

"Do you dare argue with me?"

"No, Papa." Severt winced. "I was only going to mention we have tickets for Chautauqua. The opening is tomorrow."

Joseph's face was like flint. "Enough. I do not want to hear another word from you, Severt. This conversation has ended." He strode to the door and slid it open, restraining a brief urge to slam it into the wall. "You may go and clean up now. I hope you spend some time thinking about what you have done. And tomorrow, I hope you work hard to make up for some of the harm you have caused."

Chautauqua

Anna

*T*he family returned late Saturday evening to a dark, silent house. Anna ran upstairs to find Severt's bedroom door closed, and he did not respond to her whisper, "Are you awake?" Disappointed, his sisters had hoped he would wait up to hear about the opening Chautauqua program he had missed.

Severt did not join the family for breakfast the following morning and still had not left his room when the first bell rang for church. During the last verse of the opening hymn, Charlotte nudged Anna, pointing her head to the back of the sanctuary. A few heads turned as Severt slid into an empty space on the end of the pew closest to the door. Anna saw her father glance back. Papa was not pleased.

After the sisters changed from their church clothes, they gathered in the kitchen to prepare the picnic dinner for the afternoon in Ames. Punctuating their chatter, chicken spit and snapped in the fry pan, and knives chopped against wood cutting boards.

"Do you think Severt's taken ill?" Anna carefully slid the shell from a hard-boiled egg. "He left the church right after the benediction, and he didn't wait for Cosette. He always walks her home from church."

"He didn't look that sick to me." Charlotte scraped the potato from her cutting board into the bowl beside her.

"He's had an exhausting week," Ida said. "I'm sure he's just resting up for the afternoon in Ames."

Charlotte glanced up from her cutting board. "Well, look who's here. Did you hear us talking about you?"

Without acknowledgment, their brother passed through the kitchen.

"Severt?" Olive asked. "Could I fix you a bite to eat? You must be famished. You missed breakfast, and we won't be eating again for several hours."

Severt shrugged and let the screen door bang shut behind him.

Ida resumed chopping celery. "He certainly is not himself."

"Isn't that the truth." Charlotte took a boiled potato from the pot. "It certainly wasn't like him to go back to work on Saturday. Severt despises working in the fields. Not only that, but to miss the opening of Chautauqua? The heat must have addled his brain."

"Listen to you talk about your brother," Lula laughed. "He missed quite a concert last night. Poor boy."

"Poor boy?" Charlotte diced the potato. "There's nothing wrong with Severt working hard for a change. No doubt that's what Papa would say."

"We should be proud of Severt for putting aside his own pleasure to help the renters." Olive turned a chicken leg over in the frying pan. "I think this chicken will be good."

"It smells fabulous!" Anna licked her lips. "I wish we could have some right now. I'm hungry!"

"Didn't I tell you to eat more at breakfast?" Olive reminded her.

Ida wiped her hands on her apron. "I do think it's a shame Severt missed the opening programs yesterday. It wasn't the same without him." She smiled. "I know Cosette was disappointed."

"I don't know what she sees in him. Perhaps the heat has addled her brain as well."

"Charlotte!" Ida shook her head.

"Severt would have appreciated the Trombone Quartet," Lula said. "Their rendering of Verdi's *Rigoletto* was faultless."

"And the Chicago Glee Club was simply splendid." Ida sighed. "Their voices blended perfectly. They took my breath away."

Charlotte smirked. "It seemed you enjoyed watching them as much as listening to them. I heard you whisper to Cosette how good-looking you thought the first tenor was!"

Ida blushed. "He was a fine looking man."

"What was so special about him?" Anna asked. "Mr. Dixon's impersonations were much more entertaining. And did you see the picture of the Indian in eagle feathers on the program for Wednesday? Shungopavi. Did I say that correctly?" She pushed her chair back and sprang out. "I'd rather watch an impersonator or an Indian magician than some ordinary white men singing or blowing on trombones. I can always hear Severt play the cornet."

"Spoken like a thirteen-year-old," Lula smiled. "It won't be long before you start finding tenors in tuxedos more interesting than Indians in feathers."

Charlotte shrugged. "Then again, who can tell? Perhaps Ida will find the Indian just as attractive as the Glee Club tenor."

"Charlotte!" Ida laughed. "You are scandalous!"

"Hello!" Cosette entered the house carrying a wrapped platter, which she set on the table. "I hope you have room for these cookies my mother sent. Tell me. What is so scandalous?"

"How kind of your mother," Olive said. "I've baked an apple pie, and Margretha is bringing a cake as well, so there will be plenty of dessert."

"Good!" Anna lifted the cloth to look at the cookies. "I'd love to taste one right now!"

"Such a sweet tooth you have. You have to wait until after dinner, so wrap that back up now."

"Ida is going to marry an Indian," Charlotte announced.

"An Indian!" Cosette affected an expression of alarm. "That certainly is scandalous!"

"If not an Indian, perhaps the tenor in the Glee Club," Charlotte said.

"The tenor I can understand. So handsome! And what a voice!" Cosette grinned at Ida. "I don't believe a native would be the proper match for you."

"Could you imagine what Papa would say?" Ida asked.

"Papa would never allow it." Anna shook her head insistently.

"It would cause a family uproar," Charlotte said.

Anna thought of her grandmother. "Bestemor says Indians are heathens."

"She would be beside herself if one of us married someone from another synod," Charlotte agreed.

"Enough of this silly talk." Ida turned to Cosette. "Did you see Severt on your way in?"

"No. Where is he? I missed him this morning."

"He went outside a bit ago. He didn't say, but my guess is he's working on the car." Ida called out the screen door, "Severt! Cosette is here!"

"Tell her to come out here," Severt yelled.

"Beware!" Charlotte untied her apron and lifted it over her head. "He's beginning to order you around as much as he does us!"

"He's treating her like family." Ida grinned at Cosette.

"Good!" Anna said. "Perhaps we'll get some relief from his tyranny!"

Cosette laughed as she opened the screen door. "But you've forgotten, Anna. I can escape him and run home at any moment!"

"If you're looking for an escape, you seem to be running the wrong direction." Charlotte lifted the picnic basket and placed it on the table.

"I hope she raises his spirits," Anna said. "I would tell him some jokes, but the way he's been acting, I don't think he'd crack a smile."

"If anyone could make Severt smile, it would be Cosette," Ida said.

***

They completed the trip to Ames without delay for punctures in the tires or car trouble of any kind. Beneath the cloudless blue sky, the fields of green cornstalks and yellow oats swayed, and in some stretches the air was sweet with clover.

Once they arrived at the park, the family selected a shaded spot for their picnic. Papa and Peter spotted one of Peter's brothers, and while they waited for the women and girls to set out the picnic lunch they walked over to greet him. Uncharacteristically, Severt did not follow them, but stood silently by himself, leaning against the trunk of a large oak tree.

"One more bite." Seated with her niece on a blanket spread across the grass, Anna waved a spoonful of peas at Laurentia's mouth. She laughed when the little girl wrinkled her nose and shook her head. "I don't blame you! These peas do not look in the least bit appetizing!"

Olive lifted the potato salad bowl out of the picnic basket. "Anna! Don't you give her any ideas, now. I don't want Laurentia to be a fussy eater like you."

Margretha set the coolers of lemonade and milk on a blanket. "I should say not."

"Look over there," Cosette pointed with her chin. "My cousin Walter is heading this way."

Severt straightened and stepped away from the tree.

"Severt! Where are you going?" Lula asked.

"The car."

"But we are nearly ready to eat!"

"I'll only be a few minutes. I need to check the oil."

Cosette nudged Ida. "Without Severt here, Walter can focus all his attention on you."

Ida picked up a blanket. "Charlotte, come help me spread this out."

"Well hello, ladies." Walter bent down and tickled Laurentia's nose. "Aren't you a pretty girl!"

The little girl laughed and batted his hand.

Crouching, Walter focused on Anna. "And how are you enjoying this year's Chautauqua, young lady?"

Anna beamed at the attention. "Mr. Dixon is my favorite so far. Did you see him? But the best, I think, will be Shungopavi."

Walter nodded with a wink. "You and I think alike. The dull orators don't hold my interest. I'm not much for musical programs, either. Unless, of course, it's a group of pretty ladies singing." He winked again.

Standing, his eyes swung slowly from one woman to the next until fixing on Ida. "I don't believe there is a finer group of women in attendance today."

Cosette laughed and shook her head. "Flattery will get you nowhere."

The corners of Margretha's mouth tightened.

Walter shrugged. "I only speak the truth." He scanned the park. "Where did Severt run off to?"

"The car."

"I'm beginning to think he's avoiding me."

"Now, Walter," Cosette said, "why would he want to do that?"

Walter's smile clouded. "Don't know. But it is the second time in one week. Saw him here in Ames last week, and he walked on by with hardly a hello."

"It couldn't have been Severt," Ida said. "He was threshing with one of Papa's renters south of Story City." The blanket billowed as she and Charlotte shook it before spreading it out beneath the tree.

Walter looked in the direction Severt had gone. "Threshing, huh? Not on Wednesday, he wasn't."

Ida shook her head, like a bird shaking off the rain. "It couldn't have been Severt."

Walter shrugged, smirking. "If you ask me, I think your brother took himself a break from work and didn't happen to mention it to the family."

"I would certainly hope not." Seated on a blanket, Margretha stacked blue enameled cups and saucers beside the coolers.

"Severt wouldn't do such a thing." Olive kneeled down and wiped Laurentia's mouth with a napkin. "All done, little girl?"

Cosette knelt to help Ida smooth the blanket on the ground. "Did you all know Walter won a major judging contest this year?"

"Is that right?" Ida smiled politely.

Chest out, Walter leaned back on his heels with his legs spread, hands on his hips with his thumbs hooked inside his belt. "Not just any contest, either, but the National Collegiate Stock Judging contest. Got first place judging horses, cattle, hogs, and sheep."

"That is quite an accomplishment," Olive said. "I'm sure your family is very proud. Well, here come Father and Peter. I think we're ready to eat."

"I'll leave you to your picnic." Walter nodded to the group. "Ida, it is always a pleasure seeing you."

Ida dropped her smile as soon as Walter turned away.

Cosette jumped up. "I'll go fetch Severt."

Lula passed out plates, and Margretha poured water, lemonade, and milk while they waited for Cosette and Severt to return. After they were all settled on the blankets, they passed around the chicken, beef roast, potato salad, beets, fruit salad, bread, butter, and pickles.

"Severt, Walter told us he saw you in Ames on Wednesday. Isn't that ridiculous?" Anna asked.

Severt stared at the ground and straightened the knot of his tie.

"Weren't you threshing all week for one of the renters south of town?" Peter bit into a pickle.

Severt did not look at his brother-in-law. "I was."

"I thought so."

"So Walter was mistaken." Ida smiled.

Severt coughed. "Actually, I was in Ames on Wednesday."

"You were?" Anna looked from her brother to her father. Papa stared at Severt, his expression stern.

"You weren't working?"

"I was working. But I didn't work that one day."

"Why not?"

"It was too hot."

"Well!" Margretha arched her neck.

"It definitely was a scorcher this week," Peter said. "I wouldn't have wanted to be out working in the fields either."

"Odd. You never said anything," Lula said.

Charlotte raised her eyebrows. "And we were feeling so sorry for you."

"I went back on Saturday." Severt wiped his forehead.

"So that is why!" Charlotte's eyes danced. "I knew you wouldn't work an extra day for nothing."

"Severt was taking care of his responsibility." Papa did not smile, his face hard. "As you would expect him to. Isn't that right, son?"

"Yes, Papa."

Church Schools

Joseph

*T*he following Friday, the president of the United Norwegian Church Seminary arrived in Story City. Wanting to extend a personal welcome to the distinguished clergyman, Joseph stopped by St. Petri Lutheran Church that afternoon and found Reverend Marcus O. Böckman conversing with Vangsnes in the pastor's office.

"We're pleased to have you with us this weekend, Reverend Böckman," Joseph said. "Quite an honor for us here in Story City."

"Pleased to be here." Grey-haired with a bushy goatee and small wire spectacles, the seminary president had a firm handshake and sonorous bass voice.

Pastor Vangsnes stepped forward. "Joseph Marvick is one of the leaders of our community and a strong supporter of the church. You also would be interested to know he has two daughters enrolled at St. Olaf."

"Very good. A fine school of our church." Reverend Böckman nodded. "I taught theology at the seminary there."

"Yes, I was aware of that."

"Do you have any sons?"

"One."

"He will attend St. Olaf as well?"

"He is studying at Cornell."

The seminary president's spectacles focused the intensity of his stare. "He does not attend one of our church schools?"

"No. He chose Cornell for their business program."

"Ah." Böckman lifted his brows. "The study of business and profit-making. I suggest there is more to an education than that, but I shall not expound upon the matter at this time. You shall hear what I have to say on the subject on Sunday."

Proud his son attended college, Joseph had never questioned Severt's choice of Cornell. "You will have my undivided attention. My son's education is of the utmost importance to me."

"As it should be."

"Reverend Böckman was recently in Sisseton," Pastor Vangsnes said.

Joseph nodded. "So I heard. I understand you met my brother Andrew. I trust you had a good visit there?"

"Yes, indeed. It is good to see the strong Norwegian Lutheran foundation that has been established in that territory. Your brother is to be commended for his leadership. The good news is that church membership rolls are increasing steadily there as the community expands." He stroked his thick mustache. "Their challenge is raising sufficient funds for their building needs."

"Ah, yes," Vangsnes agreed. "The needs are great. And not all members are as generous as this faithful man standing here."

"We give as we have been given." And as we are asked, Joseph thought. In addition to contributing a healthy sum to the weekly collection plate, he also responded generously when Vangsnes called upon him to support capital projects and special benevolence offerings. Joseph respected the necessity to raise money to carry out the work of the church, and, as one of the largest givers in the congregation, if not the largest, he fulfilled his responsibility. Through his own resourcefulness, he earned a good living. God helped those who helped themselves, and he gave his share back in return.

The seminary president nodded. "It is unfortunate indeed that so few follow your example. They are more interested in serving themselves than serving God. They do not share of their possessions, and they raise selfish, spoiled children. This indeed is a great sin. The future of both the church and our country depend upon these children, and there is great need to be concerned. But again, I will say no more, as this is the subject of the sermon I will deliver." He adjusted his spectacles.

On Sunday, the three Norwegian Lutheran churches held a joint service in a large tent in the park. Following the opening liturgy and scripture readings, the visiting seminary president rose from his chair. Each step slow and heavy, he crossed the wood floor of the speakers' platform, his black robe swaying like a pendulum. Gripping the edges of the pulpit, he stood silently for several seconds, sternly contemplating the assembled crowd.

"Greetings." Reverend Böckman's resonant voice rumbled loud for the old and those at the back of the crowd to hear. "Grace, mercy, and peace to you, in Jesus Christ our Lord. Today, as president of the United Church Seminary and a pastor of the Norwegian Lutheran Synod, of which you fine people are faithful members, I preach a message regarding the education of our children and the obligations of the parents among you.

"All you who are confirmed members have learned your catechism and know from memory the fourth commandment, 'Thou shalt honor thy father and thy mother' and what it means. In the Large Catechism, Martin Luther, the great founder of our church, exhorts us to preach to the parents also, as to their obligations as father and mother as it relates to this commandment. It is a strict command of God, to train children to honor and praise him, and to be heeded by every parent. I say to you, when the time comes for you to stand before God, every parent will be called to strictly account as to how you have obeyed this commandment, and you will be punished if you choose to ignore it."

Joseph did not fear punishment. He had raised his children in the church as he had been raised. The only criticism directed at him by Vangsnes was when he refused to have his youngest girls attend Norsk Skole. They had memorized the catechism; Charlotte was confirmed, and Anna would be shortly. Joseph had fulfilled his obligation as a parent, and no one could argue he had broken any commandment by insisting his children speak English rather than Norwegian. He had, in fact, led the way for change, as confirmation at St. Petri was now in taught in English.

"As in Martin Luther's time, today there is great need to be seriously concerned about the young. We must not think only how we may amass money and possessions for them."

If none of us amassed money, Joseph thought, there would be no large contributors to support the church.

"No. It is our duty as parents to raise our children, above all things, in the fear and knowledge of God, and have them learn and study according to the talents they were given, that they may be useful, well-educated citizens, chaste and domestic wives, who aid their government and the world however necessary. If you fail in this, you are doing deadly injury to yourself, and bring upon yourself sin and wrath, and earn a place in hell. Do not think you are saved if you are otherwise pious and holy? No. As Martin Luther says, we have only ourselves to blame for the problems in our homes and society, for the lack of discipline or peace in this world, which is the direct result of raising spoiled and disobedient children."

Anger flashed through Joseph as he thought of Severt's recent behavior. He had not raised his son to be spoiled, disobedient, or to lie. What had come over him?

"What, you ask, does Martin Luther admonish us to do? Is it enough to have our children attend Sunday school? Teach them their catechism? Does their education end when they are confirmed? I say not, and if Luther were before you today, he would most heartily agree that we are falling short of our obligations when we send our children to colleges and universities that have no church affiliations. Is it enough that our children study physics and mathematics, biology and chemistry, English and the romantic languages? Enough to study agriculture, education, law, science, or business?"

The seminary president briefly focused his gaze on Joseph, reminding him of their conversation the previous Friday. Sitting on his father's right, Severt failed to stifle a yawn.

"What is a liberal education without teaching them how to honor, serve, and praise God? I tell you, it is your duty to teach and educate your children, and Luther tells us that for those who are talented, it is your duty to have them instructed and trained in a liberal education. By this he does not mean a liberal education where there is no daily chapel and no study of religion. No, Luther would exhort us to send our children to a church college, where the liberal education they receive is a foundation for leadership and service in church and society. Our synod has fine colleges to this end—one in Northfield, Minnesota, where I served as professor of theology for four years, one in Minneapolis, Minnesota, and another in Decorah, Iowa. These colleges are dedicated to both faith and a liberal education. I personally know the presidents of these fine colleges. I know many of the distinguished professors. You are familiar with the colleges of which I speak. In fact, some members of your congregations have children enrolled in these fine institutions of liberal education." The bishop paused and nodded at Joseph.

Ida and Lula bent forward, looking past Severt to smile at their father. My daughters, Joseph thought, but not my son.

"Yes, I speak of St. Olaf College, Augsburg College, and Luther College. You may say the cost is too high. I ask you, how can the cost of education be too much? As Luther said, 'We must spare no diligence, time, or cost in teaching and educating our children.' I urge you. Send your sons to St. Olaf, Augsburg, or Luther. The professors are fine Christian men and women. Who can say what sentiments the professors espouse at other universities? Who can say what values the body of students hold? I say to you, send your sons to a church college, and they will learn the value of men, not machines. Feed not only their minds, but feed also their spirits and souls. Send your sons to a church college, and they will value life over profits, eternal life over material wealth."

Bowing his head, the bishop concluded in prayer.

Joseph had expected Böckman to use the pulpit to solicit financial contributions for the seminary. However, the seminary president also had incentive to promote the church colleges. Certainly the seminary depended upon those colleges to prepare men who would be future pastors. The seminary president's tacit agenda may have been to solicit financial support for the church colleges, but Böckman's message about the values taught in the church schools was persuasive and timely, given recent events. Joseph had not previously considered this aspect of college education and wondered what they taught at Cornell. It seemed Severt had forgotten what he had learned at home—the values of respect and responsibility. Perhaps the influence at Cornell was not what it should be. Perhaps this explained Severt's inexcusable behavior.

At home following the service, Joseph began the dinner conversation. "What did you think of the sermon today, Severt?"

His son looked up from his plate. "The message was a bit strong, but Bishop Böckman made some interesting points. I found it interesting that Luther expounded upon the parents' duties with respect to the fourth commandment. The bishop's intelligence seems superior, and he is quite a forceful speaker."

Charlotte laughed. "At times I thought he was about to jump out of the lectern!"

Grandmother Laurense stared sternly at her granddaughter. "Have we no respect for our churchmen?"

Charlotte took advantage of her grandmother's use of Norwegian and ignored the criticism.

Margretha cleared her throat.

Joseph continued before his sister could reprimand Charlotte. "The bishop makes a strong argument regarding the importance of a Christian environment for a liberal college education."

"I thought it was a bit exaggerated," Severt said.

"Exaggerated?" Margretha raised an eyebrow. "How can the importance of Christian values be exaggerated?"

"Naturally I do not disagree with the importance of Christian values." Severt confidently met his aunt's glare. "Or that our society depends upon them." He looked at his father. "I do, however, believe he overstated the dangers inherent in attending a college that is not affiliated with the Lutheran church."

Grandmother Laurense lifted her chin and quoted in Norwegian, "'Be sober, be watchful. Your adversary the devil prowls around like a roaring lion, seeking someone to devour.'"

"Surely you do not suggest the devil is more likely to be prowling at Iowa State or Cornell than St. Olaf?" Fighting a smile, Severt's eyes flickered and dimples appeared in his cheeks.

"Perhaps you should change your name to Daniel." Charlotte smiled slyly. "Perhaps it would save you from the mouth of the lions."

Anna laughed. "I can just imagine Severt dressed in Roman attire, surrounded by lions."

Lula choked on her water and lowered her face into her napkin.

Ida smiled. "I personally prefer the name Severt."

"This is not a laughing matter." Margretha's nose flared and chest expanded.

Grandmother Laurense's small dark eyes darted between her grandchildren. Grandfather Syvert took another bite of his dinner and chewed slowly, his long white beard bobbing.

Joseph ignored the others at the table, intent on his son. "There is something to be said for the Christian and moral influence of a Lutheran college."

"The founders of this nation had a point when they espoused the separation of church and state." Severt sat back. "There is a similar argument to be made regarding church and school."

"Surely you are not against church schools?" Lula asked.

"Certainly not. Cornell was founded by men of faith. I suggest only that a secular university not governed by a particular church offers an education for peoples of all religious faiths, Catholic and Protestant alike."

"Catholics?" Grandmother Laurense choked. "Catholics?"

"You would choose to attend a school where there is no Christian influence, then?" Margretha asked.

"I attend school to be educated in secular matters such as business, and I attend church to be educated in religious matters." Severt laughed. "And do not worry, Bestemor." He smiled at his grandmother. "I have no intention of converting to Catholicism."

Joseph set his knife and fork on his plate, the silver hard against the china. "I'm disappointed you did not hear the message this morning. I would have expected my children to place sufficient value on the importance of a Christian education at a good Lutheran school."

"But Papa." Anna leaned forward. "Both Lula and Ida go to St. Olaf. Our family is doing exactly what Reverend Böckman said we should in his sermon today."

"Not entirely, Anna. My daughters do indeed attend such a school. However, my son does not."

"I'm attending Cornell for business. Besides, they have regular chapel services." Severt shrugged. "St. Olaf doesn't offer a business program."

"You can learn what you need to know about business from me and from experience working at the bank. A church school would instill the values of respect and responsibility."

"But you have already instilled those values in all of us," Severt said.

"I had thought so as well, Severt." Joseph smoothed the coarse hairs of his mustache. "However, I might remind you of the incident last week. You acted in a most disrespectful and irresponsible manner." He did not add that he had acted like a spoiled child.

Severt colored and stared at his plate.

"Not only that, but you were disobedient and dishonest." Joseph felt the color rise in his own face as the anger of that day returned. "I had expected more of my son."

Severt did not look up.

"It seems a church school could teach you commitment to family, employer, community, and, not least of all, your church."

Severt took a sip of water and cleared his throat. "Father, Cornell offers an excellent education and certainly has a foundation of Christian values."

"Cornell is not a Lutheran school. Do you understand?"

Severt frowned.

Margretha sat straight, a piece of bread in one hand, the butter knife in the other, her eyes switching between Joseph and Severt like a cat's tail. Grandmother Laurense solemnly shook her head, clucking. Hard of hearing in his right ear, Grandfather Syvert gravely nodded at Joseph before cocking his head toward his grandson. His hands shaking, the old man gripped his knife and fork precariously over his plate. Around the table, the girls watched, silent and still, while the grandfather clock in the outer hallway counted the seconds.

"Severt?" Joseph's voice was unyielding.

Severt cleared his throat. "It is true that Cornell was not founded by a Norwegian Lutheran. But it was founded by Presbyterians. And I believe it is noteworthy that I regularly attend the morning chapel services in Mt. Vernon and take my religious upbringing seriously."

Joseph clenched his teeth and breathed in deeply. He would not lose his temper over his son's obstinacy. "Cornell may have been founded by church men, but they evidently have not emphasized responsible and moral behavior. It would not hurt you to go to St. Olaf."

Severt leaned back in his own chair, serious, his normally confident, light-hearted expression displaced. "The students and faculty I have become acquainted with at Cornell do not lack moral fiber or Christian values." Severt's voice cracked. "Surely you do not suggest this?"

"I do not question your associates, Severt. However, after the incident last week and in consideration of the message today, I have concluded my son should attend St. Olaf College." Joseph picked up his fork and knife.

"Papa." Severt sat forward, grabbing the edge of the table. "You know how satisfied I am with the program at Cornell!"

Margretha cleared her throat. "Your father has spoken, Severt."

Severt shook his head. "This is so sudden. You've expressed only approval and support of my decision to attend Cornell." He flipped the hair back on his forehead.

Grandfather Syvert's voice was low and solid. "A son does not question the will of his father, Severt," he said in Norwegian.

Clouded, Severt turned from his grandfather to his father.

"I have decided, Severt. You will transfer to St. Olaf this fall." His son's arguments had only solidified Joseph's decision. Severt did not appreciate the privilege of a college education, which his father's finances made possible. He also did not appreciate his good fortune of a position waiting for him as cashier at the bank or realize his father would know how best to prepare him for that position.

Severt coughed. "I would like to discuss this further before a final decision is made."

Grandmother Laurense lifted her chin and quoted in Norwegian, "'A wise son heeds his father's instruction, but a scoffer does not listen to rebuke.'"

"There will be no further discussion of this matter."

Severt shrunk in his chair.

Joseph began to cut his roast beef.

Gradually, the rest of the family resumed eating, scattering the silence with the gentle chink of silver against china. Severt was the last to take a bite, and he ate slowly, eyes fixed on his plate.

The lace curtains billowed with the breeze. Outside, a crow cawed.

Ida's Chosen
Joseph

As the ground thawed and the elm trees began to leaf out in the spring of 1913, Joseph finalized plans and negotiated contracts for a new two-story building on the west end of Main Street, forming a new block across the street from the current site of the Story City National Bank. In addition to the bank, construction was also planned or underway in Story City for an old people's home, auditorium, hotel, creamery, and quite a number of homes. Contractors in the area had more work than they could manage and were unwilling to discount their rates. The project would cost somewhat more than Joseph's initial estimate, but he had gone with the men he knew had the best reputations for quality and dependable work. Joseph did not complain about the increasing labor and material costs. The growth in the local economy benefited business, as reflected in the increased profits at the bank.

The *Story City Herald* published an article on construction projects planned for the year and highlighted the new bank building. The editor chose to print the bank drawings Joseph provided, including both front and side views. Good for business, the publicity pleased Joseph.

He folded the paper and checked his pocket watch. The train was due in fifteen minutes. Ida had written that she and Severt would be home for the weekend, and one of Severt's roommates, Oscar Locken, would accompany them. Joseph recalled little about Oscar other than he was a tall, young man of few words and Severt liked him.

Throughout the dinner conversation the previous evening, Joseph's two youngest daughters had peppered Lula with questions.

"What is Oscar like?" Anna quizzed.

"Tall and dark. He and Ida make such a handsome couple." Lula smiled.

"Do you like him?" Charlotte asked.

Lula nodded. "I do. Very much."

"Does Ed know him?" Anna adored Lula's fiancé.

"He does. He likes him very much as well."

"Where is Oscar's family from?" Joseph asked.

"Minnesota."

"Does he absolutely adore Ida?" Anna asked.

"Oh, but of course. Doesn't everyone?"

Anna nodded emphatically.

"Do you think Ida is in love with Oscar?" Charlotte quizzed.

Lula raised her brows. "Now that is a question Ida must answer herself."

Charlotte grinned. "Aha. You don't fool me. I know she tells you everything. She is in love with him, isn't she?"

"Now, now." The older sister laughed. "It wouldn't do to betray her confidences, would it?"

Charlotte nudged Anna. "I'll tell you what I think. Lula can't tell us, but I think Oscar is coming to ask Papa's permission to marry Ida, just like when Ed came here in January to ask to marry Lula."

Joseph wondered if that was the intent of the visit. He should have paid more attention to this Oscar. But it mattered little. Over the coming days, he would get a sense of the young man's character and could inquire as to his family.

Joseph buttoned his overcoat and reached for his hat, fitting it on his head until it felt right. He then lifted the umbrella from the basket beneath the coat rack and stepped out of his office.

"Are you gone for the day, then?" asked Clara Tokheim, the bank assistant.

Joseph nodded at the young woman who sat at the desk outside his office. "Yes." He pointed the umbrella at his office. "The article the *Herald* did on the bank was quite good. I'd like you to cut it out and file it for me."

"Yes, Mr. Marvick." Clara straightened the pile of papers before her. "Will you be in next week, or will you be traveling?"

"No travel plans next week." He tipped his head to her. "I'll be in on Monday," he said, and stepped into the afternoon sun. The dark rain clouds had blown east, but the remains of the midday downpour pooled in the low spots of the road.

One could hope for sufficient rain for the crops but not so much that it would delay the bank construction. Next week, Joseph would have Lula drive him to check on the farms he owned south of town. One of the hired hands had been into the bank the other day and mentioned there was quite a bit of standing water in the northeast corner of one of the fields. They'd had trouble there before. Perhaps some additional drain tile would be necessary.

As he headed north on Grand Avenue, tapping the umbrella on the gravel with each step, Joseph attempted to recall whether he had seen Oscar Locken at any of the St. Olaf band concerts that winter. Ida had toured with the band as a soloist, and Joseph had attended the concerts in Northfield, St. James, and Austin. He shook his head. He did not remember. His focus had been on Ida's success. The St. James concert had a large house, and a crowd of 1,400 turned out in Austin. Joseph had saved the photograph Severt took of Ida in her new winter hat and coat standing before a wall-sized promotional billboard with the headline, "Miss Ida Marvick, soprano soloist." Joseph had also saved the news clippings, which were all fine write-ups, complimenting the band, Ida, and Professor Christiansen.

F. Melius Christiansen was gaining quite a reputation as a conductor. He strove for excellence, and Joseph supported the professor's controversial decision to raise the standard for the St. Olaf Choir and invite only those with the best voices to sing. It would be interesting to see how the choir would be received during their summer tour in Norway. The tour would be an excellent experience for Ida, and Joseph had not only pledged a significant amount of money to make it possible, but also made plans to accompany the choir on the trip. Some choir members complained about the $50 cost for each person, and while Joseph and the other benefactors understood this was quite a sum for some families, they determined the amount was well worth the opportunity to sing in the land of their ancestors and before the King of Norway. Joseph looked forward to sitting in the audience while his daughter, so poised on stage, charmed the Norwegians with her beautiful voice. God had blessed her with the talent to sing. God had blessed him with such a lovely and talented daughter.

Joseph arrived home to find Charlotte and Anna practicing duets on the piano.

Anna turned her head toward him as he entered the living room but continued to play. "Hello, Papa."

"The music sounds good, girls." Joseph pulled out his pocket watch. The others would arrive shortly. There would not be time to attend to other matters. He took a seat and leaned back, observing his youngest daughters seated together on the piano bench. Both were slender, their backs straight. Anna was as tall as Charlotte, he noted. They were playing a piece he particularly liked. He did not recall the composer and would have to ask them when they finished the piece.

"They should be here any moment now!" Anna twisted around toward her father.

The music halted after several incorrect notes sounded.

"Anna, pay attention!" Charlotte jabbed her elbow into her sister's ribs.

"Gracious! I lost my place." Anna shook her hands.

They continued to play, without noticeable error, until they heard the car motor.

Leaping from the piano bench, Anna ran to the window and drew aside the lace curtains. "They're here!"

"Anna, they'll see you." Charlotte stood back.

Joseph suspected Anna did not care if they saw her and knew Charlotte wanted to look despite the fact she was seventeen.

"And here they come." Anna continued to peer out between the curtains.

Joseph stood, adjusted his tie and straightened his jacket.

"Oh, Charlotte," Anna reported. "Ida's beau is most decidedly a good looker!"

Joseph stood behind Anna and Charlotte in the hall as Lula ushered Ida and Oscar in the front door.

Oscar stood taller than Joseph, a couple inches over six feet, with broad shoulders. His long, dark gray Oxford wool overcoat was well-cut, his leather shoes worn but polished to a fine shine, his thick dark hair neatly trimmed, and face clean shaven.

Severt closed the door. "Oscar, old boy. Let me take your hat and coat." Smaller in stature and pale, Severt appeared somewhat frail in contrast to his roommate. Joseph wondered if his son was not feeling well.

Oscar removed his hat and coat and handed them to Severt. "Thank you." Standing at full height, he smoothed his thick dark hair into place with one hand and turned to face the others in the hall.

Joseph met the younger man's serious brown eyes.

Ida stepped between them and gestured to Oscar, "Papa, you remember Oscar, don't you?"

Joseph extended his hand to the young man, who did not look familiar. "Oscar."

"Mr. Marvick." Oscar's firm grip indicated self-assurance.

While the young women prepared supper, the men conversed in the parlor. Joseph noted Ida's soft smile for Oscar before she left for the kitchen, and he watched the young man's gaze follow her to the door. He focused on Oscar, who sat straight yet relaxed on the blue loveseat, wearing a single-breasted gray suit and silk necktie with a reasonably fashionable print.

"I say, it's good to finally be home!" Severt flipped the hair back on his forehead.

"Have you been to the hotel?" Joseph asked.

Severt nodded. "Lula stopped by the Nelson House after meeting us at the station so Oscar could secure his room."

"Did you find the accommodations satisfactory?" Joseph asked.

"Most certainly," Oscar nodded.

"Ma Nelson does a good business. I often recommend the hotel to business associates. They tell me the proprietors are hospitable and the rooms are clean." Joseph smoothed the edges of his mustache.

"Story City seems to be a very progressive town." Oscar commented. "Ida tells me the hotel has had both steam heat and electric lights for several years."

"We're quite proud of our town. The population is well over 1,400 now, and Story City is an excellent location for manufacturing and other business." Joseph wondered what knowledge Oscar had of business, given his interest in medicine.

"Did Ida tell you we have more painted houses than any town in the state?" Severt laughed.

Oscar smiled. "She didn't happen to mention that particular fact, but she clearly is proud of her hometown."

"My sisters certainly take advantage of the heat and electricity, but for some reason they boast more often about the painted houses."

Joseph wondered how much Severt knew of his roommate's family and background. "Lula tells me you are from Minnesota."

Oscar nodded. "Crookston City."

Joseph nodded. "Ah, yes. In Polk County."

"That's right. You're familiar with it?"

"I am. I've had some real estate business there."

"Ida told me you were in real estate business. Banking as well?"

"Yes," Joseph said. "And what business is your father in?"

The younger man glanced at Severt. "My father passed away some time ago."

"I see." The response surprised Joseph. "I'm sorry." He wondered what Oscar's father had died from and whether the mother had remarried or supported the family on her own. It would be important to know what the family's financial and social living conditions were.

All attention turned to Ida as she entered the room. She smiled first at her father and then at Oscar. "Lula said to tell you supper will be ready momentarily."

Oscar leaned forward, and Joseph saw the respectful admiration in the young man's face as he gazed up at her.

"Are you famished, Oscar?" Ida asked.

"I could eat something."

Severt nudged his friend as they stood. "Apparently she cares more about you than me!" He grinned at his sister. "Not that you asked, but I'm starving."

Ida laughed. "No need to ask you, Severt. You are always hungry. Shall we move to the dining room?"

Oscar gestured to the door. "After you, Ida." As she turned, he reached out to escort her, the tips of his fingers touching the small of Ida's back. She lifted her head and smiled up at him over her shoulder. Oscar tilted his head down toward her with a slow, small smile.

Joseph turned his head from the show of affection between his daughter and this young man he knew nothing about. At the earliest opportunity, he would ask Margretha to inquire into Oscar's family.

During supper, Oscar inquired about the bank. "Severt tells me it is to be quite a building."

"Thoroughly modern in every respect," Severt said.

Lula handed Oscar a platter of roast beef. "Please. Help yourself."

"Will the bank fill the entire building?" Oscar took a slice of beef and set it on his plate.

"Half of the first floor and some offices on the second," Joseph said. "The remaining space on the first floor will be commercial."

"The lobby will be quite grand by Story City standards," Severt added.

"We should show him the drawings." Anna said. "They were printed in the *Herald*."

"Were they?" Oscar regarded the younger girl for a moment.

"Yes. Papa was quite pleased." Anna beamed.

"I can understand why." Oscar smiled.

"There will be offices in front and a suite of living rooms in the rear." Joseph buttered his dinner roll. "The basement will have the standard rooms for heating and coal storage, as well as a space suitable for a barbershop."

"You were right, Severt," Oscar said to his friend. "It will be an impressive building. When do you expect it to be completed?"

"Depends on the weather," Joseph responded. "Should be ready to move in by fall, in any event."

"Did Ida tell you Father is going with the choir to Norway this summer?" Severt asked. "He's trusting me to supervise the construction during his absence. Can you imagine! I'll be responsible for any delays that might occur."

Ida turned to Oscar, touching his forearm. "After graduation, Severt will be the assistant cashier at the bank."

"Yes. He's fortunate to have such a good position lined up," Oscar said.

"It should keep me out of mischief." Severt laughed.

"That will be the day." Charlotte rolled her eyes.

Joseph expected that Severt would have little trouble assuming his duties at the bank. The construction supervision, however, would be a challenge for his son. Many of the contractors and their workers would take every advantage of an inexperienced young college graduate. Joseph had asked his brother Martin to step in and help in an emergency, but for the project to remain on schedule, Severt would have to pay close attention to the details and follow-up to keep the contractors on task.

"Papa," Ida said, "Oscar has been accepted to begin medical studies at the University of Minnesota next fall."

"You're going to be a doctor?" Anna gazed at Ida's beau with admiration.

"I am." Oscar smiled. "After medical school, that is."

"Quite a demand for doctors these days." Joseph wondered what a new doctor could expect for an annual income.

"Yes," Oscar said.

"Do you have any idea where you might practice?" Joseph wondered if he had family in medicine or some other connection with an established doctor or clinic.

"No."

The young man would have to rely upon his own abilities to establish himself, Joseph thought.

"We've a new doctor in town," Lula said. "More coffee, Oscar?"

Oscar nodded. "Please."

Lula pushed her chair back and reached for the china coffee pot on the buffet behind her. "Dr. Haerem and his family came here from Norway not so many years ago."

"Lula and Papa were there for dinner the other day and had quite the time." Charlotte grinned at her sister.

Lula laughed. "We did, indeed."

"Lula was quite silly by the time she and Papa returned home that evening," Anna said.

Lula laughed again and turned to Oscar. "The Haerems served a regular Norwegian dinner—wine with dinner, and that's not all. The dessert was rum pudding."

Oscar smiled. "Sounds entertaining."

"It was," Lula admitted.

"Story City has become quite the social place." Ida turned her smile to Anna. "On a serious note, how are your studies for catechization coming, Anna?"

"Fine."

"Anna is in one of the first classes at St. Petri to be confirmed in English," Lula explained to Oscar.

"Is that so?" Oscar asked.

Anna nodded.

"My father argued with the pastor for years about having confirmation taught in English," Severt said. "Lucky for Anna, he finally won out."

"Most of my friends were confirmed last year when they were freshmen," Anna told Oscar. "But as I skipped the first grade, I'm young for my grade and they held me back a year for confirmation. Seems silly to me. I'll turn fifteen just two weeks after confirmation."

"Anna, you know the church is strict about age," Lula said. "You must be fourteen when you are confirmed, regardless of how quickly your birthday comes afterward."

"I think Margretha is the one who is strict about age," Charlotte said. "She is the one who insisted that Anna wait."

"Charlotte." Joseph locked eyes with his daughter. Her comment was inappropriate, particularly with company present.

Anna shrugged. "I'm happy that I'll be confirmed in English." She wrinkled her nose. "Even though I actually started memorizing the catechism in Norwegian, which was a waste of time."

"Now, now," Lula said. "What will you do tomorrow?" she asked Ida.

***

The following afternoon, Ida and Oscar found Joseph reading the newspaper in the living room. Lula, Severt, and Charlotte had gone to town, and Anna was at church.

"Papa?"

Joseph laid the paper in his lap and looked up. Oscar stood tall behind Ida.

"May we speak with you?" Ida bit her lip.

"Yes, of course." Joseph folded the paper. So, he thought, they are going to tell me they want to be married.

Ida stepped forward, folding her hands together and smiling. "We have something to ask you."

Joseph recognized her expression—the hopeful anticipation when she was about to ask for something she wanted dearly. He set the paper on the floor beside the chair.

Joseph gestured to the divan. "Have a seat."

"Perhaps we could speak in the parlor?" Ida tilted her head and smiled at him from a side profile, which her father had always found endearing.

Oscar's expression did not betray his thoughts.

Joseph stood and nodded.

In the parlor, Ida sat on the edge of the brocaded silk seat of the red settee beside Oscar. Joseph sat across from them in the gold chair.

Ida adjusted her full, white skirt. Her shoulders rose as she took a deep breath. "So." She looked at Oscar and then her father. "Papa, we have something to ask of you." Her hands fluttered in her lap. "A most important matter." She looked back at Oscar.

Oscar smiled at her, then faced her father, at once serious. "Mr. Marvick, I have asked Ida to marry me. We would like your blessing."

Joseph studied his daughter's lovely face, radiant with affection for both her father and this young man. He wanted her happiness, yet he hardly knew this reserved young man. It had been so different with Olive. He had known Peter and the Donhowe family for years. Lula's recent engagement at the beginning of the year to Edwin Roe had also been a fairly simple matter. A personable young man, Edwin had visited the Marvicks on several occasions prior to their engagement, and he had spoken often and openly about his family. He told amusing stories of the pranks his six younger brothers played on his older sister, boasted of his mother's blueberry pies, and respected his father, who was a superintendent in a department store in Wisconsin. Joseph had no doubts about Edwin's character and knew his family to be of good standing in his community. So little was known of Oscar or his family. Although Severt obviously liked the young man.

Joseph addressed his daughter. "This is your choice as well, I assume?"

Ida leaned forward. "Oh, yes, Papa!" She reached over and rested her hand on Oscar's arm. "It would make me so wondrously happy!"

Oscar placed his other hand over hers.

"You would take good care of my daughter?" Joseph asked.

"I care very much for Ida." Oscar's expression was intense. "I would love, honor, and cherish her."

"You love this man?" Joseph asked his daughter.

Ida glowed. "Oh, I do, Papa."

Joseph faced Oscar. "I have loved and provided for my daughter. I do not want any harm to come to her."

Oscar held the older man's stare. "If you grant us your permission, I will prove to you that I will love her as much as any man could and provide for her well being."

Joseph did not know much about the young man, but he liked his serious nature. He had also seen Oscar laughing at something Ida said to him as they left the house earlier that day. It reminded him of the way Annie had made him laugh. It was good not to be so serious all of the time. Oscar's feelings for Ida appeared to be genuine, although it was impossible to know with certainty. Joseph needed to learn more about the family, but at least it seemed the young man's pursuit of a medical profession would grant him a certain amount of financial security and social respectability.

He nodded. "You have my approval."

Ida grasped Oscar's hand for a moment and then leapt to her feet and went to her father.

Joseph stood to meet her. She seemed unusually beautiful as she passed by the window, a ray of afternoon light highlighting the dark hair wound around her head and illuminating her white shirtwaist and white skirt.

"Papa." She reached up, her hands light on his shoulders. "I am so happy." She stood on her toes and kissed him on the cheek. "I knew you would give us your blessing."

Joseph held her elbows, squeezing them tenderly as she dropped back on her heels. He smiled at this beloved daughter he had rarely denied. "Your happiness and welfare have always been of utmost importance to me."

Joseph held his hand out to Oscar, who had come to stand beside Ida.

Severt's Surgery

Anna

Afew weeks later, Severt wrote home to say he had had an appendicitis attack. Anna's father immediately replied referring his son to Dr. Bockmann in St. Paul. If surgery were required, Papa would arrange his schedule to be there for a day or so. He had every confidence in Dr. Bockmann, but depending upon the seriousness of the case, Papa advised Severt to consider a visit to the Mayo Clinic.

In his next letter, Severt reported the results of his appointment in St. Paul. Papa shook his head. "An osteopath. What is he thinking?"

"An osteopath?" Lula reached for the letter. "What does he say about his appendicitis?"

"Read it for yourself." Papa shook his head again.

Anna read the letter over her sister's shoulder.

Dear Father:

I saw Dr. Bockmann but didn't make any definite arrangements with him as to an operation. He left it all to me and said I could come any time I felt like it. He said it wasn't absolutely necessary, but he would advise one sooner or later.

I called Dr. Stover, the osteopath doctor here. He is the same doctor Ida and Nellie have been going to. They both speak well of him. Dr. Stover asked me to eat lightly for a time now, that is no heavy food, but light as eggs, fruit, and milk, etc. I thought I'd try him and see what he could do. Knew he certainly couldn't do any harm. He gave me a light treatment, and I had pretty good night's rest. I went down for another treatment this morning and have been feeling pretty fair today, though I am somewhat weak and sore in body.

I don't know what he can do, but he claims that he can cure me of my trouble without an operation. I've never had anything to do with osteopaths before, but if he can do the business without operating, it sounds good to me, because although I am not afraid of an operation, I would sooner do without.

In my treatment this morning, he was trying to explain to me that the condition of the lower part of my spine, which is center of nerves and muscles feeding and governing the stomach, liver and region of appendix, showed cause for trouble in those parts.

Anyway, I do not want to go away to some hospital until I am in better condition physically than I am now and thought I would treat with him for a week or so and if it did help me, to let him go ahead with the case.

I don't know whether I am doing the right or wrong thing in going to this Dr. Stover, but as I said if he's any good at all he ought to put me in better condition soon and begin to show whether he can help my trouble with appendix.

If it should turn out to be a serious case of appendicitis, I would just as soon go to St. Paul and have Bockmann do the work if it is to be done. I think he's good enough for me. Thanks for the choice you gave me.

I don't know what you think about an osteopath in my case as I have tried to make clear to you in this letter or if you think best to go back to Bockmann soon.

Will look for a letter from you by return mail. Glad to hear that you could be there for a day or so, in case I should go. I don't think there would be any waiting before the operation, if I came up in fairly good condition.

Will keep you posted as to how I am getting along.

Hope everyone at home is not worrying too much about me.

Love to all.

> Your loving son,
>
> Severt

"Well." Lula folded the letter. "What will you tell him?"

Papa sat down at the rolltop desk and reached for a sheet of Story City National Bank stationary. "I will tell him what I thought I had made clear in my last letter. If he needs an operation, he should make arrangements for it so he does not risk his health."

Severt did not schedule the operation, responding that the osteopath treatments seemed to have helped, and with graduation approaching, he did not want to take time away from classes if he didn't have to.

***

Severt was in great spirits at his graduation, but Anna thought he seemed thinner and weaker than normal. If Papa noticed, he didn't say anything.

When Severt received his diploma during the commencement ceremony, Papa reached over and patted Anna on the shoulder, smiling broadly. "That's my son." Afterwards, Papa shook Severt's hand. "I'm proud of you, son. You've done well. You're the first in our family to graduate from college. Now you can assume your bank duties as assistant cashier at the bank. It will be good to have you there. You have a great future ahead of you."

"I don't know of what value a Bachelor of Arts degree is," Severt laughed. "But there's some satisfaction in having one, anyway."

Papa's smile disappeared. "I don't ever want to hear that from you again. I'm disappointed, Severt. I would have thought you would value your degree. You are privileged to have been given the opportunity to obtain a college education."

Severt was suddenly serious. "I was just making an attempt at some good humor. Naturally I'm grateful and appreciate the degree."

"Of course you do," Lula said.

"You might be nonchalant about college, now that you're done with it, but it's all new and exciting to me," Charlotte said. "To think in only a few months I'll be studying music theory with Professor Christiansen!" Charlotte had received an academic scholarship and would enter St. Olaf College as a freshman the upcoming fall.

"I hardly recognize you," Severt teased his sister. "You are fairly bursting with enthusiasm."

Charlotte hugged herself. "I can hardly wait to begin!"

"I'm warning you," Severt said. "You're in danger of becoming a warm, likeable person such as myself."

Charlotte batted his arm playfully.

Papa did not smile, and Anna was sorry her brother had spoiled the mood with his carefree remarks.

***

On Monday, the sixteenth of June, Papa left with Henry Donhowe for their European trip, with stops at Chicago, Washington D.C., Philadelphia, and New York en route. The family wondered how Papa would be able to leave his business for such a long stretch of time and hoped he would be able to enjoy himself. Peter's older brother Henry would certainly be an agreeable traveling companion, and Papa always took great pleasure in watching Ida perform. The trip sounded like a big adventure to Anna. Her father had traveled nearly everywhere, but he had never been across the ocean before.

While her father was away, Lula planned a two-week visit to her fiancé Edwin's home in Stanley, Wisconsin. Engaged in January upon his graduation from the Madison Short Course, they planned their wedding for the fourth of November.

Lula's train was scheduled to depart the station at 4:40 p.m. on the afternoon of the twenty-fourth of June. Anna and Charlotte watched her pack the last of her things and followed her downstairs to the front hall.

"I can't believe the day is finally here. Goodness. I have butterflies. Have I forgotten anything, I wonder?" She set her bags on the wood floor and leaned toward the beveled glass of the hall mirror, tilting her head from side to side as she examined her reflection.

"Don't spend too much time preening yourself or you'll miss your train," Charlotte said.

"You look swell, Lula," Anna said. "Just as you always do."

"How sweet of you to say so, Anna." Lula adjusted her hat and swung around to face her younger sisters. "I just can't help but worry about Severt. I should stay to look after him."

"We'll manage just fine," Charlotte said. "Now let's get your bags into the car so we can get you to the station in time."

"I have so looked forward to this trip. It's selfish of me, but I want to go."

"I wouldn't want to be the one to wire poor Edwin that you missed your train." Anna's future brother-in-law had a great sense of humor and was exactly the kind of man she hoped to marry someday. Lula and Edwin hardly saw each other, and he would be so disappointed if Lula cancelled the visit.

"He could have another appendicitis attack," Lula said.

"Severt will be just fine, Lula." Charlotte smiled and shook her head. "You know what a baby our brother is when he doesn't feel well."

Lula's expression softened to a tentative smile. "He does like attention when he's under the weather, doesn't he?"

"I do believe the weather is his problem," Charlotte said. "His abdominal cramps are most likely from supervising the bank construction outside in this horrid heat."

Anna nodded. "It is so blasted hot, it's no wonder he feels ill. His internal organs are most likely boiled up."

"We'll throw some cold water on him, and he'll recover in no time," Charlotte laughed.

"You girls!" Lula glanced back at her reflection and patted her hair. "I pity the poor boy in your care."

"He can't afford to be ill," Charlotte said. "Papa's counting on him to supervise the bank construction. Not only that, but he also leaves tomorrow for Canton, South Dakota."

Anna could not imagine her brother acting as her father's substitute as treasurer of the Stavanger Laget. "I wish I could go along to hear him speak Norsk," she laughed. "I heard him practicing with Bestemor." She shook her head. "She said his Norsk was pitiful, and all due to Papa not allowing us to speak it at home."

"I don't think it is the heat that's bothering Severt," Lula said. "More likely it is the fear of being abandoned to the two of you."

"Gather up your bags, Lula," Charlotte said. "Or you will certainly miss your train."

"Severt will be better in the morning," Anna nodded. "Not a thing for you to worry about."

***

Severt was not better by the following morning and by day's end had cancelled his trip to the Stavanger Laget. Charlotte and Anna could not coax him to eat much, and he spent less time at work with every day that passed.

After Lula had been gone five days, Severt came home at noon and went directly to bed. He complained of sharp pains below his navel, was too nauseous to eat, and was plagued by bouts of diarrhea.

That evening, in the middle of the night, Charlotte shook her sister. "Anna, wake up. Something is terribly wrong with Severt."

Anna struggled from sleep. Rubbing her eyes, she saw her sister hovering over her in the dark, long braids swaying against the white nightdress, eyes bright with alarm. Anna slowly realized that the low disturbing sounds she heard were moans from Severt's room down the hall.

"What is it?" Anna's words slurred, the inside of her mouth dry from sleep.

"Severt is in terrible pain and burning up with fever. We must do something."

Dazed, Anna followed her sister down the hall.

Pain glazed Severt's eyes. In the light of the lamp, sweat glistened on his white skin, his dark hair wet and heavy on his forehead and temples. His arms thrashed the damp bedcovers, and his anguished groans filled the room.

Terrified, Anna turned to find the same fear in Charlotte's eyes.

Severt's voice was guttural. "Doctor. Need a doctor."

Charlotte stepped back from the bed and took a deep breath. "Get a basin of water, Anna, and a cloth. Keep him cool. I'll telephone Dr. Haerem."

Outside the room, Anna clutched her sister's arm, her voice a whisper. "Is he dying?"

Charlotte stared for a moment. "I don't know. Pray the doctor is home and loses no time."

After hearing a description of Severt's symptoms, the doctor said he would make a house call within the half hour.

The cloth Anna held against Severt's forehead and chest radiated heat within moments of touching his skin, and the water in the basin was soon warm. Charlotte replaced the water several times, hoping the cool water would give him some relief.

Minutes seemed like hours before they heard the doctor's knock at the door. There was no sign of daylight, and the grandfather clock showed the time to be only half past two in the morning.

"Severt, my boy," Dr. Haerem said upon entering the room. "Not doing so well, are we?"

Severt shook his head. "The pain." He pointed to his right abdomen. "So bad. Never this bad before."

"Let's take a look." The doctor set his black bag on the floor by the bed and withdrew a stethoscope.

Severt screamed out when the doctor touched his right side.

Anna grabbed Charlotte's forearm, her fingers digging into her sister's skin.

"Appendicitis, most definitely." Dr. Haerem turned his attention from Severt to the girls at the doorway. "Fever this high, pain this intense. That appendix could burst anytime. We'll have to operate."

Charlotte pried Anna's hand from her arm. "The hospital in Des Moines?"

The doctor shook his head. "Afraid not. Too dangerous to move him." He stuffed his stethoscope into his bag and closed it up. Picking up the bag, he walked to the door. "I'll have to ring up the surgeon in Des Moines and request him to come here."

Silent, the girls followed the doctor as he swiftly descended the stairs.

"I wish Papa were here," Anna said.

Charlotte nodded.

Soon after Dr. Haerem contacted Dr. McCarthy, Olive and Peter arrived with little Laurentia and baby Joseph Oliver, who were bundled up and still asleep.

"Everything will be fine," Olive assured the girls. "You two go back to bed now and get some sleep. Peter and I can take care of Severt."

Anna and Charlotte returned to their room but did not sleep. Fearful imaginings filled the dark silences that stretched between Severt's moans and the indistinguishable hushed blend of Olive's higher pitched voice and the men's lower timbres. Would Severt die? Would the surgeon arrive in time to save him? Anna could not imagine the family without her brother. She could not imagine how terrible it would be for Papa to lose his only son.

Peter met Dr. McCarthy at the station the following morning and drove him to the house where Olive and her younger sisters waited.

Upon entering the house and before seeing Severt, Dr. McCarthy opened his bag and handed Olive several instruments. "We'll need a large pot of boiling water to sterilize the instruments. And some clean cloths."

Olive nodded. "Dr. Haerem advised me. I have the water ready."

After the frightening instruments had been sterilized and were cooling, Dr. Haerem and Dr. McCarthy assisted Severt down the stairs and into the dining room. Severt cried out as Peter and the two doctors lifted him onto the table which the girls had covered with a clean bleached sheet.

Warning that many people had a tendency to faint or become hysterical, the doctors instructed Anna and Charlotte to wait in another room. The girls left the room but watched through the open doorway as the doctor held the ether mask over Severt's mouth and nose. Anna clutched her sister's arm. She knew the ether was to put her brother to sleep, but it seemed as though the doctor was suffocating him. Beside her, Charlotte stood stiff with fear.

Olive unfolded a blanket and wrapped it around her brother's legs and feet. She stepped back when the surgeon lifted Severt's nightshirt.

"I'll need the cloths now."

Olive went to the hutch, lifted the large bowl filled with kitchen and bath towels, and returned to the surgeon's side.

Dr. McCarthy doused a washcloth in alcohol and scrupulously scrubbed Severt's abdomen. Setting it to the side, he took two dish towels, folded them in half lengthwise, and carefully laid them across Severt's body. He looked over at Dr. Haerem, who stood holding the ether bottle. "Are we ready?"

The other doctor nodded. "He's out."

"Keep a watch on him."

Anna had heard of people who died from too much ether. Worse, she had heard of people waking up too soon. She closed her eyes.

The surgeon turned to Olive. "Be ready with more towels. There will be a lot of blood."

Wondering if Olive would faint, Anna's fingers tightened on Charlotte's arm.

"That hurts," Charlotte whispered through clenched teeth as she pried Anna's fingers loose.

"Instruments, please."

Peter stepped forward with the tray.

The surgeon selected the scalpel, which glinted in the bright glare of the light as he lifted it over Severt's body.

Anna bit her lip. It reminded her of the story of Abraham laying Isaac on an altar built of wood and lifting the knife to kill him. The story of God asking a father to sacrifice his son as an offering had always terrified her, even though it had a good ending. It made her wonder what her own father would do if

God asked him to sacrifice one of his own children. She believed her father would obey God, but she also wanted to believe he would never agree to kill his own child. Anna prayed that God would not let her brother die and wished her father were home. Covering her eyes with her hands, she backed away from the doorway. Bumping into Charlotte, who had also turned away, Anna felt a stab of pain as her teeth closed on her lip. Tears spilled and she swallowed, the metallic taste of blood on her tongue.

The Christianafjord

Joseph

*J*oseph did not receive the news of his son's surgery until nearly a month later.

On the twenty-fourth of June, he and Henry Donhowe joined the St. Olaf Choir in New York and departed for Norway on the Christianafjord, the first liner of the newly established Norwegian-American steamship line. Joseph's second-class berth assignment was smaller than expected but acceptable. As he unpacked, he found the list Margretha had prepared of art institutes and notable places to visit in Norway, Sweden, Germany, and Denmark. He left the list in his bag to refer to later. Although he had some interest in sight-seeing, the objective of the trip was to hear Ida sing in Europe.

The first day at sea passed quickly. F. Melius Christiansen established a twice-daily rehearsal schedule and impressed upon the choir members that there would be no acceptable excuses for late attendance. Joseph went on deck for both rehearsals, warm in a thick wool overcoat and hat. Exhibiting discipline and rigor, the conductor demanded perfection and drilled the choir until he achieved it. Joseph understood why Ida held the professor in such high esteem.

During dinner that first evening, Joseph and Henry heard highlights from the first stops of the tour. In addition to the two men, their table for six included Ida, her cousin Lila Hansen, her friend Nellie Charlson from Story City, and another choir member, Miss Kvenes from Northfield. Having met the choir just prior to setting sail, Joseph and Henry had missed the concerts in Minnesota, Wisconsin, and New York. A man of social nature, Henry engaged the four women in an animated conversation about the success of the tour thus far.

The women complied with F. Melius Christiansen's requirement to be in their berths by ten o'clock, and Joseph returned to his own berth, having thoroughly enjoyed the evening.

The second day at sea, Joseph woke early to a thud on the other side of the wall, followed by a cry of alarm and much muttering. The room tilted and rocked about with the motion of the ship. Surveying his berth, Joseph satisfied himself that his belongings remained secured and nothing had fallen from its place.

Checking his pocket watch, he noted that he had nearly an hour before breakfast. He took his time washing and shaving, appreciating the fragrance of his shaving soap in the musty berth and steadying himself with one hand to maintain his balance. After trimming and combing his mustache, he stropped and honed his razor, rinsed the blade and shaving brush, and replaced them in the satin-lined morocco shaving case. He dressed slowly, donned his coat and hat, and leisurely strolled the deck, nodding to a few passengers he passed and politely ignoring those retching over the side of the railings.

When he knocked on Henry's door at the agreed upon time, his fellow traveler was feeling the effects of the sea and in no hurry to rise for breakfast. It seemed many shared Henry's discomfort, as there were very few in the dining room.

Joseph had sliced the top off his second soft-boiled egg when Ida joined him. The first egg had been a bit overcooked. The second was just as he preferred, with the yolk soft but the white firm throughout.

"Good morning, Papa!" Ida took a seat beside him. "Did you sleep well?"

"I did." Joseph asked, "And you?" Ida's face had good color, which he took as a sign she did not suffer from seasickness.

"I did as well." Ida reached for the small silver pot of coffee. "Much better than poor Nellie. I'm afraid my berth mate is one of those who have fed the fishes."

"Ah. A shame." Joseph scooped a spoonful of egg from inside the shell. He wondered if he had passed Nellie on the deck during his stroll.

"Did you look at the sea this morning?" Ida asked. "The waves are the color of pewter and quite amazing in size. I'm thankful we're on such a large ship. I can't imagine braving these seas on a smaller vessel."

"I agree. I have a greater appreciation of how ships have succumbed to storms on the seas."

Ida leaned forward and rested her hand on her father's. "Please don't mention sinking ships or I shall think of the Titanic."

Joseph regretted his mention of disasters on the seas. He did not want to alarm his daughter.

Tilting her head with a serene smile, Ida patted his hand. "Not that I worry. This ship seems perfectly safe to me, and I doubt we will encounter any icebergs."

"No." Relieved, he returned her smile. "I'm certain safety precautions have been taken after the lessons learned from the Titanic."

Ida set a slice of bread on her plate and spread it with a thick layer of lingonberry jam. "With all the people feeling sick on board, I was thinking of Severt. Did you say he was feeling better when you left home?"

Joseph frowned and took a sip of coffee. The coffee was stronger than he preferred. "He wasn't complaining." Though his son seemed to lack energy and color, he retained his normal humor and enthusiasm.

"It's a shame he's been under the weather so much the past year. It seems he has had one thing or another without much time to recover in between."

"I must say, I wish he had followed my advice and had the surgery on his appendix."

"He was so hoping Dr. Stover would help him."

"Unfortunately, those treatments appear to have been a waste of time and money." Joseph wiped his mouth with his napkin. "If Severt is not the picture of health when I return, I will send him to see a doctor at the Mayo Clinic. I spoke with Margretha before I left about making an appointment. Your brother is optimistic and believes his health will improve during the summer."

Ida wiped a dab of jam from the corner of her mouth with her napkin. "Let's hope he is the picture of health when we get back. Isn't it grand having him at the bank?"

"It's good to have him there. Particularly with the building project in process." Joseph hoped there had not been any difficulties or delays in his absence. He wondered how Severt was dealing with the construction crew. His son had no experience managing other men. He thought of the construction manager, a hard-working man but also hardheaded and often belligerent.

"I'm so anxious to see the new building."

Joseph nodded. "It will be a fine addition to Main Street." He folded his napkin and set it on the table.

"With all the changes in town, it will be a wonder if I recognize it when I return." Ida smiled. "I imagine Severt doesn't much like working outside in the heat during construction, though, does he?"

Joseph had not thought much about the working conditions at the bank or their effect on Severt. He was more concerned about the construction crew. It had certainly started out to be an unusually hot summer, but Severt was merely overseeing the project and not performing hard labor of any kind.

A server appeared at the table. "Are you finished with your breakfast, sir?"

"I am." Joseph leaned back to allow the server to remove his dishes.

"And you, miss?" The server lifted the lid of the pot of coffee and peered inside. "Could I bring you some fresh coffee? Eggs? Or would you prefer a sweet pastry?" He was young, near Ida's age. He did not smile and was not familiar, but his eyes did not leave Ida.

Ida beamed with delight. "How did you know I adore sweets? Yes, I would love a sweet roll or whatever you have. And more coffee would be wonderful."

"I'll get that for you straightaway, miss." Smiling, he nodded and picked up the tray.

"Thank you." Ida focused a smile on the server and then leaned toward her father. "Speaking of Severt, isn't it grand he and Cosette are engaged? Have they set a date yet?"

"I can't say what their specific plans might be. I believe they are waiting until after Cosette graduates from Grinnell next year."

"What a big summer it will be for our family. Two weddings—Severt and Cosette, and Oscar and me." Ida pushed her half-eaten slice of bread to the edge of her plate. "I shouldn't waste this, but I think I'll save my appetite for the pastry that is coming." She lifted her coffee cup to her lips and, before sipping, said, "And to think Lula will be married this fall. Ed Roe is perfect for Lula, don't you agree?"

"He's a fine man."

"They must be counting the days to the wedding." Ida waved to some choir members across the room. "Soon you will have your second daughter married. And moving away." Her brow creased for a moment, then cleared just as quickly. "Although I suppose Wisconsin isn't as far away as some places, is it?"

Joseph studied his daughter as she poured herself more coffee. He had not considered the effect Lula's move would have on Ida.

He recalled the day he and Annie moved from Illinois to Story City. Her sisters sobbed as they said their farewells. Tears welled in Annie's eyes that day, but the excitement of the move balanced her sadness. Only later, after a few months in their new home, did Annie's homesickness surface. One evening before bed, as she brushed her long hair at the dressing table, her body trembled in the white lace and embroidery-trimmed yoke of her Cambric gown, the tears reflected in the mirror before her. Fearing something was terribly wrong, he asked, "What is it, Annie?" Eyes red and swollen, she shook her head. "Oh, Joseph, forgive me for my foolish tears. I have you and the children, and I love you so, but how I miss my family. Mama and Papa, and little Linnie, but especially my dear sister Serena. She and I have always been so close." Grateful that nothing more serious was the matter, he patted her back. "There, there, my dear. We shall plan a trip to visit your family next summer and take baby Anna to meet them." It was a promise to his wife he failed to fulfill. Annie died before they reached her parents' home and never saw her sister again.

Joseph studied Ida as she glanced around the room. Ida and Lula had the same relationship that Annie and her sister Serena had. He wanted to spare them the pain of separation or illness. "Transportation is not so difficult these days," he said. "I trust you and Lula shall visit each other often."

Turning her attention from the room, Ida smiled. "I suppose it won't be much different than it is now, with Lula in Story City and me in Northfield, will it? Until now, I hadn't thought much about one of us getting married and moving away." She paused to sip her coffee. "It's fortunate Olive is in Story City, isn't it? So perfect that she and Peter will move back in with you to keep house after Lula is married so both Charlotte and I can attend St. Olaf."

He would not have asked Ida to leave St. Olaf to manage the household, but it had never been a consideration. Olive and Peter offered to rent out their house and move in with Joseph and Anna after Lula's wedding just as they had while Lula was at college. "I must say, it will be somewhat of an adjustment having the little children living in the house again."

"I suppose so, but you do travel so much of the time."

"True." It was also true that Laurentia was a well-behaved little girl and Joseph Oliver a good baby for the most part.

"Anna will be a big help. She adores those children." Ida shook her head. "Time does pass quickly, doesn't it? It seems Anna was just a baby and now she is a senior in high school already."

"The top of her class."

"And popular as well. Always playing pranks and having such fun."

Joseph's witty youngest daughter carried laughter with her and on occasion even drew a smile from her grandmother. He had never been so lighthearted himself. He recalled doing farm chores under his father's direction with little time if any left for play. Unlike his younger brother Andrew, the most sociable son of the family, he had not minded. He respected his father and, as a responsible son, did as he was told. He worked hard and as a result accomplished much with the grace of God.

Living under the same roof as his son-in-law would be an adjustment. There could be only one head of the household, and Peter had become accustomed to heading his own. "Peter found a renter for their house."

"Oh?"

"Halvar Kloster. I expect Peter got a good rent from him." His son-in-law would have negotiated the highest rent possible.

"Kloster? He and his wife are fortunate. Olive has decorated her home so tastefully and is such a good housekeeper." Ida twisted the hair on the side of her face around her finger. "I can't imagine a nicer place to rent."

The server returned to the table, china and silver clinking on the large silver tray. He replaced the coffee pot and set a plate of pastries before Ida. "I brought a selection for you. I trust you will find one you like."

"So many to choose from." Ida face radiated delight. "Now I will be tempted to have more than one!"

"Our aim is to please." The blond waiter smiled down at her as he lifted the tray from the table.

"Well, these certainly make me happy." Ida handed the plate to her father. "Would you like one?"

He shook his head. "No. Thank you."

"I can't tempt you?" Ida laughed. "You have had your sensible breakfast of eggs and toast, and I shall have my sweets." She examined the selection of pastries and chose one with chocolate drizzled across the top.

Ida had a weakness for sweets. How many times he had heard Margretha say, "That girl eats too much sugar. It isn't good for her. Her teeth will rot."

Ida cut into the pastry. "Oh look. It's filled with chocolate. How divine!" Holding her fork midair, she paused. "Speaking of Olive, I mustn't forget to find something for little Laurentia and baby Joseph Oliver in Norway. Not to mention a wedding gift for Lula and Ed."

"Your grandmother is giving Lula a set of spoons and asked me to buy them for her in Norway."

"What a wonderful gift!"

Shopping with Ida would be a new experience. He often purchased gifts for his children on his travels, but relied upon the shop owner to assist him in the selection. "You could help me choose my wedding gift for them."

"That would be fun. Do you have something in mind?"

"I was thinking of some silver serving pieces. A coffee and tea service, perhaps. And a nice piece of jewelry for Lula." He would also gift the couple property, as he had with Olive and Peter.

"Lula would like that." Ida scraped chocolate from her plate with her fork.

It occurred to him that soon he would be choosing a wedding gift for her as well. He wondered where Oscar would eventually settle to practice medicine. The young man would likely prefer Minnesota, near his own family, but it would be nice to have Ida closer to home. Joseph would have to see what opportunities there were for doctors near Story City. He had time to exert his influence before Oscar completed his medical studies. He also had time to look into the young man's family. Perhaps when he returned home, Margretha would have made some inquiries.

"Oh, my!" Ida said.

"What is it?" Joseph focused on his daughter.

"Didn't you see? Our waiter nearly dropped a tray full of dishes. I don't see how he managed to keep it balanced."

"I didn't notice."

"You didn't? It is rather frightening how much the ship is being tossed about."

"We'll be fine, Ida. I don't want you to worry. This ship will not sink."

Dreams
Joseph

On the fourth of July, the ship reached Bergen, Norway, where the choir sang the opening concert of the European tour. Of the eleven pieces on the program, Joseph particularly liked "Still, Still with Thee," sung by Ida and the Ladies Quartet, and F. Melius Christiansen's arrangement of Nicolai's "Wake, Awake," which the choir sang at the conclusion of each concert.

Following the concert, the Anglo-American Club sponsored a banquet for the choir in the Grand Hotel. Toward the end of the evening, Paul Schmidt, the St. Olaf professor responsible for planning and managing the choir tour, sought out Joseph and shook his hand. "I wanted to take a moment to thank you once again. Without your generous contribution, we would not be here this evening."

Joseph nodded. "Based on what I have seen so far, it was money well spent. I must commend you for the effort you expended in planning the tour and making all of the arrangements. You seem to have considered every detail."

"Thank you. I must admit it was a difficult assignment, but I was fortunate to have good help. Without the funding you provided, however, we could not have even considered undertaking this tour to Scandinavia."

Joseph had no reservations about the large sum of money he had contributed, but it annoyed him that only a few of the thirteen named guarantors actually agreed to provide financing. Professor Schmidt had solicited them all, but when he failed to raise sufficient financial aid to proceed, he had approached Joseph for a larger commitment. After calling upon each of the vocal supporters himself to no avail, Joseph had increased his own contribution and provided the funds necessary.

From Bergen, the ship continued to the capital city of Christiana, where a crowd of thousands cheered the ocean liner as it completed its maiden voyage from America to Norway. Standing beside her father, Ida waved from the deck. "Have you ever seen so many people in one place? How grand to have such a welcoming reception. I'll never in my life forget this." Joseph had not seen such a large crowd before. Surprising himself, he waved at the crowd, causing Ida to laugh with delight.

The reception at the pier proved to be a prelude to the concert that evening. When they arrived at the university auditorium for the performance, thousands of people who had not been able to get tickets thronged the streets outside. Not only was the concert completely sold out, but King Haakon VII and Queen Maud were in attendance. Ida said she had never been more nervous for a performance.

The following day, many members of the Norwegian cabinet and city elite attended a banquet in honor of the choir at Holmenkollen, and several approached Ida to praise her soprano solo. Watching from across the room, Henry lifted his glass to Joseph. "The Norwegians seem to appreciate your daughter's lovely voice as much as we do. She's always been a charmer, hasn't she? Given this audience, it is quite impressive, I'd say." Joseph lifted his glass and drank to the toast, thinking what a rich return he had already received on the investment he made to make the trip possible. He had never been more proud of his beautiful, talented daughter.

The tour continued by train, with concert stops in Gjovik, Lillehammer, and Hamar, to the city of Trondheim. The brightly-painted wood houses and gabled buildings charmed Ida. "I was so proud of our white-painted houses in Story City," she said, "but now they will seem so drab compared to this. When we return home, you should have our house painted a deep Norwegian blue. Wouldn't that give people something to talk about?" Imagining the attention a blue house would attract and how horrified his mother and Margretha would be, Joseph chuckled.

From Trondheim, they traveled south for two weeks by boat along the coast. Going ashore to Merok in the Geiranger fjords, Ida sat between her father and Nellie on the wood bench of the rowboat. "This must be what heaven looks like," she sighed. Snow-capped mountains towered the blue glacial waters, the steep, deep green hillsides streaked with white waterfalls and dotted improbably with dark brown mountain farms. It may be what heaven looked like, Joseph thought, but it was not a place to make a living. The flat, black, tillable earth of the Midwest must have looked like heaven when his father emigrated from Norway.

As they approached the landing pier of each tour stop, the captain announced their arrival to the cheering crowds by detonating small bombs in the water. "I'll never forget this, Papa," Ida said. "It all seems too grand to be true. I keep thinking I'm going to wake up and discover it was all just a dream."

Between the welcoming festivities, evening concerts, banquets and receptions, and some time for sight-seeing or shopping, the days passed quickly. After the final concert on the sixth of August in the City Hall of Copenhagen, Denmark, many of the choir members, including Ida, returned home. Though she wanted to see more of Europe, Ida felt such a hurried trip would be too tiresome. Joseph stayed on as planned with Henry, Professor Schmidt and his wife, and several others.

The rest of the trip proved interesting, but he missed Ida's company, and when Joseph boarded the Lusitania on the twenty-first of August, he was anxious to return home. On ship, a bundle of mail awaited him. After unpacking, Joseph sat down at the dressing table in his berth and sorted through the pile of letters.

The first letter he opened was Severt's. His son mentioned his appendicitis attack, but wrote there was no need to worry, as he was now recovered. Severt did not mention surgery. Construction was well underway and bank matters taken care of. As Joseph refolded the letter and replaced it in the envelope, he considered his son's health. Severt had been ill so often the past year and now another attack. He would discuss the matter with Margretha upon his return and have Severt examined as soon as possible at the Mayo Clinic. A young man of his age should not be ill so often.

Joseph relaxed in his chair as he read the first seven pages of Lula's letter, which included detailed accounts of her visit to Edwin in Stanley, the family's two-week stay at the cottage at Lake Okoboji, wedding preparations that had been made, and Joseph Oliver's first birthday party. When he read the last pages, Joseph stiffened and sat forward.

> I suppose Severt wrote to you all about his operation. We had quite a scare. I received the news by telegram while I was in Stanley. Although I was not scheduled to return for several more days, you can imagine that I took the first train home straightaway to help care for him. Can you imagine, having the operation in our house on the dining room table? Charlotte and Anna will not soon forget the experience. But of course the doctors didn't want to risk moving him to the hospital. Severt recovered quite nicely and was feeling fine when the nurse left on July 11th. By now, naturally, he is fully recovered and working diligently at the

bank in your stead. Although he did take a week to join us at the lake for some relaxation.

We are so looking forward to seeing Ida and hearing first hand about the tour. She wrote that we should have angel food, burnt sugar cake, fudge, etc., for her when she gets home.

Well, you shall be home soon. It will be interesting to hear your observations of the choir tour and of the other countries you have just visited.

Your loving daughter,

Lula

An emergency operation at home? What doctor performed the procedure? He could have lost his only son while he was beyond reach across the sea. He had enjoyed himself on this trip, unaware his son had been close to death. He had not taken Severt's complaints about feeling under the weather seriously enough.

Joseph searched through the remaining unopened letters for Margretha's familiar handwriting. Since Annie's death so many years ago, his sister had looked after his children's welfare and kept him informed of family matters when he was away on business. Joseph slit the envelope with the mother of pearl inlaid letter opener.

Dear Joseph,

It will be good for you to be home. I trust from your letters that you have enjoyed your trip.

Severt had another appendicitis attack at the end of June, and an emergency surgery was performed at the home. We are fortunate that Charlotte and Anna had the presence of mind to call Dr. Haerem before it was too late. We are also fortunate that Dr. Haerem did not risk moving Severt to the hospital and that such a fine surgeon as Dr. McCarthy of Des Moines was able to come on such short notice. The doctors believe that if they had waited a few hours more the appendix would have burst, and we likely would have lost Severt. Lula arranged for a nurse, who remained with Severt through his recovery. Severt has since returned to his duties at the bank, although he seems to lack vigor. When you return, I suggest we arrange for him to be examined thoroughly. Perhaps he should go to the Mayo Clinic as we have discussed, as they have the finest doctors and most advanced testing equipment.

The summer has been filled with the usual events. Severt was unable to attend the Stavangar Laget as he had taken ill at that time. This will come as a disappointment to you, but I know you care more for his welfare and will understand the situation.

I am confident that the girls have written more than you care to know about the remainder of the summer activities, so I will not belabor the details.

Our mother and father are well, as are the rest of the family.

Your sister,

Margretha

Margretha's words confirmed his concerns. The small berth suddenly felt confining, and the ship slow. It would be two weeks before he would be home and could take Severt to be examined at Mayo. He should have sailed home with Ida on the earlier ship. He should not have continued on with Henry. He would have been home by now and could have taken the proper actions.

That evening, as the ship surged in the swells of the sea, Joseph tossed sleeplessly in the hard bed of his berth. When exhaustion overcame him, he dreamed he was traveling across the country by train. From his window, he saw a man in white shirt and dark pants standing alone in the midst of a field of clover. The steel wheels of the train turned along the tracks toward the thin figure, and as they drew nearer Joseph realized it was Severt standing in the field. Confused, Joseph could not recall his destination and wondered what part of the country they were passing through and why his son would be standing alone in the middle of a field when he should be at the bank. Storm clouds swirled above Severt. Suddenly, a churning dark funnel cloud appeared behind him on the horizon. Joseph leaned out the window to yell for his son to run, but as he opened his mouth, the deafening train whistle blew, and his warning went unheard. Oblivious to both his father passing by and the danger overtaking him from behind, Severt remained rooted to the ground, swaying with the wind. Joseph rang for the bellman. He opened the door of his stateroom and yelled, "Stop the train!" But the bellman did not appear, and the narrow hallway of the car remained empty. The whistle sounded again, the train unstoppable. There was nothing he could do to save his son.

Family Secrets
Joseph

*J*oseph arrived home in Story City on the first of September and sent Severt to the Mayo Clinic the following week.

The doctors did not find anything during testing, which both relieved and frustrated Joseph. Severt continued to perform his duties at the bank, but he lacked vitality, ached with fatigue even after resting, had little appetite, and caught one cold after another. The fall of 1913 was unusually wet and cold, and Severt developed a persistent cough and sore throat, complained of a constant but dull, aching pain between his shoulder blades, and had difficulty breathing when he climbed stairs or walked briskly. Dr. Haerem diagnosed an obstinate case of bronchitis.

To his dismay, Severt did not regain his health before Lula's wedding on the fourth of November. Particularly fond of Edwin Roe, he had been looking forward to the event for months.

"Well, old boy," Severt remarked to Edwin on the wedding day, "it's a good thing this cough had me down and out all week. It kept us both out of trouble."

Lula laughed and kissed her brother on the cheek. "Thank the Lord for small favors." Standing back, her eyes serious and smile tender, she patted his cheek. "Take care of yourself, Severt."

Severt's cough grew worse after the wedding, and when he began to complain of pain in his heart region, Joseph told Margretha to schedule another examination with the Mayo doctors.

A few days later, Joseph was at home reading the paper when he heard the front door open.

His sister stepped into the house, turned, and shook her umbrella out the door, stomping her feet on the hall carpet. Pulling the umbrella closed, she set it in the hall tree. She shrugged off her dripping coat, shook it over the rug by the front door, and hung it on the coat rack.

Chilling rain pelted the windows. "What brings you out in this weather?" Joseph folded his paper and set it on the floor.

Margretha examined herself in the hall mirror, her mouth drawn tight. "I had a letter today." Her navy skirt whipped rhythmically as she stepped across the living room.

"Did you?" Joseph rubbed the sides of his mustache. "From the clinic?"

His sister sat down on the divan, reached beneath the sleeve of her white shirtwaist and pulled out an envelope. "You remember Sigrid Hansen."

"Sigrid?" His interest faltered. A friend of Margretha's, Sigrid moved from Story City after her marriage. Joseph could imagine no correspondence between the two women being of interest to him.

"Sigrid knows Oscar Locken's family." Her lips drew together.

Joseph pulled in his outstretched legs and sat forward. "How so?"

"I wrote Sigrid after you asked me to make some inquiries. Ida mentioned that one of Oscar's older sisters attended St. Olaf before him." Margretha gripped the envelope with both hands.

"I see."

"It turns out Sigrid and his sister were friends."

"And?"

"The news is not good."

Joseph's eyes narrowed. His sister tended to be overly critical of others, and he wondered what concerned her about Oscar's family. But perhaps he underestimated his sister and the matter was serious. He considered the possibilities. Financial troubles. Lawlessness.

"Tuberculosis." She glanced down at the envelope and back at her brother. "His father succumbed some time ago."

Joseph felt a chill—tuberculosis in Ida's fiancé's family. A contagious, deadly disease of unsanitary tenement houses, saloons, and beer halls. A disease of poor immigrants, criminals, and other unsavory sorts with personal moral failings. Anger flashed through Joseph. Oscar had withheld the cause of his father's death.

"Worse yet, it seems he did not go to a sanatorium." Her black eyes narrowed. "The family cared for him in the home until his death."

Alarmed by the family's negligence, Joseph considered the risk. Not only was Oscar engaged to Ida, he had been one of Severt's roommates. Mercifully, the Mayo doctors had found nothing when they tested Severt.

"The family was infected, Joseph."

Joseph pictured Oscar, so tall, so healthy. He thought of Ida, so in love with him. Perhaps there was some mistake, some misunderstanding. "You're certain?"

"Yes, I'm certain." Margretha's dark eyes flashed. "Sigrid knows this family, Joseph." She thrust out the letter. "Would you like to read it for yourself?"

"That is not necessary."

"You must insist that Ida call off the engagement." She sat back in the chair, clutching the letter in her lap.

Joseph thought of Ida standing before him after he had given his approval to marry, happier than he had ever seen her, smiling up at Oscar. It was a smile he had not seen her bestow upon any other man, and he had felt an odd twinge of jealousy.

"Well?" Margretha cleared her throat. "Did you hear what I just said?"

Joseph wished his sister would leave him to digest the news by himself. "Is Ida aware of this?"

"I would imagine not." Margretha lifted her chin. "If she is, she certainly did not mention it to me. Severt must not be aware of the family history either."

Joseph pushed the thought of Severt's cough away. "Surely if there was tuberculosis in the family, Severt would have known and said something."

"One would certainly think so."

Joseph could not imagine Ida marrying a man exposed to and possibly infected with tuberculosis. He also could not imagine breaking her heart. "Ida is quite in love with Oscar."

Margretha stiffened and exhaled through her nose. "Oscar is not the only man in this world." Her black eyes darted. "Ida has always had her share of admirers. Walter Henderson for one."

Joseph studied his stern sister. As a spinster, she could not understand. He knew what it was like to lose the woman he loved. Certainly, he had found some women attractive after his wife's death, but none had ever compared to his beloved Annie. There was no doubt Ida would find another man to marry, but she was in love with Oscar. "Perhaps he was not infected."

"Joseph." She shook her head. "His father expired in the home. The entire family was exposed."

Joseph rubbed his thumb along the smooth curved walnut end of the armrest. Oscar seemed healthy, but there was no way to know how sanitary their home had been or what kind of man his father had been. "I want Ida's happiness."

"And what happiness would she have if she were to suffer and die? Or if she were left a young widow?" She shook her head. "Joseph, come to your senses."

The fear of losing Ida to tuberculosis and the sharpness of his younger sister's words provoked him. "I have not taken leave of my senses, Margretha. I simply do not wish for Ida to be hurt."

"You have always been too soft on her."

His jaws ached from clenching his teeth. "I have always held Ida to the same standards as the others."

Margretha shrugged. "I disagree. You have always had difficulty saying no to that child. Believe me, I understand. She is very much like her mother. And I admit she has always been an easy, loving child."

Joseph sighed. He had nothing more to say to his sister and rose from his chair. "This is quite a serious matter and requires more consideration."

Margretha stood and faced him. Her nostrils flared as she drew in her breath, her eyes glowing embers. "Very well." She turned as though to leave, then wheeled around to face him once again. "Consider what is best for Ida."

His youngest sister's desire to have the last word irritated Joseph. He measured his words. "You need not doubt that I will do what is best for my daughter. I am her father, and I love her."

"And I do not?" Pain sharpened the anger in Margretha's eyes. "I love your children as my own." She pointed her chin at the ceiling.

He reminded himself that his sister had sacrificed her prime marriageable years to care for his children. "I have no doubt of that, Margretha."

Margretha's heels struck the hardwood floor as she strode to the front hallway.

Joseph watched her throw her coat on and jerk each button through its buttonhole. He did not question her love for his children, but he was their father and their welfare was his responsibility, not hers.

Umbrella in hand, she paused at the front door and faced him. "I do not wish to lose Ida, Joseph. And you. Are you willing to risk losing her, as you did your wife? I'll say it again. Consider what is best for Ida." Her boring eyes narrowed. "But also consider yourself. Consider the burden you would feel if Ida were to marry Oscar and we were to lose her to tuberculosis."

She stared for a moment, opened the door, snapped open the umbrella, and marched into the cold rain.

***

The conversation preoccupied Joseph the remainder of the day. In bed that evening, the disagreeable considerations and damaging consequences surged through his mind like a swelling river, rising ever higher, overflowing the banks, a flood of murky water beneath which he could not breathe. Hours before dawn, he threw the bedcovers aside, pulled on his dressing gown, stepped into his night slippers, and paced through the damp darkness. Periodically he paused at the living room bay window, staring into the night through the deluge of water that pelted and streamed down the glass.

When he first heard the baby cry, it blended with the wail of the trees bending to the fall wind. Joseph had forgotten that Olive and Peter had moved back into the house earlier that week with their two children. Thinking of four- year-old Laurentia and one-year-old Joseph Oliver safe in their beds on the second floor, he realized he had made his decision.

Margretha was right. Ida would have to break off with Oscar. He could not risk her health or her life.

The floorboards moaned above him, and Joseph noticed that the house was beginning to brighten with the dawn. Olive would be rising to fix breakfast.

Olive shushed Joseph Oliver as she carried him down the stairs and did not see her father until she nearly bumped into him. "Papa! What are you doing up so early?" she whispered.

Joseph Oliver blinked at his grandfather, his right hand in his mouth, not quite awake.

"Trouble sleeping."

"Come. I'll put the coffee on."

Joseph sat at the kitchen table while Olive fed Joseph Oliver his breakfast. "Thanksgiving will be upon us soon."

Olive spooned food into the baby's mouth and looked up. "It will, won't it?"

Joseph Oliver reached for his cup.

"Swallow your food, and then you can have some milk." Olive wiped the corners of the baby's mouth. "I haven't yet planned for Thanksgiving. I've been so occupied with Lula's wedding and moving between houses—not to mention the children."

"When do you expect Ida and Charlotte home?"

"Joseph Oliver, what a mess you are making." Olive pulled the baby's hand out of his mouth. "Thanksgiving Eve." Taking a cloth from her lap, she wiped the food from her son's fingers.

Joseph took another sip of coffee. He would speak to Ida at Thanksgiving.

Olive wiped off Joseph Oliver's mouth. "I think you've had enough now. It's time for Mama to make your grandfather his breakfast."

"Coffee is all I need today." He did not have much of an appetite.

"Nothing more? An egg perhaps or some bread with preserves?" She set the child on the floor beside the small wood blocks painted with letters. "Now stay put, little one, and don't make me chase you."

"Not today." Joseph lifted his empty cup. "I could use a bit more coffee, though."

Joseph watched his grandson reach for a block with a blue letter B.

"More coffee, then." Olive set the silver baby cup in the bowl and carried them to the sink. "This rain doesn't seem to want to let up, does it?"

"Quite a downpour."

"I hope the children don't catch cold in this weather. It's enough to chill your bones, isn't it?"

"That it is."

Broken Engagement
Joseph

*I*da and Charlotte took the last train from Northfield and did not arrive in Story City until late on Thanksgiving Eve. Severt collected them from the station, and Joseph joined the rest of the family in greeting them when they arrived at the house. The girls had not been home since the beginning of the school year.

"I hope you plan to stay up awhile—we must hear all about college life!" Anna reached for one of Charlotte's bags.

"I've written letters." Charlotte arched her eyebrows. "Haven't you read them?"

"Of course I have. But now you can tell us everything."

"I'm a bit tired, but I would like to catch up on St. Olaf news myself." The skin beneath Severt's eyes was dark and his cheeks flushed.

"Are you hungry?" Olive asked. "I have some lefse I could put out."

"That sounds wonderful," Ida smiled. "Do you have anything sweet to add to the plate?"

Joseph found it difficult to look at Ida.

Charlotte laughed. "All I heard during the train ride was 'I hope Olive baked some angel food cake or made some fudge.'"

"Good you are home, girls," Joseph said. "I'll see you in the morning. I must get to bed."

"Tired?" Ida reached up and touched his shoulder. "Professor Christiansen sends his greetings. He still speaks of how enjoyable it was to have you on the Norway tour."

Joseph nodded. The imprint of her fingertips remained on his shoulder after she removed her hand. "Tomorrow."

"Good night, Papa."

"I'm off to bed myself." Peter walked toward the stairs.

"We'll try to keep the noise down so you can sleep," Severt said.

"Do that." Peter paused at the bottom of the stairs. "Although I suspect that is easier said than done. See you in the morning."

As Joseph walked into his bedroom in the southwest corner of the house across from the living room, he heard Severt ask, "And how is Oscar liking medical school?"

"He finds the subjects quite fascinating," Ida responded. "But quite difficult, as well. Between the classes and studying, his time is spoken for."

"No time for any fun and games?" Anna asked. "It sounds positively dull to me."

Ida voice lightened. "I must admit, I don't at all mind that he has no time for fun and games when I'm not with him."

Joseph latched the door to his room and slowly prepared for bed, his body heavy.

Long after the rise and fall of voices and laughter had died out and the floorboards and box springs on the upper floor fell silent, Joseph lay awake, unable to find the peace of sleep.

***

Following the Thanksgiving morning church service, the St. Petri Ladies Aid served a dinner of lutefisk, chicken, lefse, potato cakes, cranberry jelly, buns, pie, and cake. The strong smell of lutefisk permeated the entire church, drawing the congregation into the basement for the traditional meal, and the fellowship hall filled quickly. Toward the end of the line, Joseph stood at the door waiting for seats with his older brother Martin and his wife Mary.

Across the room, Laurense beckoned with a crooked finger. "Joseph. Martin. Over here."

Martin and Mary took the chairs across from Syvert and Laurense, leaving the empty seat beside Margretha for Joseph.

"Coffee?" Margretha lifted the pot.

"Please." As his sister filled his cup, Joseph scanned the crowd for his children. Charlotte and Anna shared a table with a group of laughing young people. A few tables away from them, Severt sat beside Cosette, across from Ida and their friend Jenny Donhowe.

"You will speak with her this afternoon?" Margretha had been watching him.

Joseph clenched his teeth. He did not need to be reminded of the task ahead. "Yes."

Margretha nodded. "Good. It is about time."

"Ja." His mother nodded solemnly.

Joseph reached for the platter of lutefisk, which appeared overcooked.

"About time for what?" Martin asked.

Joseph took a small portion of fish and placed it on his plate. "Nothing we need to discuss here." He passed the platter across the table to his brother.

Beside him, Margretha's voice had a sharp edge. "Well."

Martin examined the fish, shaking his head. "This looks like jelly. We should have made it to the first seating. I don't like eating the bottom of the barrel."

Joseph wondered if the lutefisk had looked any better at the first seating. "Did you hear the latest about that seven-story building that collapsed last week in Cedar Rapids?"

Martin nodded.

"I can't imagine being buried like that," Mary said. "To think it took a week before they could pull the last body out."

"It would be a rough way to go," Martin said. "Mother, could you pass us the chicken?" he asked in Norwegian.

"Terrible," Margretha said. "What a tragedy for the families of those seven men who were killed."

"And for it to happen just before Thanksgiving." Mary shuddered. "They certainly aren't celebrating today." She spooned some cranberry jelly onto her plate.

Laurense's bony forefinger rapped the table as she quoted in Norwegian. "As it is written in Ecclesiastes 3, 'For everything there is a season, and a time for every matter under the heaven: a time to be born and a time to die; a time to plant, and a time to pluck up what is planted. . . . All go to one place; all are from the dust, and all turn to dust again.'"

"You think it was the concrete?" Joseph took a fried chicken breast from the platter. It looked much better than the lutefisk. "I read in the paper they called in a professor of structural engineering from the University of Iowa to investigate. Seems the building was unusually well designed, so he's thinking it might be the concrete."

Martin shrugged. "Could be. They're looking to see what the weather was like when they poured cement. What they should look into is the falsework. If those forms were faulty or insufficient, the structure wouldn't be safe. That's the most likely reason the building collapsed, if you ask me."

"What a terrible shame," Mary said. "To think it might have been prevented."

"There's no excuse, whatever the case," Joseph shook his head.

"I agree," Martin said. "They probably got a low bid on the concrete and hired some inexperienced or lazy workmen."

"I wouldn't want that on my conscience," Margretha said. "How could you live with yourself if you knew you could have done something to prevent a tragedy? Don't you agree, Joseph?"

Ignoring his sister, Joseph took a large bite of chicken and chewed slowly.

"'For God will bring every deed into judgment, with every secret thing, whether good or evil,'" Laurense quoted in Norwegian.

"Well," Margretha said. "Here come the girls."

Joseph looked up to see Ida and Charlotte approaching the table.

"We thought we'd come say hello." Ida's smile circled the table.

Their grandmother stiffly nodded to each of the girls.

"I hear you are enjoying St. Olaf, Charlotte," Mary said.

Charlotte grinned. "I am."

"Professor Christiansen gave her a tremendous compliment the other day." Ida tilted her head toward her sister. "Said she is the most advanced student he's ever had in Music Theory class."

"Did he?" Margretha's brows lifted. "Very good, Charlotte."

Charlotte blushed. "Christiansen is an excellent teacher."

"Your father speaks highly of him." Martin wiped his mouth with his napkin.

"He's building quite a reputation for himself and the choir," Margretha said.

"Yes, he is." A sly, smug smile spread across Charlotte's face. "In fact, Jennie Donhowe was just telling us during dinner that after the Norway tour, she thinks the reputation of the St. Olaf Choir surpassed that of Grinnell's Glee Club."

"Charlotte, I'm not sure she said 'surpassed.'"

Charlotte shrugged. "If it isn't what she said, Ida, it's what she meant. She was clearly jealous. Both Jennie and Cosette chose Grinnell for its superior music program." She tossed her head. "Seems it may not be so superior after all."

"Pride cometh before a fall." Laurense pursed her lips and stared at Charlotte.

"Speaking of Cosette," Ida looked at her father. "She and Severt have gone to the bazaar."

The Ladies Aids of the four churches in town and the Young Peoples' Society of Immanuel Church were holding their fourth annual bazaar. Joseph did not care for these events, having no interest in the items for sale or the milling crowds of women and young people.

"You girls must go see your grandmother's quilt. It's on display at the quilters' booth," Margretha said.

Mary nodded to her mother-in-law. "I do believe it is the nicest you've ever made." She looked up at her nieces. "It won first prize again this year."

"I'm not surprised." Ida smiled at her grandmother. "You make the most beautiful quilts."

"Well," Charlotte said, "I'm going to go catch up with Jennie. Are you coming along, Ida?"

"I haven't quite decided."

"Are you still thinking of going home to write a letter to Oscar?"

Ida smiled. "I just may do that."

Joseph felt Margretha's hard stare. He did not need her to remind him that the time had come. "If you are leaving now, I'll accompany you."

During the walk home, Ida chatted about Professor Christiansen and some of the choir members who had been on tour the previous summer.

After they had hung up their coats and hats, she followed her father into the living room.

Joseph cleared his throat. "Ida."

"Yes, Papa?" Ida smiled softly.

He sighed. "I have a difficult matter to discuss with you."

Ida tilted her head. "Difficult?"

"Regarding Oscar."

Searching his face, Ida's smile dissolved. "Oscar?"

"It seems there is a problem with his family."

Ida frowned. "I don't understand." She shook her head. "What kind of a problem?"

"Tuberculosis." Joseph watched for her reaction, hoping to see surprise.

"His father?" Ida's hand went to her hair, nervously brushing back the fallen curls from her face.

She had known and had not said anything. He had not thought her capable of withholding information from him.

"Where did you learn about his father?"

"Margretha had a letter from Sigrid Hansen." It would have been better to have heard the news from Ida herself.

Ida squinted. "Sigrid?"

"She attended St. Olaf with Oscar's sister."

Ida hesitated, her expression shifting from understanding to wounded surprise. "Margretha was checking into Oscar's family?"

"Are you aware his father did not go to a sanatorium?"

Ida focused at the floor and shrugged. "Oscar hasn't spoken much about it, other than to say how hard it was on the family."

"Oscar was exposed, Ida."

Ida raised her head and leaned forward. "Oscar is fine, Papa. You saw him yourself."

"He could be infected."

She shook her head. "I don't believe it."

"The risk is too great, Ida."

"I don't understand." Her brows pulled together, her eyes searching his.

"I cannot allow you to be exposed to tuberculosis."

Ida froze, her eyes wide. "Papa." She swallowed, her voice broken. "What are you saying?"

Joseph took a breath and held it. He had dreaded this moment. "You must break off the engagement, Ida."

His favorite daughter sat back with a stunned stare. Blinking slowly, she swallowed, shaking her head. "No, Papa," she whispered.

Joseph steeled himself against her pain. "It is for the best, Ida."

"No." She shook her head again. "You cannot ask this of me."

Joseph looked away. This was not a time for weakness or hesitation on his behalf, but he wanted her to understand he had not made the decision lightly. "I have considered the matter and have thought of little else." He forced himself to face her once again. "I am afraid there is no other choice."

Tears flooded Ida's eyes. "But I love Oscar. I couldn't bear to lose him."

Disconcerted by the display of emotion, Joseph studied his hands. "I wish I could spare you this pain, Ida. But I am your father, and I cannot allow you to risk your very life."

"I'll take the risk, Papa." She swallowed, choking on the tears. "I beg you." She smothered her nose and mouth with her hands. "Please." Her head fluttered. "Do not make me do this."

"I could not bear to lose you, Ida." Surely she understood the love of a father for his daughter.

Ida gasped. Tears flooded her face.

"If you break with him, I'll send you to any of the finest music schools in the east." He would do anything to compensate for what he was demanding. Anything to help heal her heart.

Anger flashed through her pain. "That is not what I want." She coughed, choking on the tears. "I only want to marry Oscar." She closed her eyes, crossed her hands over her breast and bowed her head.

"I am sorry, Ida. Truly sorry."

He remained seated as his daughter rushed from the room and ran up the stairs, sobbing uncontrollably.

When the door of Ida's room slammed shut, Joseph's heart felt the impact.

III

1914 – 1917

"Better off poor, healthy, and fit
than rich and afflicted in body.
Health and fitness are better than any gold,
And a robust body than countless riches.
There is no wealth better than health of body,
And no gladness above joy of heart."

SIRACH 30: 14-16

Diagnosis
Joseph

*I*da broke her engagement with Oscar. When she returned home from St. Olaf College for the Christmas break, she spent much of her time alone in her room and avoided conversation and eye contact with her father. She refused his offer to visit the east coast, but wrote in March that she had applied to and been accepted at the New England Conservatory of Music. She would move to Boston immediately after graduation and would not return home.

While Ida's distress and detachment concerned Joseph, he expected her studies in Boston would absorb her attention and take her mind from Oscar. Ida's heart would heal.

Considering his daughter's emotional state a temporary matter that had been addressed, Joseph shifted his attention to his son's physical health. Severt had not regained his energy and seemed to contract one ailment after another. By spring, he had lost quite a bit of weight, and his clothes appeared to be a good size too large. A cold settled in his chest, and his labored breathing was often broken by a hoarse cough. Suffering periodic fevers and exhausted from lack of sleep, Severt was unable to work much of the month of April.

Though Dr. William J. Mayo had not found anything the matter with Severt the previous September, the doctor had recommended a return visit if his patient's health showed any deterioration. By May, even Severt could not deny his condition had worsened, and Joseph accompanied him to the Mayo Clinic for a follow-up examination. Joseph would hear what the doctor had to say himself. The lack of a diagnosis the previous fall had been good news and particularly reassuring after Margretha discovered the history of tuberculosis in Oscar's family. As the months passed, however, relief that Severt had not contracted tuberculosis was obscured by renewed concern. A young man of twenty-three should not suffer from incessant ill health. Surely the good Mayo doctors could perform some additional tests to isolate the trouble and recommend a cure.

Father and son arrived at the clinic a quarter of an hour prior to the scheduled appointment time, only to discover the building vacated and in process of being remodeled. A notice posted at the entrance directed them to the new address.

The unexpected delay perturbed Joseph. "I would have thought the doctor's office would have notified us of this in advance."

Severt shrugged. "Perhaps I received a notice in the post. I seem to recall something about a new building." Turning, he scanned the street. "I most likely tossed it out, not expecting to return." He attempted a laugh. "Wishful thinking on my part, it seems." He struggled to suppress the cough that rose from the aborted laugh and gestured to an impressive new structure down the street. "I should think that is it."

Joseph clenched his teeth. It was incomprehensible that Severt could have neglected to recall or mention that the clinic had moved. The new building did not look particularly like a clinic, but with any luck it was the site of their appointment. If not, they would be late.

Just as they were about to turn away, the door before them opened, and Joseph and Severt stepped back to allow a ruddy workman carrying a can of paint to exit the building.

Reeking of perspiration, the worker spewed a stream of tobacco from the gap between his stained front teeth onto the grass. "Lookin' for the new buildin'?" He lifted his chin and waved his paintbrush down the street. "That's it, all right. Worked on it myself. Everything under one roof, they wanted. All the offices, laboratories, and whatnot. Quite the place, I'll say. Nothin' ordinary about it, no question about that." He peered for a moment at Joseph and then his gaze crawled down Severt's thin body. "You'll see for yourself. Doesn't look nothin' like a place for sick folks, if you ask me."

Irritated by the rude behavior and anxious to get to the appointment, Joseph nodded curtly. "We'd best be on our way."

Spitting again, the workman stared after them as they crossed the street, appearing in no hurry to return to work.

Joseph watched the painter from the corner of his eye, stepping with care to avoid the low spots slick with mud. "The clinic should forbid its workers from spitting as a public health measure."

"A rather unsavory sort, isn't he?" Severt glanced back. "Nice of him to point us in the right direction, though."

"The man would be better off talking less to passersby and working harder to improve his lot."

The smell of the damp earth hung in the heavy air. Foraging robins hopped through the sprouting grass in the surrounding yards, pausing to cock their heads from side to side. Oblivious to the flitting movements and tuneful warbles of the birds or the contorting worms he crushed underfoot, Joseph focused on the appointment ahead, annoyed that they would arrive with mud splatters on their pants.

The stately clinic structure, constructed in the shape of a U, towered six floors above the street. Joseph and Severt stepped from the muddy street onto the white stone courtyard spread before the building where several laborers were planting flowers and shrubs, their voices raised to compete with the scrape of shovels against wheelbarrows.

After climbing the stairs to the carved stone entrance, Severt paused, out of breath. Joseph considered the building. He had expected a purely functional construction, lacking ornamentation of any kind. It did not have the appearance of a medical institution, and when they entered the interior design gave the impression of a fine hotel rather than a clinic. An open, white Rookwood tile staircase with elaborately carved railings curved up toward a landing overlooking a spacious waiting room, then split and continued upward on either side to the floors above. Rookwood tiles also covered the walls and square pillars. In the center of the waiting room, beneath a Tiffany stained skylight ceiling, a carved Rookwood tile fountain rose above the cushioned cane armchairs casually spread out across the terrazzo floor.

The personable front desk receptionist confirmed Severt's appointment with Dr. Will, as she referred to him, and instructed them to take a seat, telling them they shouldn't have to wait long. The father and son chose two chairs at the edge of the quiet waiting room. Folded into a chair nearby sat an elderly, large-boned man with a bandage wrapped around the top of his shaved skull. Beside him, a slight woman—presumably his wife—nervously rearranged herself in her seat, smoothing her skirt over her knees with one hand and clutching a handbag in the other. Near the fountain, a young woman with black circles beneath her eyes stood rocking an infant in her arms, swaying and humming softly. A small girl sat on the floor near the woman's feet, playing with a cloth doll.

Within a few minutes, a nurse called out Severt's name and directed them to Dr. Mayo's office down the hall to the right. Joseph noted the brass name-plates on the doors as they passed: Dr. Donald Balfour, Dr. Melvin Millet, Dr. Christopher Graham, Dr. Louis Wilson, and Dr. Henry Plummer. Some of the doctors in the clinic specialized in particular areas. Joseph's confidence increased; there was no better medical facility in the nation. The doctors would soon diagnose what ailed Severt and recommend a treatment to restore his health.

They found Dr. William J. Mayo's office at the end of the second hall they entered, next to his brother's, Dr. Charles H. Mayo. The doctor welcomed them into his office, introduced himself to Joseph, and gestured to a large upholstered davenport centered on the wall to the right of the desk. "Please. Have a seat." He shut the door behind him and strode to the black leather chair behind the desk, which was centered in the room facing the door.

Severt sat down at the far end of the davenport near the heat register. He leaned forward and adjusted the stuffed pillow propped against the arm of the davenport. Joseph considered sitting in the oversized, ornately carved arm-chair by the door, but seeing the large space his son had left for him, took a seat at the opposite end of the davenport, leaving the space of a full cushion between them. He too found the pillow uncomfortable but did not move to adjust it.

A thick wool carpet with a deep jewel-toned oriental design covered the floor from wall to wall. The doctor's desk was mahogany, the sides inlaid and edges carved. The quality of the office furnishings equaled that of the exterior and lobby, but the room itself was plain and uncluttered, with painted white walls and ceilings. The Mayo doctors had invested quite a sum in the building. Perhaps an excessive amount, Joseph thought. Evidently, the progressive group medical practice approach generated quite a profit. It certainly provided superior care for the patients, and was worth the cost.

Joseph thought of the local doctors who traveled the countryside with their black leather bags, the doctors who could not save his precious Annie. Perhaps the Mayos could have saved her. He had not paid attention to her infection, had not acted immediately. But he had learned. Never again would he allow any ailment, however small, to go unchecked. He would not lose a child as he had his wife. He would take them to the best doctors and have them reexamined until a treatment was prescribed. Yes, he had done the right thing bringing Severt back to the Mayos.

"Quite an impressive clinic you have here," Joseph said.

The doctor glanced up from the open file lying before him. Pausing, he rolled his chair back a bit and turned toward them. "This new facility is quite an improvement. Our own Dr. Plummer came up with the design, understanding the particular needs of integrating the various aspects of a group medical practice. We finally opened here the beginning of March and are quite pleased with the new arrangement. A benefit both to us as physicians as well as to our patients, as your son will soon experience."

"Everything under one roof, a laborer down the street informed us!" Severt grinned at his father.

Joseph did not find humor in his son's remark and did not smile.

Dr. Mayo rolled his chair back toward the desk and tapped the file with his pen. "Dr. Plummer has been of great service to us. He came up with the idea of the dossier medical records system we use today. Helps tremendously to organize all of a patient's information in a single file to share with the entire team working on the case." He peered down at the file before him. "Now let's see what we have here."

Under different circumstances, Joseph would have been interested to hear more about the design and architecture of the new building. Today, however, he was anxious to get on with the matter of Severt's diagnosis and pleased the doctor did not engage in unnecessary conversation.

As the physician scanned the file, Joseph studied the man before him. The eldest of the two Mayo sons, Dr. William J. Mayo appeared to be near Joseph's age. The physician's hands were large, his handshake solid. Large of stature, he was neither thin nor overweight, a man who did not drink or eat to excess. A full head of neatly trimmed, coarse white hair framed a large, square face. His features were equally strong and in proportion. Large mouth set in a thin line, probing eyes deep set beneath bushy black eyebrows, his expression did not betray his thoughts.

Severt fidgeted while they waited for the doctor to review the file. Impatient to hear what the doctor had to say, Joseph studied the room. The surface of the doctor's large desk was clear except for a large green marble bust of a bald man, several reference books between two green marble bookends of what appeared to be kneeling or bowing figures of some sort, and the file. Behind the doctor, on the wall opposite the door they had entered, several different sets of volumes filled the three shelves of a maple bookcase. On a stand beside the bookcase, an oversized book with fine white pages lay open.

A second book of similar size lay on its side on a shelf below the open book. Like the Bible on the altar, Joseph thought. The guiding principles and judgments for the physicians. The gift of life. Above, prominently displayed near the ceiling, three photographs of solemn men hung in a triangle. One of the lower photographs was of the man seated at the desk before him. Joseph supposed the others to be the doctor's brother and their father, who had founded the practice.

"We last examined you on September 18, 1913, I see." The doctor did not look up from the file.

Severt nodded. "Yes."

"At the time, your symptoms were fatigue following an appendectomy and a period of general ill health."

His face flushed, Severt glanced at his father. "Yes."

Joseph wondered if the color was due to embarrassment or fever.

"The examination did not reveal any abnormalities, and laboratory tests were negative. Nothing to indicate we were dealing with a chronic illness." He paused and looked up. "The sputum and X-ray tests were negative." Dr. Mayo picked up the pen. "How is your energy level now?"

"I tire quickly."

"Explain. What types of activities do you find difficult to perform?"

"Well, that seems to be the problem. Even a short stroll seems to leave me breathless, not to mention walking up a flight of stairs. Like an old man." Severt attempted a laugh but instead began to cough. He quickly pulled out his handkerchief and placed it over his mouth.

The physician's thick eyebrows lifted, and he jotted a few notes in the file. "Sleeping at night?"

"Not well." Severt folded his handkerchief. "The past few weeks or so."

Joseph shook his head. "More than the past few weeks. Several months, I would say."

Severt shrugged. "Perhaps."

Dr. Mayo nodded. "Coughing keep you up?"

"Not coughing so much as the fever and chills." Severt studied his handkerchief, twisting the edges with both hands.

"Sweat at night? Enough to soak the bedcovers?"

"Yes." Severt tried to laugh again. "Causes quite a bit of extra laundry, I'm afraid."

The doctor nodded without expression. "Is your cough productive?"

"Productive?"

"Does your cough produce any sputum?"

Severt colored. "Some."

The doctor stared intently at his patient. "Some meaning frequency or amount?"

Severt frowned, staring at the handkerchief in his hands. "It seems to happen more often than before." He squinted. "I would say whenever I cough, I cough something up, but I wouldn't say it is a great amount."

The doctor added to his notes. "Does the sputum have a color, or is it clear?"

Severt shrugged. "Clear, I would say."

The doctor's eyes narrowed intently. "Have you ever noticed it to be white, or appear to have any blood?"

"No." Severt emphatically shook his head. "No, certainly no blood."

Joseph's stomach twisted. "Why do you ask about coughing blood?"

The doctor's penetrating eyes met Joseph's briefly before refocusing on Severt. "Any pain? Joints? Limbs? Chest? Muscles? Spine? Head?"

Severt shrugged again. "My chest aches at times when I have overexerted myself or at times during a coughing spell."

The doctor nodded, added a few more notes, and sat back, pen still in hand. "I shall examine you and will have a few more questions for you at that time. I shall also request a few laboratory tests." Leaning forward, he flipped a few pages in the file, searched the page, and tapped an entry with his pen. "You weighed 155 pounds on your last visit. We will weigh you again, but it appears you have lost some weight."

Severt stiffened, clutching his handkerchief in one hand. "I dare say I have lost a bit. My clothes are rather big at the moment." He forced a smile. "I always have been smaller than I would like. I'm not on the right trend, am I?"

Joseph cleared his throat. "After the Mayos treat what ails you, you'll gain your weight back." He turned to the physician. "What do you suspect is the problem, doctor? You must have some idea." He didn't intend such a harsh tone, but in response, Dr. Mayo's stern expression seemed to soften rather than harden.

"Yes, I do have some idea." He set his pen on the table. "But I shall wait for the results of the examination and laboratory tests before I pronounce a diagnosis." He stood, and gestured to the door. "Shall we proceed?"

Joseph wanted to press the doctor further but understood and respected the man's refusal to speculate. The wait would require more patience, but the time would pass quickly enough with the examination and tests soon to be underway.

✳✳✳

Later that day, Dr. William J. Mayo delivered the diagnosis in his office. Severt and Joseph had chosen the same seats they had earlier, at opposite ends of the large davenport.

Tuberculosis.

Fear emanated from Severt. He responded to the diagnosis in silence, clutching the arm of the davenport beside him as he turned toward his father.

As the blood drained from his son's face, Joseph's own blood surged and pounded to a roar. He turned to the doctor, but found his gaze drawn upwards, toward the ceiling, where the physician's father stared down upon him from the photograph. Below, the volumes of medical knowledge stood firm. On the stand, the great heavy book lay open. The words of judgment had been spoken.

Unnerved, he looked at the clock on the bookshelf. Joseph did not immediately focus on the hands of the clock or even then comprehend what they represented.

How much time would Severt have?

Severt cleared his throat.

Perhaps there was a mistake. Earlier tests had been negative, had shown no sign. The pounding in Joseph's head subsided, and anger filled the void.

Dr. Mayo waited, his chair rolled away from his desk, facing them, expressionless.

"How can this be?" Deep within, Joseph contained a dark desire to rush forward and seize the doctor. His hands fisted, the nails pressing hard into his palms. "My son was tested here not long ago. The tests showed nothing."

The physician did not speak immediately. His expression remained stern and unreadable. "Mr. Marvick. You are both technically correct and incorrect. The tuberculin skin test result from your son's last visit was positive. The analysis of the . . . "

Joseph heard nothing more the doctor said. Positive. The meaning of the word did not register immediately. In all other contexts, positive would mean a favorable result. "Excuse me, doctor. Did you say one of the tests was positive?"

Dr. Mayo nodded. "Yes. The tuberculin skin test was positive."

Taken aback, Joseph faced his son in disbelief. "Severt? Did you know of this?"

Severt shrunk back into the davenport. He shrugged, winced, and glanced at the doctor before replying. "They said it did not indicate I had tuberculosis, just that I had been exposed to it."

Joseph took a deep breath, attempting to retain his composure. Had Margretha known this? Surely not. He could not believe his own son had kept this information from him.

Severt shrugged again. "I didn't want to trouble you with it when the other tests showed nothing."

Joseph smoothed his mustache. This was neither the time nor place to chastise his son. He could imagine what the doctor was thinking. How could a son withhold such critical information from his own father? Joseph knew his face betrayed him as his blood surged in anger and embarrassment.

"As I was about to explain." His voice measured, the doctor's expression revealed neither judgment nor compassion. "The tuberculin skin test was positive, but the culture sample we obtained during Severt's last visit was negative. Severt is correct in saying that he was not diagnosed with the disease of tuberculosis. A positive culture from the sputum is the only way to positively diagnose the disease. A positive tuberculin skin test indicates exposure to the microorganism mycobacterium tuberculosis, but not disease. We have seen patients who have had a positive skin test but who have remained disease free for years. We also know that tuberculosis develops very slowly. The sputum sample we took during Severt's last visit did not include any of the tubercle bacilli. Perhaps Severt's body was strong enough to fight off the disease, in other words, to wall off the bacillus, and it was in an inactive state at that time. Perhaps it was active at the time, but the sample we obtained was from an uninfected area of tissue." He paused. "In any event, my diagnosis today is definite. The sputum sample we analyzed contained several bacilli, and the chest X-ray revealed two infected areas in Severt's lungs. Severt has pulmonary tuberculosis, meaning it resides in his lungs, which is the most common form of the disease."

"What does this mean for me?" Severt winced and swallowed. He avoided his father's eyes.

The question settled into the shadows of fear and uncertainty.

Joseph focused, searching for the way leading out of darkness. Severt would have the best care available. Joseph would make the arrangements himself. Severt would be cured, as others had been. "My son shall have the best treatment available, Dr. Mayo. What do you recommend? The cost is of no consequence."

The physician nodded. "It is imperative he be admitted to a sanatorium, both for his own health as well as the health of others. To arrest and prevent the disease from spreading, it is necessary to build the resistive power of the tissues of the lung. The sanatorium provides a hygienic and dietetic regimen under the supervision of a physician, designed to support and increase the patient's strength."

Severt paled. "A sanatorium? For how long?"

The doctor paused. "It is not possible to say. Every patient's case differs."

Joseph did not want to imagine Severt in a sanatorium with infected patients, and focused on the doctor. "Which sanatorium do you recommend?"

Dr. Mayo leaned back in his chair. "There are several fine sanatoriums in Colorado."

"Colorado?" Severt's voice cracked. He turned to his father, panic palpable in his wide eyes. "It's so far away."

"The priority is where the best care is, Severt, not how close it is to home." Joseph looked away. The last time he and Severt had disagreed, Severt wanted to remain at Cornell, but Joseph insisted he transfer to St. Olaf College. He had acted in his son's best interest. He could not have known Severt would be exposed to tuberculosis at St. Olaf. By one of his roommates. Joseph focused on the doctor. "Colorado is the best place for a cure?"

The doctor nodded. "The research does seem to indicate that the climate there contributes to the healing process. I will not say that a cure is guaranteed. However, the prognosis for recovery is improved in a sunny and dry climate, such as the Colorado area provides. Perhaps you know of F. O. Stanley, the inventor of the steamer. He was a patient here, and after moving to Colorado Springs he appears to have made a complete recovery. Severt also has the benefit of having been diagnosed in the early stages of the disease and at a relatively young age."

Joseph made his decision. "Colorado, then. Which sanatorium is the best?"

As Dr. Mayo informed them of the better sanatoriums in Colorado Springs and Denver, Severt's shoulders dropped and his gaze fell to the floor.

Joseph wished he could spare his son the sanatorium, but resolved that Severt's time there would be temporary. His son would be cured, just as F. O. Stanley and others had been. Joseph would do everything possible to ensure it.

Agnes Phipps Memorial Sanatorium

Joseph

*I*t was snowing when Joseph arrived in Denver in early March 1915. The flakes floating from the heavens were as light as ashes, shrouding Joseph's robust frame as he walked from the station, suffocating the sound of his feet upon the earth. His warm breath misted in the cold while his chest expanded. Severt had been a patient at Agnes Phipps Sanatorium for nearly a year now, and Joseph hoped to find his health improved. Visits from family and friends were discouraged, and it had been months since Joseph had last seen his son.

On the train to Denver, Joseph warily kept his distance from his fellow travelers, knowing many were tuberculars seeking the cure in Colorado. The hopeful arrivals would soon find that while the climate would be indiscriminate and seemingly uncompromising in its cleansing, the community's tolerance of them would depend upon health and wealth. Many boardinghouse keepers turned away those who admitted they were sick or were betrayed by their coughs. The penniless took their blankets and joined others of their kind in the tent colonies. Several miles outside the Denver city limits, the train wheels rumbled along the Kansas Pacific railway line past a camp of tents spewed across the flat, barren land. The first time Joseph noticed the camp from his stateroom window, he had not understood why so many people would choose to live in tents or why the leaders of the fairly progressive city of Denver did not act to improve or remove such an unsightly settlement so close to the city. He learned that those who lived in the camp, commonly referred to as "Bugsville," were diseased, destitute, and dying. Living in filth and contamination, they followed no sanitary measures.

Some of the sick went into the city to beg. On his last visit, Joseph saw two men lingering outside the entrance of the Hotel Broadway, eyes sunken and staring, their frayed layers of stained clothing hanging on shrunken frames. As Joseph watched, the doorman ushered a couple from the hotel, extending his arm to guide the couple in the opposite direction of the skeletal men. One of the men began to cough violently, making no attempt to turn his head or cover his mouth. The cough was bigger than the man, raw, rough, a rumbling steel locomotive ripping from his chest and splintering his wooden frame. When the cough subsided, he spit on the sidewalk and wiped his chin with his bare hand. Loathing lined the doorman's face. "Away with you, I say!" The visiting gentleman wrapped his arm around the woman, shielding her with his body. Aghast, she covered her nose and mouth with her gloved hand and turned her head into his chest, her hat brushing the shoulder of his coat. "I told you to leave the area," the uniformed doorman shouted at the men. "We don't want your kind here. You're dangerous. Bad for business. Filthy bugs, you are. You'll find no charity here. Go back to Bugsville or whatever hole you came from. I'm warning you, if you don't move off now, I will call the authorities. I will. Not that they want to touch you, but they'll remove you if necessary." Sneering, the man who had been coughing leaned back against the building. The other stepped forward, lifted his chin, and spit at the doorman.

Joseph crossed the street to avoid them. The absence of a breeze minimized his risk of contamination, but he turned his head and held his breath as he passed as an added precaution. Reprehensible lower class men like these imperiled society by failing to use spittoons. The city should enforce the ordinances that prohibited spitting to prevent such men from wandering the streets and spreading their infection.

It seemed half the people in Denver had come for a cure, whether for themselves or someone in their family. Throughout the city's less affluent residential areas, invalids with proper hygiene and moderate resources rented rooms in boarding houses or cure cottages, distinguishable by the disfiguring large porches that swelled from every wall, from every floor. In the mornings and afternoons, invalids taking their rest cures lined the porches. Enclosed in blankets, they lay stretched out on reclining chairs, silent and unmoving.

Only the most well-to-do could afford the strictly supervised medical care at Agnes Phipps where the weekly rates ranged from $9 to $12. On the thirty-minute ride by electric car from Denver, Joseph considered his choice of Agnes Phipps. Drs. Charles and William Mayo had provided referrals to several sanatoriums in Colorado, but did not recommend one over the others. The staffs of all included equally eminent physicians, and all provided good care. Despite the testimonial by Stanley, Joseph decided against Colorado Springs, preferring the convenience of Denver. Cragmor and Glockner accepted patients in any stage of the disease, including the most advanced cases; Joseph did not want Severt exposed to the very ill. Nordrach Ranch did not accept patients in far advanced stages, but patients slept outdoors in octagonal tents, which seemed extreme. He finally settled upon Agnes Phipps Sanatorium, seven miles from the smoke and dust of Denver, a convenient thirty minutes by electric car. Agnes Phipps accepted only early cases of pulmonary tuberculosis, and each patient had a spacious private room with a view of Cherry Creek and Pike's Peak.

Situated on 160 acres at the highest elevation on the plains east of Denver, the seven buildings at Agnes Phipps faced south, maximizing exposure to the sun while providing protection from east and west winds. Designed in the old Spanish mission style of architecture, large open arches extended the lengths of the structures, which, though particularly suited to the open air requirements of a sanatorium, gave the facades a hollow and porous impression from a distance.

Walking paths traversed the grounds, leading to attractive gardens with shelters, arbors, and benches where patients could rest. Two open air pavilions optimized exposure to the fresh air, and the patients resided in two additional separate pavilions for men and women, where each invalid's private room opened to a wide open air porch, divided by canvas partitions for sleeping purposes. A three-story administration building housed reception rooms, board room, offices, dining rooms, kitchen, and library. The medical building contained reception and consultation rooms, complete laboratory and treatment rooms, and an infirmary with a well-equipped operating room. A power house, which provided electricity, ice, and refrigeration, also housed an electric laundry and a cremation device for sputum, garbage, and sweepings.

Joseph arrived at the sanatorium shortly after noon, and the receptionist directed him to the dining room complex located on the first floor in the southeast wing.

Blinding sunlight reflected from the white painted pillars, the white painted walls, the white china set on the white linen tablecloths, the white uniforms of the nurses. Joseph's own skin absorbed the purified light, his hands pale against the dark brown sleeves of his suit. His warm breath steamed in the drafty air. All of the floor to ceiling arched windows that filled the southeast wall were wide open, and the temperature in the room was not much above freezing.

Conversation and laughter interspersed the clinking of silver against china. The well-dressed diners in the room, seated on dark stained formal wood chairs, seemed in good spirits.

Severt stood and offered his father an empty chair at the table. "Sorry, but you will have to sit here until I'm finished. The rules are that I cannot leave the table until I have eaten every bite and drunk every drop."

"The rules are the rules," one of the men at the table said.

"More rules than Aunt Margretha had!" Severt laughed.

"Am I taking someone's seat?"

"Not at all. Today we have an extra chair at our table. You have Pete's assigned seat. Unfortunately for him, they dropped his up time, and he isn't allowed to join us until he is reclassified."

"Up time?"

"Time out of bed. I've moved up to six hours a day. An hour for each meal, an hour mid-morning, another mid-afternoon, and one in the evening before bed."

Severt reintroduced his father to the others at his table. Joseph had met two of the men previously. Mr. Merriweather was Severt's porch mate. Mr. Elmerdorf was from Albuquerque.

"You seem to have put on some weight since I was here last."

"What do you expect?" Severt laughed. "Three-course dinners and a quart of heavy cream every day. They bring the cream in the morning, and I can drink it whenever I choose, but I must say, I still have trouble getting it all down."

"You've no reason to complain." Mr. Elmerdorf shook his head. "How many eggs you on now? They still have me on 28 eggs a day. Can't seem to get my weight up." The young man stood close to six feet tall, but Joseph guessed he didn't weigh much more than Severt.

After Severt finished eating, Joseph walked with him around the grounds. Though his son made light of the rules in the dining room, he resisted the rigid rules that had become the repetitive rhythm of his life. "The mountains may be a great view," Severt said, "but they remain the same, day after day, just like life here at the san. Rules, rules, rules. The bell rings, and I rise at seven o'clock. I take my temperature and record it. I eat a full breakfast, and afterwards I walk outside for an hour. I don't know what I would do if they didn't allow me outside. I couldn't bear it if I was limited to lung gymnastics in my room. I take my temperature again after exercise and then lie on my porch before dinner and wait for the doctor to make his visit. Nothing changes there, either. He can't tell me when I'll be released, only what the measurements are.

My chance for recovery depends upon my obeying the rules, he says. So I follow the rules. I eat all of my dinner. I drink my quart of heavy cream each day, however much it makes me gag. I take my two-hour rest cure on the porch in the afternoon. I've become quite adept at wrapping myself up in my blankets to stay warm and dry. Quite an accomplishment, wouldn't you say? Ha. They didn't teach me that at St. Olaf. Naturally I realize it isn't a skill required at the bank."

Severt's attempt at humor expired in a coughing paroxysm. "I recline on my chair without reading or writing and try not to talk to my porch mates for fear of losing the few privileges I've gained. I could lose my outside passes, or—worse—they could extend my sentence here. Although in actuality, they won't tell me what my sentence is, so I wouldn't know if they extended it or not. And so I lie on the sleeping porch with nothing to do but stare at the mountains. It is a good day if there are some clouds to add variety to the view. I'm not sure if I like the dark storm clouds best or the white calm clouds. Not a matter I contemplated before the san, I tell you! I try not to listen to the coughs, which is the only sound we're allowed. It's the graveyard coughs that are the worst. If they could, they would silence that too. We are here to get better, and a graveyard cough has a depressing effect on the rest of us, which is against the rules. We must be cheerful, the nurses tell us. The most cheerful time is when we're allowed outside passes, and we can leave the san and go into town. Our cheerfulness would be guaranteed if we knew we didn't have to return. But return we do, like the good lungers we are." Severt paused. "At least Dr. Tygard increased my exercise time in the afternoon, so I am outside more now. I take my temperature afterwards, have my supper, and by 9:00 I'm back in bed with the lights out. The san goes silent again except for the coughing and occasionally the choking and bustling of nurses in the halls when someone throws a hemorrhage. When I can't sleep, I lie in the dark waiting for the bell to ring again in the morning so I can repeat the routine all over again. Sometimes I have the urge to scream, but my throat would hurt too much." Severt stopped at the top of a hill to catch his breath. "Look at me, Father. I may not be cured, but I've gained weight and am certainly much improved. You must get me out of here."

"I'll speak with your doctor, Severt."

"Well, that is the end of it, then." Severt resumed walking, shaking his head. "He'll never agree to it."

It was not Severt's condition that convinced Joseph his son must leave the sanatorium. When he accompanied Severt to his sleeping porch, the canvas partitions were pulled back, exposing the other patients. Joseph glanced down the length of the sun-filled, narrow porch. Each patient had a white painted metal bed and a rocking chair. Many of the men sat in their chairs reading, dressed in their dinner clothes. Several had blankets wrapped around their shoulders or draped across their legs. Some lay shrouded in their white painted metal beds beneath the white sheets. Seemingly unaware that the curtains between them remained tied to the wall, each man appeared emotionally isolated. Joseph thought it odd that none of the patients conversed, particularly given their close physical proximity, but recalled Severt's complaints.

Seated in his chair, Mr. Merriweather lifted his hand in greeting, breaking the rules of silence. "You've deposited our good man Severt just in time. The nurses will soon arrive to put us to bed. We need our rest, you know, and no exceptions granted."

"I won't be long." Despite the open arches and absence of bars, Joseph felt confined on the porch. Anxious to escape himself, he sympathized with Severt's desire to leave.

On the other side of Mr. Merriweather, what appeared to be a skeleton stared at Joseph from his bed. Only the pain-filled, pleading eyes, sunken in dark pits of his skull, seemed alive. Pale, transparent, paper-dry skin stretched over the protruding, nearly fleshless bones of his cheeks, nose, jaws, and forehead. Broken lines of blue veins marked his temples, and a blotch of brilliant red burned in the midst of his cheek. With every breath, his chest crackled and rattled through the silence of the porch. Suddenly, a hard, hollow cough ripped from deep within the consumptive. The lids closed over his eyes, and he turned his head to the side, weakly raising his skeleton arm to cover his mouth with a paper handkerchief.

The cold mountain air swept into the open spaces of the porch, swirling around, entering one set of diseased lungs only to be spewed out to enter the lungs of another.

Joseph held his breath, realizing that Severt breathed in that disease-laden air day and night. Agnes Phipps did not accept patients in advanced states of the disease. Why was this man still on the premises? Why wasn't he in the infirmary? If he were to remain at Agnes Phipps, Severt could become even worse.

Severt caught his father's eye. He stepped toward his father, with his back to the man on the bed and whispered in a low voice. "Don't worry. His days are numbered, and they'll be taking him out of here any day now. They couldn't find a place for him. Otherwise he'd be out of here before now. He begged them to let him see the mountains one more time. You might not believe it, but a month ago, he was a regular fellow. Quite charming. All of us will be sorry to see him go." Severt leaned back against the railing on the edge of the porch. "You will speak to Dr. Tygart before you leave, won't you?"

"I'll see what he has to say." Severt had not recovered enough to return home, but Joseph knew he did not want his son exposed to consumptives who were dying of the disease, even if it were an isolated case. Worse, he did not want his son to speak of a man dying of a contagious disease as a harmless acquaintance or friend.

The doctor strongly advised against Severt's discharge. "The breath is harmless. The germs from consumptives are carried by the sputum, not the breath. If the sputum is properly collected and destroyed, no danger results, and the patient is neither threat to nurse nor porch mate."

"That may be, but I will not have my son lying on the porch beside a dying man. Your policy is to remove patients long before they reach an advanced stage of the disease."

Dr. Tygard leaned forward. "This patient's condition deteriorated rapidly. He will be removed soon. You have no idea how difficult it is to find a place for them when they reach this stage, and we will not put him out on the street."

"Why isn't he in the infirmary? Why would you allow him near the others?"

The strain on the doctor lined his forehead and weighted his eyes. "He has been confined to the infirmary for several weeks now, and we believe all patients should have time outdoors. The canvas partitions should have been closed—not because of any physical danger, but because patients in his condition have a depressing effect on the others. We do our best here. Sometimes it is not optimal."

Despite himself, Joseph sympathized with the doctor's challenge.

"Your son has a better chance of recovery if he remains at Agnes Phipps."

Joseph hesitated, weighing the risks. He had chosen Denver for the benefit of the cool, dry climate, and Agnes Phipps for the quality of the physicians and treatment. He would not, and need not, compromise on that. Severt would remain in Denver under the care of his physicians, and Joseph would arrange for someone to provide sanitary care in a home, away from the dying patients. "I would like him to remain under your care but move into a private residence. Some place nearby."

The doctor raised his eyebrows. "Good luck finding a place. They're hard to come by."

"He could remain under your care?"

Dr. Tygard shrugged. "Of course. His care extends beyond appointments with me, however."

"I'll hire a nurse."

The doctor shook his head. "I doubt you will find a nurse. There aren't enough of them to fill the positions in the institutions as it is."

"I'll advertise and make inquiries. If not a nurse, then someone with experience."

"You must be very careful about who you hire. Sanatorium methods must be strictly employed."

"I understand."

"It is quite a bit of work, you know." The doctor leaned back in his chair.

"We will do everything required. Whatever you advise."

Dr. Tygard sighed. "You are a determined man, Mr. Marvick. I wish I could change your mind, but I see you have made it up." He paused. "Most important, as I said, is to contain the tuberculous discharges. The person who uses a sputum cup is safe; the person who spits on the floor is dangerous. I recommend the use of paper cuspidors which are burned over metal or glass ones that require disinfection."

Joseph stared intently at Dr. Tygard. He did not wish to hear the details, but wanted to impress upon the doctor that he had made his decision and was prepared to proceed. "Go on."

"Severt must have his own room to sleep in, preferably with a southern exposure and with large windows. The larger the windows the better. Windows on two walls, if possible. He should sleep with both top and bottom windows open. Fresh air is critical. The house should have a porch where he should sit or lie as much of the day as possible. Some type of reclining chair will be required. All chairs should be constructed for comfort rather than beauty, with coverings that can be disinfected and washed. The walls of the house should be painted, so as to allow for frequent and proper cleaning. Similarly, wood floors should be painted or waxed for ready cleaning, and any carpets removed and replaced by a few rugs. Floors must be swept only with a broom bag dampened with five percent carbolic solution, and rooms dusted with a cloth similarly dampened. Broom bags and dusters must be washed and boiled frequently. Bed linen must be boiled. He should use only paper napkins at the table and gauze or paper handkerchiefs, and both must be burned. He must have his own knives, forks, spoons and all other utensils, which must be kept separate and scalded after use."

Joseph nodded. As soon as arrangements could be made, Severt would move out of the sanatorium.

Brother's Keeper
Joseph

*B*efore leaving Denver, Joseph funded the required deposit to secure a house. Not only had it taken more time than he expected, as Severt's doctor had warned, but the house would not be available until early August. Of the homes advertised for rent, many included restrictions against tenants with tuberculosis. Some landlords considered excessive coughing alone as grounds for eviction. Available homes without restrictions were in objectionable neighborhoods, in disrepair, or had not been properly sanitized after the death of a previously infected tenant. Finally, Joseph found the property at 2518 Bellaire Street, within a few blocks of the electric car line and featuring both a bedroom and porch with south exposure. The three additional bedrooms would be sufficient to accommodate Severt's caretaker, Joseph, and visiting family.

If the dying patients at Agnes Phipps were not dangerous to live with, as Dr. Tygard insisted, Severt would not be a risk to family or friends. It was a matter of proper sanitary methods. Nothing had been lost having Severt at Agnes Phipps, and he had learned the hygienic, dietary and other daily disciplines of treatment. He would have the same treatment at home in the rental house, and his frame of mind would improve.

The challenge in finding a suitable house proved inconsequential to that of finding a caretaker, however. The growth of sanatoriums and hospitals in the Denver and Colorado Springs area led to a shortage of nurses. Inquiries led to a few interviews, but the women were either unsuitable to Joseph or unwilling to provide live-in care for a tubercular patient.

Perturbed, Joseph returned home.

Margretha's resolute opinion was that Severt should remain in the sanatorium where he had the best possible care and "where a person infected with tuberculosis ought to be." Responsible for their aged parents, she could not consider assuming the role herself. "Not that I would agree to go. He should be in a sanatorium, where Oscar's father should have been. I don't care what the doctors say. If others had been prudent and been confined, the disease could have been contained and our own Severt would not have been infected. To think his other roommate was infected as well. We can only be thankful Ida was spared. One day Ida will be over that young man and grateful you made her break off with him, although I must say it has been a long time coming. Come to your senses, Joseph. You mustn't place Severt above all else, even if he is your only son. I most certainly would not want to be responsible for spreading the dread disease—particularly not within my own family—and I would think you would be of the same mind."

Joseph did not wish to be reminded that Ida was not over Oscar, despite nearly a year in Boston. Nothing he had done had regained her favor or made her happy, and the space between them seemed as vast and turbulent as the ocean they had traveled to Norway.

In her last letter, she had written,

> ". . . You inquired as to when my recital will be and indicated that you would make arrangements to attend. As for the date, it is scheduled for the 17th of June at 7 p.m. I would rather that you not trouble yourself to make the trip out east, however, as my commitments are such that I do not have time for play or visitors. . . ."

Nor did he wish to be reminded that Severt had contracted his illness at St. Olaf. The family had since learned one of Severt's other roommates also had tuberculosis. Margretha was convinced that Oscar spread the germs and infected both Severt and the roommate. Given what he knew now, Joseph thought it more likely that the other roommate had infected Severt. Oscar seemed healthy, whereas the other roommate, in retrospect, was thin and suffered from one illness or another whenever Joseph saw him. In any event, Severt had been exposed at St. Olaf. And the truth was that Severt would not have attended St. Olaf or become ill if Joseph had not insisted that Severt attend a Lutheran church school. Joseph acknowledged his own responsibility for his son's condition. He had done what he thought was best but had inadvertently and undeniably put his son in harm's way. He could not undo the error of the past, but he could ensure Severt had the best treatment and care.

For Severt to be cured, he could have no further exposure to the lungers at Agnes Phipps. Margretha had not been to visit Severt and refused to comprehend the situation at the sanatorium.

"Severt lives with tuberculosis as though it were a normal state," Joseph told his sister. "I'm beginning to think this conditioning of his state of mind is contributing to his physical failing."

"Perhaps you would be well to condition your own mind." Margretha rose from her chair. "Whether we like it or not, Severt has tuberculosis. Better to accept it and deal with it appropriately." Arching her neck, she stared down at him. "And now you must excuse me, as I am going home to my darkroom to develop some photographs."

Joseph watched her leave, thinking his sister cared more for her carefully composed black and white images of healthy family and friends and her water-color paintings of pastel landscapes than she did the welfare of her flesh and blood nephew.

***

It was Peter who suggested Charlotte.

That evening, the men retired to the living room while Olive and Anna washed dishes after supper.

"Certainly cooled off." Peter shoved the windows closed against the evening breeze. "A cigar?" The younger man unlatched and offered the box.

Joseph took a cigar and rolled it slowly with both hands. The soft caramel wrapping caressed his fingertips.

"Quite a predicament about Severt." Peter lit the end of his cigar and inhaled deeply. Tipping his head back, he exhaled and extinguished the flame with a snap of his hand.

Joseph squinted as he inhaled the rich tobacco. The tension in his neck eased somewhat as he slowly released the scented smoke. "It is. I intended on hiring a nurse, but there aren't enough in Denver to fill the demand. My advertisements and inquiries produced a few leads, but failed to turn up any-one conscientious, trustworthy, and willing to live with a patient."

"I suppose it should be no surprise, what with the risk of infection."

Joseph stared at the glowing end of his cigar. "There is no danger if the germs are collected and destroyed."

"You don't fear contagion?"

"No." Joseph squinted through the smoke. "Not from Severt. There is a greater risk of picking up germs on the street."

Peter raised his eyebrows. "You wouldn't fear living in the same house with him?"

"No. Severt is not a poor immigrant. He does not spit carelessly about."

"But he is infected."

"There is no chance of catching his germs if he uses sputum cups and paper handkerchiefs, and disinfectants are used."

"Oh?"

"I spoke with the doctor. He declared Severt poses no risk, as long as sanatorium methods are strictly employed."

"Such as?"

"As for sanitation, there is quite a bit of rigorous cleaning involved— boiling sheets and washing with solutions. Fresh air is important, so the windows would be open at all times. Severt would sleep alone and have his own utensils."

Peter inspected the glowing end of his cigar. "You truly believe there is no risk living in the same house with him?"

Joseph exhaled, squinting from the smoke. "I do."

Peter shrugged. "I don't know that I would risk sending anyone, but if you must, it seems Ida is the best choice. The only option, really."

Joseph coughed, shaking his head. "I hadn't considered her." He would not ask Ida to leave Boston. He had forced her to break off with Oscar and offered the New England Conservatory in exchange. He would not take that away from her.

Ashen smoke hung above Peter like an early morning fog. "Ida is free. Unmarried."

"There are her studies." Ida's letters described days filled with lessons, practice, and the added responsibility of directing the choir at a local church. Not a Lutheran church, but that did not concern Joseph. He did not believe she would lose her faith, as her grandmother prophesied.

"What does she need further study for?" Peter crossed his stretched out legs and leaned back with a sidelong glance at his father-in-law. "She's had more than most women. And I would think you would be concerned that she might be influenced by the women suffragettes there in the east."

"No. Not Ida." With what little free time she had, she chose to attend recitals. She wrote that she feared the other women in her boarding house found her to be quite unsociable, as she refused to accompany them when they went out to enjoy themselves. In time she would get over Oscar. In time the smile for her father would return.

Within the soft darkness, smoke drifted in a dance to the ceiling of the sitting room. Beyond, in the bright lights of the kitchen, the clanging of iron pots and china punctuated the women's chatter.

Joseph owed no explanation to his son-in-law. "Ida will remain in Boston."

Peter shrugged. "I suppose you could leave him in the place."

"No." Joseph gripped the cigar as he tapped the ashes into the brass stand beside him. "That is not an option. He will not be cured there and is at risk of getting worse." He did not describe the skeletal man on the porch. To erase the image, Joseph regarded Peter. His son-in-law had put on weight as a married man. He was not a heavy man, but his features had become more substantial with age. A man who ate well. A man who had his health.

"Do you doubt the competence of his doctors?" Peter leaned forward to tap the ashes from his cigar.

"No. I would move him elsewhere if that were the case. I'm confident they are as good any. Severt will remain in Denver and continue under their care."

Olive appeared in the doorway, reaching behind her back to untie her apron. "We've finished with the dishes. Anna has gone up to her room to read a bit, and after I check on the children I will be off to bed myself. I'll leave you two to your cigars. Good night, Papa."

"Good night." Joseph watched his eldest daughter lift the apron over her head as she left the room.

"Charlotte, then."

Joseph had not considered Charlotte. He had not considered any of his daughters. How could he possibly risk exposing any of his other children to the disease? But if, as he had assured Peter, he truly believed Dr. Tygard's medical opinion that Severt posed no risk if his sputum was contained and destroyed, perhaps the risk was not as great as he had once feared.

***

Joseph welcomed the strong southwest wind as he advanced up the hill from the Northfield station to the St. Olaf College campus. The temperature was warmer than normal for the end of May, and he touched his handkerchief to his moist brow. Scattered across the gently sloping grounds, sunlit students lounged on blankets, some absorbed in textbooks or writing in notebooks, others conversing and laughing. A few rested in the cool dappled shade of the maple trees. A couple strolled slowly, waving occasionally when others called their attention from their inclination toward each other. A roar arose from a group of young men playing catch. The baseball soared over the hands of the intended receiver, who leaped, grasping air as he fell to the earth in a tumble of limbs while the ball plummeted toward a group of reclining women who were saved at the last moment when another player dove and the ball deflected from his mitt. In the distance, the band played.

Severt had once played trumpet in the band. Now he exhaled a contagious cough.

Charlotte rushed along the path toward her father, her smile as full and fresh as the flowering crabapple trees in town. The afternoon sun sprinkled gold in the fluttering oak and maple leaves, and dusted the chestnut braids loosely woven around Charlotte's head.

"Papa, I have had the most incredible news."

Joseph smiled despite himself. "Oh? And what could that be?" With Charlotte's untempered enthusiasm, perhaps the impending conversation would proceed more smoothly than he had anticipated. He had been prepared for her usual tartness.

"You could not have chosen a more opportune time to visit."

"Is that so?"

"Papa, just this morning, Professor Christiansen proposed I teach his freshman music theory class next year. I was so stunned, I was speechless, and I do believe he mistook my initial reaction to be disinterest. Naturally I recovered myself and expressed to him what an incredible honor it was to be considered qualified to assist him, and I assured him I would do everything to my best ability to not disappoint him." Tossing her head back, she paused to catch her breath. "Papa, this is possibly the greatest day of my life."

Joseph swallowed his smile and clenched his teeth against her unavoidable coming disappointment. "I was not aware Christiansen had student assistants."

"Papa, that is what is so astonishing—this is the first he has considered it." She closed her eyes. "At times, I think I must be dreaming. I have already posted a letter to Ida—you know how highly she regards him! She will be so pleased for me. Tomorrow I must write to Severt." She laughed. "I can just imagine what my older brother will have to say about this! Before he tells me what a great opportunity it is, he will most likely feel compelled to say

Christiansen has lowered his standards or doesn't know what he has gotten himself into with me."

"Quite an honor." Joseph had always appreciated Charlotte's quick wit and musical ability, but the highly esteemed F. Melius Christiansen had no time for anything less than exceptional. He regretted that she would have to decline the offer.

"Will you be staying in Northfield this evening, or are you just passing through?"

"On my way to Sisseton on the six o'clock."

Charlotte suggested that they get something cool to drink. For the next hour, she chatted about her studies, recent and upcoming events, and commented on various students and faculty her father knew.

Drinking the last of her lemonade, she pushed the glass aside. "And how was Severt when you saw him last?"

"Gained a little."

"That's good to hear. Will he be coming home soon?"

Joseph methodically smoothed his mustache along the corners of his mouth with his thumb and forefinger. "Actually, that is the matter I wish to discuss with you."

Charlotte's eyes searched his, a question raised between them in silence. Severt's health was not a matter he would visit Charlotte to discuss.

"Severt cannot remain at the sanatorium. I've rented a house for him."

Charlotte sat back, the question settling between her brows. "Rented a house? Where?"

"In Denver."

"He doesn't need to be in a sanatorium?"

"No. He will continue under the care of his physicians, but I've decided he should no longer be confined there."

"Who will care for him?"

Joseph smoothed his mustache. "I have considered and pursued all the alternatives. I had planned on a nurse from Denver but was unable to engage one." He frowned, uncomfortable with the sudden need to provide explanation. "It seems I have no alternative but to send you."

The questions deepened in her brow and wariness stiffened her shoulders as she struggled to absorb the implications. "Me? Denver?"

"Yes."

"When?"

"The house is not available until August, but I would like you there in June."

"The beginning of June. For the summer, then?" Her shoulders relaxed. "Who will care for him when I return to school next fall?"

"There is no one else."

Joseph watched the light fade as Charlotte realized that she would not return to St. Olaf in the fall, that she would not teach the freshman music theory class for F. Melius, that the happiest day of her life had been snuffed out.

Silent, Charlotte's sorrow streamed from the corners of her eyes down the curve of her cheeks. She turned her head to the wall and held her open hands to her face, pressing her forefingers tightly to the corners of her eyes to halt the tears. Her eyes closed and she swallowed, holding in and shutting out.

Joseph turned his head in pretext of examining the room. Seeing the waitress turn toward their table, he held his hand up and shook his head. The elderly woman smiled and turned back to the counter. Fortunately, she gave no indication that she had noticed the tears.

Taking a deep breath, Charlotte opened her eyes and blinked. Her hands slowly fanned away from her eyes to her temples. She gathered the tears as though they were loose pearls that could be lost or blood that could stain, and carefully held them in her lap.

Swallowing again, Charlotte cleared her throat. "Papa," she whispered, her voice hoarse. "Papa, please do not say anything to Severt about the theory class. I will write to Ida and ask the same." She cleared her throat again and raised her head. "He would not want me to come if he knew. I wouldn't have him know it for the world. We must have him believe that this was my decision."

Joseph nodded, both in acknowledgment and admiration of this daughter he had underestimated, who would be her brother's keeper.

City Stories

Anna

*T*he bell on the door caused the four men in the post office to glance at Anna as she entered, but they continued their discussion without any further acknowledgment of her. Hearing mention of President Wilson's second note to Germany after the sinking of the Lusitania and the resignation of Secretary of State Bryan, Anna sighed. She set the letters to be mailed on the counter, hoping she would not have to wait long. During the past month, her father and Peter had discussed the news from Washington and possibility of war at length. Anna did not want to think about Americans joining the war or imagine the horror of the people who died at sea. To think her own father crossed the ocean on the Lusitania! But that was in 1913, before the Allies and Germans had gone to war with each other. Safe now, he had no international travel plans. All of his travel during the past year had been out west, and that would not change. Her father would not leave the country until Severt's health improved enough to return home again.

"Yes, I do believe Wilson has taken the proper approach." Cradling one lens of his glasses between thumb and forefinger, A. M. Henderson stood centered behind the counter, the postmaster's feet planted a good distance apart to evenly support his stocky frame. "A shame Bryan had to resign. It seems the tone of the president's second note is not so threatening as the first, so I don't know why the secretary thought it would lead us to war. The president moves to avoid war with the Germans but seeks vindication for the wrongs committed, as he should. And he insists on the rights of neutral American shipmasters and citizens to travel without jeopardy in the war zone proclaimed by Germany." Glasses adjusted, the postmaster massaged his chin and nodded at the other three men in the office.

A. L. Bartlet, one of the attorneys in town, leaned against the counter, *The Story City Herald* spread before him. "No doubt the second note is less provocative than the note on May 15, which is a relief. The secretary resigned in principle. He contends the difficulties between Germany and the United States should be investigated by an international commission, and Americans should be warned to keep off belligerent ships or those carrying ammunition in the danger zone. I'm not so sure I agree about the international commission, but I do agree Americans should be warned. Based on the Germans' reply, it seems unlikely we will be vindicated or safe on the seas. The Germans maintain they have the right to destroy any ship carrying contraband to an enemy belligerent without violation of treaty obligations. Furthermore, they contend it is the obligation of the belligerent to pay any compensation fixed by a prize court."

Reverend T. T. Heimark, one of the Lutheran pastors in town, stood beside him, peering at another section of the paper. "The tone of Wilson's second note may, in the opinion of some, be less threatening, but I say to you, as he alloweth the blood to spill forth, the cries for vengeance shall rise up and surely he shall lead us into war."

The owner of the department store, S. R. Corneliussen, sat in the only chair for customers, his legs stretched out before him. Sucking his breath, he took hold of his suspenders and slid his thumbs behind as spacers. Exhaling deeply, he appeared more comfortable. He raised his eyebrows. "Three years with Wilson has been enough for us to know the man, and I tell you, my friends, my opinion of him has not improved with the recent developments. Is not the federal income tax legislation he pushed through last year evidence of his misguided domestic policy? And is not the Mexico debacle evidence of his mishandling of international relations? I ask you, is not the resignation of Bryan, Wilson's own secretary of state, an indication of a lack of leadership?"

Anna focused on the letters she had brought, aligning the edges of the envelopes, creating an island of order in an attempt to ignore the sea of tension surrounding her. She considered leaving to attend to her other errands, but as it was late morning, did not want to risk missing the postmaster when he closed up during the noon hour. She did not want to listen to the men argue. She heard more than she cared to about politics and the war at home. The general idea of war and loss of life disturbed her, and the details of politics bored her.

The owner of the department store cleared his throat. "My friends, Wilson is entirely the wrong man to address international conflicts. What this country needs, at this moment of grievous torpedo attacks on Americans at sea, is a man with a big stick like Roosevelt. Wilson should have acted when the Germans unlawfully attacked the steamers Cushing, Gulflight, and Falaba—all merchant ships sailing under neutral flags—attacks that resulted in the loss of not only property, but also the life of one of our own American citizens. I tell you, if the president had responded firmly and without delay to those losses, as any president of strength would have, he could perhaps have averted this disaster. Instead, he has allowed it to go beyond the jeopardy of merchant ships—to the unthinkable destruction without warning of an unarmed British vessel and the loss of more than 1,000 innocent souls—souls who perished within minutes and many of them women and children like this young woman standing here at the counter." He paused and gestured at Anna.

All of the men looked at Anna. Anna hung her head in sympathy for those who had perished. She hoped the conversation would end now, and the postmaster would acknowledge her and take care of her business so that she could finish her other errands.

Instead, the store owner continued, "The United States has no choice but to insist on retribution for the deaths of noncombatants in the name of humanity, and for the more than 100 Americans who were among the dead. I mean no personal offense to you or your honored profession," he said, nodding to the attorney. "But we do not need a lawyer and academic man as president. Wilson may know his way around the law, but he does not know how to uphold and protect the rights of the people in a world of aggressors. No, I tell you, my friends, we need a bull moose like Roosevelt who has been victorious on the battlefield and is not afraid to show the world that the United States is a mighty nation that will not be threatened or harmed."

The pastor began to speak but inhaled so quickly that he choked and was overtaken by a coughing fit. He dropped the newspaper section on the counter and clamped his handkerchief over his mouth, his face crimson behind the white cloth.

Anna lowered her head, squeezed her eyes shut, and bit her tongue to keep from laughing.

"Former Secretary Bryan does not seem to be of the same mind," the attorney said, tapping his long finger on a headline at the top of the page. "I must say, his seems to be the most reasonable method to employ to reach a peaceful solution. Surely, you do not suggest that we conduct ourselves as belligerents?"

The postmaster shifted his weight between feet and then settled back on his heels. "Some say the recent course of the imperial German government is in fact nothing less than war against the United States, and they have thrust upon us the status of belligerent. I wouldn't say I agree with that aggressive point of view. No, I maintain Wilson has taken the proper position. He neither declares war rashly, as some would urge, nor does he compromise our rights."

The pastor stuffed his handkerchief in his pocket. He reached for the newspaper and held it up with both hands. "May God grant mercy upon us at this time of strife and loss. May he transform the hearts of men everywhere that they may exalt peace above war, service above gain, and righteousness above glory, whereby justice and order may be established and the differences of peoples be resolved in equity. I urge you to join with the ministers of the Northern District Synod of the church, representing 12,000 peace-loving, law-abiding and loyal citizens, in our protest. The resolutions, passed last week in our session at Preston, Minnesota, and sent to President Wilson, are printed in this very newspaper." The pastor jabbed at the paper. "We protest against the export of arms, ammunition, and contraband of war to those nations involved in war, which aids in the shedding of human blood, blood which cries to heaven for vengeance. The Lord said, 'You shall not hate your brother in your heart, but you shall reason with your neighbor, lest you bear sin because of him. You shall not take vengeance or bear any grudge against the sons of your own people, but you shall love your neighbor as yourself.'"

The reverend paused as he jabbed at the paper again, his eyes darting from one man in the room to the next. "We also protest against the custom of receiving passengers on ships containing high explosives, the persistence of which conjectures the ghastly specter of possible war, the greatest calamity which could befall our nation, from which God in his grace may preserve us."

"The Germans would support your resolution on the sale of arms," the attorney said. "It would save them hundreds of millions. Their solution to stop the flow of contraband to Great Britain and her allies is to purchase the great gun and munitions-of-war plants in Pennsylvania and Connecticut that are supplying them. Attorney General Gregory and the department of justice have taken up the question with a view of interposing legal obstacles to prevent the sales."

The postmaster stepped toward the counter. "I cannot say I approve of the intervention of the federal government in the affairs of business." He reached for Anna's letters. "But in this instance, I would support the move. Now, gentlemen, you must excuse me for a moment while I take care of postal business."

Relieved to have one errand taken care of and the dark conversation of war behind her, Anna left the post office only to find black storm clouds fast approaching from the southwest. Thunder rumbled in the not-so-far distance. Trees trembled, and flags flapped in the gusting wind. There had been no rain for weeks, and Anna struggled to keep the blowing dirt and gravel from her eyes. She would have to hurry if she was to have any chance of avoiding the rain.

Within the week, Anna would be in Denver, Colorado. It had happened so quickly it seemed a dream. The past week, she had graduated first in her high school class, and now she would be the first of her friends to travel west of the Dakotas. It would be a grand adventure with Charlotte.

Charlotte's decision to leave St. Olaf to care for Severt had completely astonished Anna. "But Charlotte," Anna said when her sister came home for the summer. "It's good of you to want to help Severt, but how can you possibly think of leaving St. Olaf? You just wrote to me that last year was the best ever, and next year would be even better. And I was so looking forward to being college girls together and having a grand time together, like Ida and Lula and Severt. It won't be the same there without you."

"Do you think I could pass on the opportunity to take control of Severt's life and enforce his doctor's orders?" Charlotte laughed. "When Papa told me he rented a house, I told him no one else would be able to put up with Severt. Not only that, it's an opportunity to experience the wild west. Naturally I'll miss St. Olaf, but I learned a tremendous amount last year. I see no sense in amusing myself as a college girl when I could be doing something useful."

Anna bit her lip. "Are you worried at all about getting sick?"

Charlotte shook her head. "I'll admit I thought about it, but the doctor told Papa there is no danger at all living with Severt as long as sanitary measures are taken. Papa wouldn't allow me to go otherwise. Agnes Phipps will provide all the necessary training on how to care for him, and they'll test me twice a year. The rental house will be thoroughly disinfected before we move in, just to be safe. Severt will have his own utensils that I'll need to thoroughly boil to kill any germs. I'll also need to learn how to prepare healthy meals for Severt—lots of eggs and cream and rare meat, it seems." Charlotte made a face. "Papa insists I eat the same meals Severt does, to make sure I stay healthy, but surely I'll gain weight, which will be a fright."

"It sounds like so much work." Anna thought it sounded like a maid's job.

"It will be good for me, especially after how lazy I've been this past year."

"I wouldn't say you were lazy at all," Anna said. "You had a very demanding schedule with your classes and practicing."

Charlotte smiled. "Oh, but it was all so much fun. It didn't seem like work at all."

"You're not scared at all, then?" Anna asked.

Charlotte shook her head. "The only thing that concerns me is how difficult Severt can be." She laughed. "He'll try to order me around, so I'll have to put him in his place right away. I'll need to take plenty of warm clothes, though. He needs fresh air for his treatment, so the windows will be open even in the winter months, and we'll spend as much time as possible outside resting on the porch."

Intrigued by the adventure, Anna impulsively decided to defer her freshman year at St. Olaf and spend the year with Charlotte in Denver.

At first, Papa did not approve. "I won't allow it."

"But why not?" Anna asked.

"There is no need to have more than one of you out there."

"But with all the cleaning and disinfecting that must be done and the special foods to cook, it will be so much work for Charlotte. I could help so it won't be such a burden on her."

"It won't be too much for me, Anna," Charlotte said. "I told you. It will be good for me to work a little after enjoying myself at St. Olaf the past year."

"Well, then, it will be good for me to work a little to earn the fun I will have when I go to St. Olaf the following year." Anna grinned.

"I don't want to risk it." Papa shook his head.

"But there's no risk at all, Charlotte says, if we do as the doctors say. You wouldn't let Charlotte go otherwise."

Papa looked at Charlotte and did not immediately respond.

Anna charged forward. "Besides, poor Severt needs someone to cheer him up after being away so long without us. He wrote that the doctors say a positive attitude is important in getting well. Charlotte will order him around ,and he'll think he's gone from the sanatorium to a jail. He'll need someone there to make him laugh instead of cry."

"A jail? Don't you think that is rather harsh?" Charlotte shook her head, smiling.

"You always have been able to make him laugh," Papa admitted.

"Before you know it, the year will have passed, Charlotte and I will be back at St. Olaf, and Severt will be working in the bank." Anna snapped her fingers.

Papa agreed.

Margretha was beside herself, but Papa made it clear it was not her decision to make. He would not subject his daughters to danger. They would strictly adhere to the same safe practices used at the sanatorium. Olive seemed worried but did not say anything. Peter raised his eyebrows when the topic arose but also held his tongue.

College housing and registration plans were cancelled, piano instructors notified, roommates advised to find replacements, clothing and personal items selected and packed, travel schedules discussed and arranged, and instructions obtained through multiple correspondences with the doctors and nurses at Agnes Phipps.

Severt wrote that he was thrilled.

Papa, who had seemed increasingly distant and brusque after Severt entered the sanatorium, became quite good-humored. Olive gave lessons on how to manage a household and helped the girls make arrangements for the trip west. Occasionally she remarked how much she would miss the girls. Denver was so much farther away than Northfield, too far to come home for the holidays. Peter reassured her that a year was not such a long time at all and reminded her she had her own children to care for. Little Laurentia and baby Joseph Oliver would keep her occupied, and her youngest sisters would be home before she knew it.

As she hurried from the post office, Anna considered how much she would miss Olive and the children. It wouldn't be so bad, she thought, since she would be with Charlotte and Severt. It wouldn't be like Severt going away by himself to live at Agnes Phipps.

Anna dashed to the dry goods store to complete her errands. A horn blared in the street, muting the bell over the door. She wondered whether someone had honked to draw her attention and hesitated for a moment, catching the door just before it swung shut. Considering Olive's reminder not to dawdle and the time already lost in the post office, Anna released the door. She extracted the list tucked in the weave of her shopping basket and unfolded it. Hair pins, a clothes brush, a complete needle case, thimbles, thread, earache drops, Willow Charcoal tablets, witch hazel extract, lavender smelling salts, tooth powder, talcum powder, White Lily face wash, shampoo, cold cream soap, antiseptic soap sheets, and writing paper. Items for the trip to Denver.

Women's voices ascended from behind the shelves in the rear of the store, where the bolts of material, thread, and sewing items were displayed.

"I would not have believed it possible. Asking for trouble, if you ask me." Emelia Henryson's Norwegian accent was unmistakable.

"I should say so." Anna recognized the second voice to be Tillie Donhowe's.

"It isn't right, I tell you."

"I'll say it isn't."

"Sending lambs to the slaughter."

She smiled, amused the women would be discussing the international situation so passionately when they were more often concerned what their neighbors were or were not doing. Spotting the White Lily face wash on the shelf, Anna added it to her basket.

She thought it odd they believed war was so likely. Despite the tragic sinking of the Lusitania, even the men in the post office were in disagreement as to whether the president's note to Germany would lead to war.

"Not everyone in the family agrees, I'll have you know."

"No?"

"I heard it with my own ears."

"Oh?"

"Margretha herself told me."

Anna slowly dropped the cold cream soap into her basket. Silent, still, she realized the women thought they were alone and were not talking about President Wilson.

"The long and short of it is that she talked herself blue in the face, but Joseph Marvick won't listen to reason."

"She spoke out against her own brother to you?"

"Margretha has a mind of her own. Always has."

"Isn't that the truth. She must be sick, watching him send those young girls off. She raised them like they were her own."

Anna frowned and she bit her lip, her stomach twisting.

"Of all people. Joseph always made sure his children had the best of everything. Nobody in town can imagine what he is thinking."

"I presume he is thinking of Severt."

"Well, he certainly isn't thinking of the girls. Heaven knows he could lose all three of them now. And what is done cannot be undone."

The blood surged to her head, and Anna determined to hear no more. Hands shaking, she emptied the few items in her basket on the floor and rushed out of the store, letting the door slam shut behind her.

Opening her umbrella to the downpour, she hid her face from the rain and the street and dashed home. She did not turn as a horn sounded in the street behind.

The burning rush of discomfort was new to Anna. The Marvick family was above reproach, and no man in town more respected than her father. Any criticism sprang from envy. Anger flashed for a moment at the thought of Margretha speaking out.

"No bags?" Olive asked as Anna rushed in from the rain. "Here, let me take the umbrella so you can get out of that coat!"

"It took quite some time at the post office. There were several men from town in there having a lengthy debate."

"Ah. And then you were caught by the rain."

"But what harm is a little rain? I'll dry off in no time!"

Anna shook off the dripping coat and with it the talk she had heard in town.

Denver

Joseph

While they waited for the rental house in Denver to become available, Charlotte and Anna rented a room on a month-to-month basis from Mrs. Farrington, a lovely, jolly widow. The other roomers in the large boarding house included another widow and her son, two doctors, three nurses, and another girl whose mother was in a sanatorium. The address at 1537 Marion Street was in one of the nicest residential areas of the city and only three houses from the home of Mr. Phipps, the wealthiest man in Denver and former partner of Andrew Carnegie. Lawrence Phipps built the Agnes Phipps Sanatorium in memory of his mother who died of tuberculosis.

After Charlotte and Anna moved to Denver in June, Severt's mental and physical condition both steadily improved. Visits to the sanatorium were limited to an hour each day, but enough to reconnect their brother to the healthy world outside Agnes Phipps. By mid-September, he recovered from the cold that had settled into his lungs in the spring, and his physicians reluctantly permitted him to move out of the sanatorium into the rental house with his sisters. In a few months, Severt gained four pounds and seemed in better health than he had since his diagnosis. The doctors, however, refused to provide any opinion as to his chance of a cure and cautioned that he could have a relapse at any time.

Conceding that Severt would likely be in Denver for another year, Joseph made Denver his temporary residence in the summer of 1915 and spent most of his time pursuing real estate opportunities in Montana, Wyoming, Idaho, and the western half of South Dakota. Campbell's "Scientific Farming System" had gained acceptance, and the vast semiarid Great Plains he had once viewed as useless in terms of growing crops were now being cultivated and producing wheat. The Northern Pacific Railroad was selling off much of the land it had been granted by Congress in exchange for building its transcontinental track, and extensive promotional advertising by the railroads had created a homestead boom. Seeking opportunity, settlers from the Midwest and East Coast and immigrants from Britain and Europe came west by the trainload, eager to file claims on 160-acre parcels in Montana.

The advertising promised prosperity, but the plains of central and eastern Montana did not compare to the fertile black soil in Illinois and Iowa. Even with the mechanized equipment being used by more and more farmers, the land in Montana required extensive work before any crops could be planted, and most of the new sodbusters Joseph met lacked farming experience and arrived unaware of the challenges before them. He knew many would fail in their dryland farming endeavor and, when they were forced to sell out, their failure would create opportunity for others.

At the end of October, Joseph purchased 160 acres from Fred Howell, a former teacher from Pennsylvania who had enthusiastically moved his family west to seek the opportunity promised in the promotional advertising. Fred not only could not tolerate the physical labor required to work the dry land, but he also lacked business sense. Accustomed to city life, his wife Luella was ill-suited for the adversity and isolation of the Montana plains. Sixty-five miles from the nearest supply store and church and miles from the nearest neighbor, Luella bitterly complained to Joseph about the loss of social and cultural activities and how she struggled to care for her four young children without the support of nearby family.

"Now, now, Luella," Fred said, embarrassed by his wife's outburst. "No need to air your grievances to Mr. Marvick."

"Who else do I have to talk to?" Luella fumed. "Certainly not you. I didn't want to come here in the first place, but you didn't listen to me. Oh, no! You dragged us out to this godforsaken place and now look at us. We've lost everything." Bursting into tears, she ran from the room.

Fred hunched in his chair. "She's had a rough time of it, I'm afraid."

"I understand." Joseph would never have moved Annie to such a remote place. Luella Howell had married her husband for better or worse, and it appeared she had gotten the worst of it.

"Now. Back to the matter you came to discuss." Fred stared at the empty coffee cup he held with both hands. "I've thought your offer over and have decided to accept it." He sighed. "I was hoping for something better, but it doesn't look like I'm going to get it."

Joseph regarded the financially and mentally broken man before him. The former teacher suffered from an unrealistic outlook, which had led to his predicament. Joseph had offered the Howells a reasonable price. Unfortunately for Fred, it would not be enough to cover his debts. Joseph was in the business of real estate to make a profit, however, not to perform acts of charity.

The expansion of Montana's economy also created banking and lending opportunities. Not only was the population multiplying as settlers moved into the state, but established farmers were aggressively investing in land, livestock, and equipment. Joseph recognized the opportunity to open a bank or land and loan company in the territory, but if he were to do so, he would need to hire a cashier or manager he could trust implicitly, preferably someone he knew. His son-in-law Peter had no experience in banking and was already established in Story City at the clothing store. Likewise, Lula's husband Ed had his roots in Wisconsin and also worked in sales. As Joseph considered other potential candidates, Peter's nephew, Jack Donhowe, came to mind. Jack had taken the position Severt was to have had as cashier at the bank in Story City and exhibited a good head for business. If he and Charlotte were to marry, which appeared a strong possibility based on their daily correspondence, Jack would be a candidate to move west to manage a bank. It would be an excellent opportunity for the young man and would compensate Charlotte for her commitment to Severt. Now was not the time to establish a new bank in the western territory, however. Joseph would wait until the territory had stabilized more and Jack gained more experience in his position in Story City.

As president of two banks, co-owner and active manager of a land and loan real estate company, and with personal holdings of large tracts of farmland throughout the Midwest and western states, Joseph had more than enough demands on his time without taking on a new business venture. Generally, Joseph partnered with local landowners who farmed their own land but were interested in expanding, and in all cases he shared the crop and livestock profits on a fifty percent basis with his tenants. He believed the cash rent arrangement generally favored the tenant rather than the landowner during good years, and he did not believe in wage arrangements in which the tenant did not share the risks. Joseph sought out tenants who had a proven history of high productivity, practiced sustainable soil management, and demonstrated sound financial sense. Though he relied upon his tenants to operate the farms, he maintained regular correspondence with them and inspected each of the farms at least once a year between spring planting and the fall harvest.

To Olive's disappointment, Joseph scheduled as little time as possible in Story City. While he enjoyed seeing his eldest daughter and grandchildren, he could not return home without thinking Severt should be working at the bank. Instead, his son remained ill in Denver with an uncertain future. It was not what he had planned for his son. By entrusting John Donhowe, Peter's older brother and Jack's father, to manage the bank on a daily basis, Joseph could dispatch most of his responsibilities through correspondence. With one long day in the office each month, he reviewed the ledgers and significant transactions, gave instructions regarding investments, adjusted the rates to reflect market conditions, and approved lending decisions. The bank continued to be profitable, and there were no indications they had lost any share of business to the competition.

**

After traveling most of the fall, Joseph arranged to be in Denver for Thanksgiving. He took the streetcar from the station and walked the short distance to the rental house, passing through the long afternoon shadows on Bellaire Avenue. As he neared the house, the source of the general din he had been hearing for several blocks became apparent. A group of boys were playing ball in the vacant lot across the street. Both teams screamed as the catcher scrambled after a wild pitch and the runner at first base stole to second and then to third. The second pitch was high, and the screaming resumed as the catcher reached to stop it, holding the runner at third base. On the third pitch, the batter leaned back, holding his bat over his head, and let the ball pass. "Ball!" Tossing his bat to the side, he jogged to first base. The catcher jumped to his feet, threw his hat on the ground and kicked the dirt. "For the love of Mike! You know that was a strike!"

Disquieted by the irrepressible energy of the children, Joseph turned up the sidewalk to the house. Apprehension as to how he would find Severt counterbalanced the cautious optimism he had felt since his son left Agnes Phipps.

Anna and Charlotte sat on the front porch with Severt. Reclining and wrapped in a blanket, Severt appeared to be sleeping, despite the clamor across the street. Joseph wondered where Ida was, as she had arrived the previous week to celebrate the holiday in Denver.

Absorbed in writing, the girls did not notice their father until they heard the porch stairs creak beneath his feet.

Anna jumped up, dropping pen and paper on the seat of her chair. "How was your trip?"

"Fine." Joseph watched his son unwrap his blankets. "No need to get up, Severt."

Anna turned to the house and stuck her head inside the door. "Ida! Papa's here!"

"I've had enough of this porch for today. Time to get up and move around." Severt stood, seemingly strong, in a spotlight of sun. His face had good color and lacked any strain of discomfort.

"We were scribbling as fast as we possibly could, hoping to be finished with our letter writing before you arrived," Charlotte said.

"I don't understand what takes you so long," Severt said. "My letter was sealed an hour ago."

"Cosette has my sympathies. She writes you pages every day, and you respond with such short notes. It's a wonder she continues to write." Charlotte said.

"Save your sympathies for Jack," Severt said. "I write about the significant matters, and don't ramble on about anything and everything. I cannot imagine what you write to Jack about that can fill so many pages. It's a wonder he even reads them."

Charlotte rolled her eyes. "As you can see, Papa, Severt is feeling well. Unfortunately, when he has nothing better to do, he becomes quite argumentative."

Joseph smiled. "Peter and Olive send their greetings, as did your Uncle Andrew and Aunt Linnie. I had some time with them on the way through Sisseton." Relieved to find Severt looking well and Charlotte in good spirits, he glanced at the doorway, hoping Ida's frame of mind had brightened as well.

Anna grabbed her father's arm. "You must tell us all about the new baby! Is little Joseph Oliver jealous? Olive wrote that dear Laurentia wants to help as much as she can and adores baby Herbert. Such a little lady she is now that she is in school. How I miss them so! To imagine not being with them for the holidays! Is Olive completely exhausted?" She released his arm and sighed.

Charlotte shook her head at her sister as she held the door open for her father. "Anna! Save your twenty questions until Papa has had a chance to catch his breath."

Joseph's animated youngest daughter was so like her mother. It was good she had come to Denver. Her presence guaranteed laughter. Ironically, for years it had been Anna's health that had concerned him. She had been the child prone to sickness, suffering from frequent ear infections which seemed so serious at the time. If only Severt's diagnosis had been as inconsequential.

Ida met them inside the door, wiping her hands on her apron. "Welcome back, Papa. Severt certainly seems to be thriving under his sisters' care, doesn't he?"

"That he does." Joseph smiled at the soft light in his daughter's eyes.

***

Severt invited three of his friends from the sanatorium for Thanksgiving dinner, and Ida planned a roast duck with all the fixings. Joseph did not express his reservations about having Severt's friends to dinner. He knew the doctors at Agnes Phipps enforced strict rules and would not allow patients to leave the facility if their health or behavior fell below specific standard levels, and they would eat with Severt's utensils. And while Joseph did not like his daughters socializing with infected people, he knew Severt's friends presented no greater risk of contagion than their brother.

Ida placed the platter of duck on the table. "I hope this tastes as good as it looks." She smiled at Severt's friends. "I must admit, it is my first duck."

"It may be your first duck, but this is the last supper," Charlotte said.

Severt laughed. "Charlotte. None of us is that sick."

Charlotte blushed. "That is not what I meant."

"Not to worry." Severt's former porch mate Mr. Merriweather chuckled. "Our sense of humor at the san is quite dark."

"Quite right," Mr. Elmerdorf nodded. "I must say, that is a good line. I must remember to use it."

"Just don't let the staff hear you," Severt said. "You could lose your privileges. Bad attitude."

"I was referring to Ida's imminent departure." Embarrassment colored Charlotte's face. "I don't know if Severt told you, but she is returning to Boston next week, and I'm taking over as chief cook and bottle washer."

"Boston!" Mr. Elmerdorf said. "How grand!"

"Grand for Ida, perhaps, but not so grand for me." Severt sighed heavily. "I shall once again be at the mercy of Charlotte's experiments."

Charlotte laughed. "If you don't like my cooking, feel free to take all your meals at the san. And if my housekeeping doesn't meet your approval, you could always move back to the san entirely."

"Ha. I won't be taken in by your scheme to get out of work."

Mr. Merriweather raised his hand. "I'll gladly swap places with you, Severt. I'm certain Charlotte is a wonderful cook."

"I'll consider that offer," Severt said.

"You do that," Charlotte said. "Mr. Merriweather, you would be a most welcome substitute for this cantankerous, ungrateful brother of mine."

Severt remained animated throughout the meal. When Anna helped herself to a second helping, he teased her about how much she was eating.

"But I had no breakfast this morning."

Mr. Merriweather laughed. "You wouldn't be happy in the san, I say."

"Quite right." Mr. Elmendorf wiped his mouth with his napkin. "You would never be permitted to miss a meal there. No choice involved whatsoever."

Anna grimaced and shook her head. "After all these months, I just cannot seem to adjust to eating such a large breakfast of protein and cream. I'm not sure I ever shall get accustomed to it. However, I must say," lifting her eyebrows, she grinned, "I would have no difficulty eating breakfast every morning if there were fresh baked sweet rolls with frosting or cinnamon and caramel."

Severt laughed. "I fear Anna would live on a diet of sugar if she were left to her own devices."

"I would indeed."

"I must say, I have a sweet tooth myself," Ida said.

Joseph said little as he listened to the young people converse, somewhat irritated that Severt's friends from the san could be so lighthearted about their condition and the cure but pleased to see his son in such good spirits. Severt's color was better than it had been; his shirt and pants did not hang as loosely, and he recovered from coughing spells in less time. Severt's health had certainly improved. Removing him from the sanatorium had proven to be the right decision, although Joseph worried about the girls' health and looked forward to the day when Severt no longer required their care.

After dinner, Severt hired a seven-passenger Pierce Arrow. Joseph offered to stay home, as did Ida, but Anna insisted it would be great fun if everyone went for a ride together. The group joked while they discussed how best to squeeze everyone into the car. Charlotte elbowed her father and remarked how much space his 220-pound bulk required. Infected by the levity, Joseph chuckled and winked in response. Severt reminded Charlotte that she seemed to have put on some weight herself after coming to Denver. Blushing, Charlotte said she needed to start eating less.

"I'd love to have that problem," Mr. Merriweather said. "Although I must say, after we've bundled ourselves up in coats and blankets to avoid a chill, your brother and his scrawny friends from the san seem to require as much space as anyone."

The group rode around Denver for most of the afternoon. An expanse of unbroken blue stretched across the sky, and though the temperature did not quite reach fifty degrees, there was relatively no wind. After circling City Park, they drove through the downtown area. From there, they proceeded to the boarding house where Anna and Charlotte rented rooms when they first arrived in Denver. As they drove by the large home, they waved at the group gathered on the porch.

Ida suggested they drive to Inspiration Point, where they got out to stretch their legs. Mr. Elmerdorf remarked that the view of the surrounding countryside and mountains surpassed the view from their porch at the san. Mr. Merriweather suggested that may have something to do with being confined to bed with a thermometer. Everyone laughed with him except Joseph. The laughter, however, was thinner than it had been earlier in the day, etched by the recognition that the next stop would be to return Severt's friends to the san. As they stuffed themselves back into the Packard, the sun fell into the mountains, and the infusive golden light expired.

Estes Park

Anna

*C*osette surprised Severt with her first visit to Denver the week before Christmas. Anna and Charlotte congratulated themselves at keeping the secret.

When the door opened, Severt expected to see only Ida, returning from Boston for the holidays. Anna would never forget the elation that filled her brother's face when he saw Cosette walk into the rental house behind his sister.

When Severt asked whether her parents had objected to the visit, Cosette responded, "But how could they? After all, your sisters are here. Your father wouldn't permit them to be with you if there was the slightest danger of getting sick. And your doctors released you from the sanatorium. They wouldn't have done that unless they thought your health had improved and you were on the mend, would they?" Her voice was smooth. "I also reminded them that we are engaged to be married, and I haven't seen you for over a year."

Anna couldn't help but think of Ida and how she had broken with Oscar, who had never been sick at all. If it was safe to live with Severt, surely Oscar posed no danger. But of course Papa hadn't known that at the time. Anna avoided looking at Ida, whose heart remained broken. No one ever mentioned Oscar, but there were times when Anna knew Ida was thinking of him. Her sister's focus would fade as her soft smile expired. A few times tears pooled, but Ida closed her eyes and swallowed them. Anna wondered what Ida would have done if Oscar had gotten sick like Severt and whether she would have stuck with him like Cosette had with Severt. Anna thought it would be hard to marry if they could never kiss or live in the same bedroom as man and wife. Although she had never mentioned it to anyone, she had not expected Cosette to stick by Severt after his diagnosis. Now she realized how wrong she had been about her brother's fiancé. Cosette wrote to Severt nearly every day, and now here she was visiting. Evidently her father had not objected like Papa had. But then, visiting was one thing. Marrying and sharing the same bedroom with someone who had been infected was something altogether different. Perhaps Mr. Henderson expected they would wait to marry until Severt was pronounced cured, which surely was only a matter of time.

Cosette stayed through New Year's Day, and her presence energized Severt throughout the visit. He stayed up late, rose earlier, required less rest during the day, coughed fewer times throughout the day, ate heartily, and sustained a positive outlook.

When Cosette returned to Story City, however, Severt relapsed. As the weather grew colder, the sharp edges of Severt's disease ravaged his lungs and his character and Charlotte's patience. The worst days were when there were no letters from Cosette and Jack, and the house girl had the day off. On those days, Anna's futile attempts to humor her brother and sister elicited only sarcastic retorts.

On a particularly trying day, the girls had just reached the kitchen when Severt called out. "Charlotte!"

"Hark!" Anna said. "The king summons you."

Charlotte dropped Severt's silverware into the pot of boiling water. "I wonder what he wants now. He just ate. Can't he wait for us to clean up after him? Not to mention the fact we haven't eaten ourselves yet and I'm starving."

"Perhaps he would like some entertainment before his afternoon relaxation. We could send the court jester."

"Ha. His idea of fun is watching me wait on him while he orders me around. How many times have I run up and down those stairs for him already, and the day is only half gone."

"I'll go see what he wants," Anna offered. "I'll tell him a few jokes." Running up the stairs, she hoped this would be one of the days when she could make Severt laugh.

Charlotte and Severt regained their senses of humor as the days lengthened and the earth warmed. The re-emergence of emerald lawns, lime green tree buds, yellow jonquils, red tulips, and warblers seemed propitious. Renewed hope bloomed from the depths of the dark undeclared doubts, and Charlotte persuaded their father to rent a cabin in Estes Park for the summer season.

Severt's cough improved in the pine-scented higher altitude, and by the end of July he had gained several pounds. For the first time in months, his recovery again seemed a possibility.

When Papa arrived in Estes Park, the family visited the Stanley Hotel Casino where they made acquaintance with F. O. Stanley. Both Papa and Severt considered Stanley a genius. Not only had he invented the Stanley Steamer but also a photographic process he sold to George Eastman. When he contracted tuberculosis in 1903, he was told he had one year to live. He moved to Colorado on the advice of his doctor and said the beauty of the mountains gave him his life back. He went on as though he had never been ill. He designed and built the hotel, along with the hydroelectric power plant and water pipe system that provided electric power and running water for the entire village of Estes Park. Stanley told Papa the hotel cost a half-million dollars, paid for in cash because he didn't believe in credit. If a man couldn't afford it, he shouldn't buy it, Stanley said. More impressive to the Marvick family than Stanley's inventions and fortune, however, was that the man was living proof a cure could be found in the mountains of Colorado.

***

That summer, several relatives and friends traveled to Estes Park. Jack Donhowe arrived the second week of June. Anna's Uncle Andrew and Aunt Linnie came from Sisseton on their way to San Francisco. Henry Donhowe visited at the end of a business trip. Margretha, who had not been to Colorado, wrote that she wanted to see the Rocky Mountain National Park and would spend two weeks with them in the middle of July. Cosette would be on the same train and planned to stay on in Estes Park for the remainder of the summer.

The day of Margretha's arrival, Anna sat on one of the boulders surrounded by wildflowers outside the cabin, elbows on knees, chin in hands. No car in sight yet, and no sign of dust rising above the tree line in the distance. She would have liked to have gone to the station, but someone had to stay with Severt.

Anna's eyes wandered from the graveled road that wound down the steep hill and disappeared behind the pine trees. Longs Peak rose in the distance. Anna thought the area spectacular but had not traveled to the mountains and fjords of Norway like Margretha had, and she wondered how they compared. Surely her aunt's artistic eye would appreciate the Rocky Mountains, and she would capture the beauty of the place in her watercolors and photographs.

Anna wondered if Margretha and Cosette spent much time together on the train, or if they had kept to their separate berths. Her aunt did not like to be unproductive, and likely spent much of her time reading, writing, or perhaps painting. Anna thought about her trip to Denver with Charlotte the past summer. Embarking upon their adventure to the west, the sisters had talked and laughed into the night in their shared private sleeping compartment. It seemed a lifetime ago. At the time, they had planned on being in Denver for only a year, until Severt was cured. The year had passed, but only Anna would return home at the end of the summer. Severt and Charlotte would return to the rental house in Denver.

The screen door slapped shut behind Anna.

"Not here, yet?" Severt spoke softly, his voice continually hoarse.

Anna twisted her head toward her brother. Margretha had not seen him since his diagnosis nearly two years ago. Severt stood on the porch, his pants gathered awkwardly beneath his belt, his jacket hanging loosely from his sloped shoulders over his white shirt. Dark circles below his eyes and a red brush of fever colored his otherwise pale face. Despite Severt's recent improvement, he was not the picture of health.

Anna stood, brushing the dirt from her skirt. "You couldn't sleep?" She focused on the brother she loved, softening the image of illness she didn't wish to see.

Severt smiled. "No. Too excited, with Cosette and Margretha due to arrive."

"Now why would you be excited to see Cosette? She was just here to visit in May, and she writes nearly every day."

Severt opened his mouth to respond, but instead began to cough. Holding his paper handkerchief to his mouth with one hand, he leaned to grip the porch railing with the other.

Anna stiffened as Severt fought the cough that racked his body, his face contorted. She ran up the uneven wood stairs and held the door open. "Let's go inside, Severt. I'll get you something to drink."

Her older brother's eyes met hers as the coughing subsided. She recognized the apology, but smiled as though nothing had happened. "Imagine—soon we will be hearing all the news from home."

Severt grinned. "Indeed." Wincing, he turned and limped toward the door.

Within minutes, Anna heard the car doors from the kitchen. "Severt. They're here." She dashed to the door.

Their aunt wore a beautiful hat and smart suit.

"Aunt Margretha, how wonderful to see you." Anna sprinted down the porch stairs. "Here, let me help you with your luggage."

"Hello, Anna." Margretha nodded. "You are looking well."

Anna knew the moment her aunt saw Severt.

The older woman's eyes flashed before freezing. "Severt. How good to see you."

Severt stood on the deck in front of the cabin. "Aunt Margretha." Gripping the railing, he wheezed as he hobbled down the stairs. "Welcome to my summer retreat—such as it is."

Cosette dropped one of her bags beside Severt. "Your letters didn't do this cabin justice." She surveyed the property. "What a pleasant change from the house in Denver!"

Anna stepped between her aunt and brother. "Which of these bags are yours, Aunt Margretha? I'm anxious to show you our cabin."

"I do hope you packed some things to wear for hiking and riding," Charlotte said.

"Oh, yes." Anna nodded. "We plan to take you out on a few trails to see the sights while you're here. Aunt Margretha, I'm certain you'll find plenty of places you would like to sketch or paint."

***

Anna suggested, and Charlotte and Severt agreed, that Big Owl Hill should be the first place to take Margretha and Cosette. Charlotte drove, and Margretha sat in the front passenger seat. Anna shared the back with Ida, Severt, and Cosette, insisting that Cosette sit on one end to take advantage of the view.

"It's a great place to hike," Anna said. "And you must meet K.G."

"Oh?" Margretha turned to face Anna. "And who might he be?"

"Actually, K.G. is a woman. Her name is Katherine Garetson, but she prefers to be called K.G. She owns the Big Owl Tea Place. She came out here from St. Louis for vacation with friends a few years ago and decided to stay and homestead."

"By herself?" Cosette winced.

"Yes. Hard to believe, isn't it?"

Charlotte leaned as she turned the wheel around a sharp curve in the road. "I admire her nearly as much as the women who climbed Longs Peak. Can you imagine climbing that mountain?"

"Longs Peak is the mountain you see from the cabin," Anna explained.

"I find strong independent women like K.G. simply fascinating." Charlotte shifted gears.

"Is she a single woman?" Margretha continued to stare straight ahead.

Severt nodded. "She is."

"I imagine she's rough." Cosette held the brim of her hat against the wind.

"Actually not." Ida leaned forward to look across at her friend. "She will surprise you. I expected her to be big and brawny like a man. Especially with a name like K.G. But she is nothing of the sort. She is slight of frame and appears delicate almost. Quite feminine, in fact."

"And pretty. The first time I saw her, she reminded me a bit of you, Cosette." Anna laughed. "Not dressed the same, as you will see, but she does have a refined air about her and has the same sort of coloring as you."

"Really." Cosette arched her eyebrows.

Anna knew Cosette could not reconcile the image of a mountain homesteader with a feminine woman, but she would soon see for herself.

"K.G. is a strong young woman," Charlotte said. "She does as she pleases and is not afraid of what other people will think."

Severt laughed. "Sounds like you, Charlotte. Are you considering taking up homesteading yourself?"

"I said I admired her, Severt. The cabin we are renting is as rough as I choose to live, and then only for a few months."

"It's a relief to know you won't be abandoning Severt to clear some land and build your own place, Charlotte," Cosette laughed.

Twelve miles south of the village of Estes Park, the moraine west of Big Owl Hill was a favorite hiking spot of Anna's. Both Margretha and Cosette commented on the beauty of the place and had the good fortune of sighting a beaver swimming across a lake.

After hiking, they stopped at Big Owl Tea Place for something hot to eat and drink. Usually spent by the exercise, today Anna felt restless, as the group had walked at a leisurely pace so as not to overly stress Severt.

K.G. lifted the kettle of boiling water from the small cook stove in the middle of the tea room. "Have a seat while I make you some tea. Or take a look around in the gift shop."

Cosette lifted a doll from the display. "How adorable!" The doll wore a scarlet skirt, white blouse, blue jacket trimmed in gold braid, high button red kid shoes, and a wreath of flowers in her hair.

Severt pointed at a neatly written card lying on the table in front of the dolls. "She's a Russian peasant bride. I'll buy one for you if you like."

"How sweet of you." Cosette smiled at her fiancé. "I'd love one. It will remind me that you plan to marry me one of these days."

"Just as soon as my health improves," Severt said.

Behind the couple, Margretha raised her eyebrows and turned away.

Anna ignored her aunt and picked up one of the dolls dressed in khaki-colored bloomers, middies, cloth outing hats, and brown kid shoes. "I like the hiker doll best. I suppose that is because I don't have any wedding plans. Will you buy me a doll too?" she teased her brother.

"I suggest he buy each one of you something," K.G. said.

Severt chuckled. "I wouldn't want to spoil them all."

"We'll be fortunate if he buys us something to eat." Charlotte sat down at a table and picked up a menu. "I must have some of your tiny chocolate cakes. I ordered them last time we were here and loved them."

In the gift shop, Margretha unfolded a table runner with a Scandinavian design in red, black, and salmon. "My, this is very fine cross stitch work."

"It's real Russian crash," K.G. said. "Hand woven by the peasants."

"Very nice. I noticed the curtains." Margretha gestured at the windows. "Did you cross-stitch those as well?"

K.G. nodded.

"You are a woman of many talents, I see," Margretha said.

"Isn't that what we told you?" Anna had known K.G. would impress her artistic aunt.

"However do you find time to sew?" Cosette asked.

"I try to get as much done as I can during the winter."

"Admirable of you." Margretha refolded the runner. "Few women would have had the staying power. I dare say, few men, either."

Anna wondered whether her aunt was thinking of Severt. "I don't know how you survive up here by yourself." She sat down beside her sister. "It must be very hard work."

K.G. set a teacup in front of Charlotte. "I'll admit, while we're snow-bound here in the dead of winter, it is a bare existence." She laughed. "When I first arrived, I thought I'd have plenty of time on my hands to sew, but I didn't think of all of the necessary work that needed to be done—chopping ice, hauling water up the hill, shoveling drifts of snow, bringing in wood and coal oil, and then breaking through two and a half miles of snow to get the mail. Not to mention cooking and washing and scrubbing to keep the place clean after dragging in wet snow and soot."

"Oh, my!" Cosette exclaimed. "I wouldn't last a day."

"It sounds like more work than keeping house for Severt." Charlotte sipped her tea.

"Oh, but to have someone to talk to!" K.G. said. "A person who lives in solitude soon learns the laughable trait of talking to one's self. The worst was a time this winter when the weather was bad and I didn't see a soul for weeks on end. Not only did I talk to myself, but I began talking to things in the room as though they were members of the family." She patted the stove. "I assigned personalities to the stove, my shoes, water pails, and even the broom."

Anna laughed. "Did they talk back?"

K.G. grinned. "No. Lest you think I'd gone mad, the only voice I heard was my own."

"That's a thought." Charlotte said. "Severt, if you were a broom, you couldn't talk back."

Severt pulled out a chair. "Don't get any ideas, Charlotte. I'm never going to let you do all the talking. If you are so anxious for solitude, perhaps you should consider homesteading yourself."

***

The day after the hike at Big Owl Hill, Margretha announced she wanted to paint some scenes and needed to purchase some art supplies. Cosette agreed to drive her into Estes Park to see what they could find, as she and Severt wanted to spend some time in the village together.

Watching the car drive away, Ida stood at the window with her back to her sisters. "The view here really is quite spectacular, isn't it?"

"It is," Anna nodded. "I expected Margretha would want to paint it. It seems a perfect scene for watercolor, don't you think?"

"I find it rather amazing that Margretha came to visit, don't you?" Ida turned from the window.

"But of course she would want to visit. She is like a mother to us."

"I wouldn't think she would want to expose herself." Ida turned back to the window. "She certainly made it clear she didn't want any of us exposed."

Startled by the sharp edge of her sister's voice, Anna glanced at Charlotte.

Charlotte frowned. "You can't blame her. She was only looking out for our best interests. She didn't understand how safe we would be and believed Papa was risking our lives by sending us to be with Severt."

Anna could hear the critical voices of the Story City women in the dry goods store and shook her head to clear the memory. "I can't imagine how lonely he would be if we hadn't come to be with him."

Ida left the window and scanned the titles of the books on the shelf. "He's happiest when Cosette is with him. Severt is fortunate Papa for once didn't take Aunt Margretha's advice about what is best for us. If he had, none of us would be here, and Severt would still be in Agnes Phipps."

Anna looked to Charlotte, hoping she would change the conversation.

Charlotte lifted her chin. "You should have stood up to him, Ida."

Ida turned, her eyes dark. "Oh?" She paused. "Like you did? I know how important it was to you to teach F. Melius' theory class. You were so happy in your studies at St. Olaf and had such an opportunity. Why didn't you stand up to Papa?"

Staring in stunned silence, Anna closed her eyes to the words that touched the pain of both sisters. She did not want to think about Ida's heartbreak over Oscar or hear about the opportunity Charlotte lost but never mentioned.

Charlotte's voice remained cool and calm. "I didn't do this for Papa, Ida." She looked down at her hands. "I did it for Severt. He was more important to me than studying with Professor Christiansen or teaching the theory class or practicing for a recital no one will remember years from now." She looked up. "It is not much to ask to sacrifice a few years when Severt has lost so much."

Ida's head and shoulders folded as she turned and faced her sister. "Forgive me, Charlotte. I don't know what got into me."

Charlotte paused. "Cosette told us that her cousin Walter paid you a visit in Boston in March."

Ida nodded and turned back to the bookshelf.

"You never mentioned it," Charlotte stared at her sister's back.

Ida shrugged. "Didn't I?"

"Walter told Cosette he's always known you were the girl for him," Anna said. "He said he'd do anything to win your attention."

Ida pulled a book from the shelf and glanced at the cover. "The girls at the conservatory thought him very charming. He filled the room with roses. There were so many that I gave some of them away."

Anna wished her sister sounded more enthusiastic. "Did you attend any recitals or concerts when he was there?"

Ida shook her head. "No. Walter isn't much for sitting inside listening to music." She returned the book to the shelf.

Anna wanted to hear more about Walter's visit, but Ida clearly did not wish to speak of it.

Ida wandered back to the window.

"You don't care for Walter, do you?" Charlotte asked.

Ida turned. "I wouldn't say that."

"No, you wouldn't," Charlotte said. "But he isn't Oscar, is he?"

Ida winced.

"You still aren't over him, are you?" Charlotte asked.

The question shocked Anna.

Ida bit her lip and sighed. "I know everyone thinks I should be, after all this time." She shook her head. "However much I've tried, I can't forget him. I loved him with all my heart."

Anna looked at the floor. She could not bear to see her sister suffering.

"You could write to Oscar," Charlotte said. "Tell him you made a mistake."

Ida shook her head. "Oh, no. I couldn't."

"Why not?" Charlotte asked.

"I couldn't."

The suggestion horrified Anna. "What would Papa say?"

Charlotte shrugged. "It seems to me Papa wants us all to be happy. He asked Ida to break off with Oscar because he feared for her life. We were all afraid of the disease before we came here." She looked at Ida. "Papa was afraid you would get sick if you married Oscar and we would lose you. He was afraid Oscar was infected. But we all know now if we are careful and take the proper hygienic measures, there is nothing to fear. Oscar might have had a father who was infected and died, but that doesn't mean Oscar was infected. He could be tested, like we have been, to know for sure." She stared intently at Ida. "I may be wrong, but it seems to me you would be happier with Oscar than you are now, and there is no doubt that Papa wants your happiness. If you still love Oscar, Ida, write to him. What harm could a letter do?"

Hemorrhage
Joseph

*J*oseph had agreed to Charlotte's suggestion to rent the Estes Park cabin for the summer season more for her benefit than for his son's.

The year caring for Severt in Denver had demanded much from Charlotte, and Joseph recognized the stressful winter had drained her energy. In retrospect, allowing Anna to spend the year in Denver had been a good decision. Charlotte needed her sister's lighthearted presence as much or more than Severt did. Though Joseph considered any risk of contamination unacceptable, he acknowledged the risk was not as great as he had once feared. Severt and the girls meticulously followed the sanitary procedures recommended by the doctors, and both times the girls were tested for tuberculosis at Agnes Phipps the results came back negative.

In August, Anna took the train back to Story City, packed for college, and moved to Northfield to begin her freshman year at St. Olaf College. Charlotte remained in Denver to care for Severt another year. Rather than return to the New England Conservatory, Ida decided to study with a voice teacher at the Wilcox studios in Denver and took a music position at the Congregational Church.

Severt's health did not improve much during the summer in Estes Park and was little better than when he left Agnes Phipps. Periods of deterioration followed every interval of progress, and Joseph knew a relapse could occur at any time. To ease the burden on Charlotte, he instructed her to hire both a full-time maid and a nurse. After making a profit of $4,000 on the sale of some land in Cheyenne, Wyoming, he succumbed to her appeal to buy a car. Charlotte requested $950, but Joseph knew they could find a good used car for less, and authorized her to spend no more than $850.

In early September, Joseph traveled to Billings, Montana, where he rented a room at the Northern Hotel through the end of the month. Conveniently located in the heart of downtown, the hotel was near the Union Depot and across the street from the Federal Building, which housed the post office, courthouse, and U.S. Land Office.

After filing some deeds at the courthouse one afternoon in mid-September, Joseph returned to his hotel.

"Good afternoon, Mr. Marvick." The desk clerk lifted Joseph's room key from the wall.

"Good afternoon."

The clerk handed Joseph his key and then reached below the counter. "I have some mail for you today."

Joseph flipped through the envelopes as he climbed the stairs to his room. In addition to a thick envelope from the bank in Sisseton, he had personal letters from both Olive and Charlotte. Once in his room, he slit open the envelope from Charlotte first.

> Dear Papa,
>
> Thanks to you, we are the proud owners of a new "used" car. We tested a four-cylinder Reo, an Olds "eight," and a Buick "six." We settled on the Olds. The Reo was in very good condition but a long ways from coming up to the Olds. I can't get used to such high seats any more. I drove it awhile but not for very long because shifting was too hard on my knee. Severt seemed to want to get the Buick, but after we test drove the Olds he found it rode much easier than many other cars. Well, the Olds "four" came out, and it looked just like new. It had only been run 3,000 miles and was owned by a banker here who left the city and of course he had to sell it. The salesman was the queerest fellow—I'm sure he's just been over here from Germany a couple years. Severt dickered a long time with the salesman about the price and at last he said he'd call him up later. Sure enough, early Friday morning he called Severt and said, "Vell, I tink ve can get togedder," and sure enough they did, and we got the car for $850.
>
> Violet Cherry, a friend of Ida's from Boston whose home is in Boise, Idaho, stopped off here with her mother and sister Saturday. They were on their way to Kansas City. It was nice to have a car to meet them in, show them around the city, etc. Violet's

younger sister, Madeline, has a splendid voice so with Violet playing the violin, and Ida, Madeline, and Cosette singing, we had a regular concert here that evening.

We hired a maid, and she surely is fine. I'm afraid you will regret it and change your mind once you see how lazy I'm getting. I'm so glad, though, because with Ida's lessons and practices and performances, she's often gone morning, noon, and night, and this gives her time to rest when she's home.

We also hired a nurse, Mrs. Markley. It's a good thing we did. Last night we girls were sitting downstairs reading when we heard Severt start to cough. We got nervous when he kept on coughing and pretty soon we heard him call out, "Mrs. Markley." She came and then we heard her run to the bathroom for medicine. We all ran upstairs and the nurse told us Severt had a hemorrhage. Cosette fell on the floor nearly fainting, and Ida flew to the kitchen for a glass of water for her. Of course many patients that get well have hemorrhages, but I always hoped Severt never would. Some exciting time! I feel so bad because now he has to lie flat on his back all the time—without even a pillow. Eggs, milk, orangeade, ice cream, jello, and butter are all the doctors will allow him to eat. I must say, Severt is taking it well and is wonderfully brave and patient.

Joseph closed his eyes. Charlotte's amusing account of the car purchase and pleasant social report of Violet Cherry's visit were the deceptive calm before the storm. The news that Severt had a hemorrhage touched down with the violence of a funnel cloud, shattering the illusions of safety and strength.

**

The hemorrhages continued intermittently, and Severt spent the fall in bed, much of it on his back. Frustrated by his confinement, he craved and demanded constant companionship. The positive outlook he maintained during Cosette's visits disintegrated during her absences, and Charlotte bore the brunt of his demands and irritability, as did the nurse and maid. The maid grumbled, the nurse shrugged, and Charlotte lost her patience.

When in Denver, Joseph spent as much time as he could with Severt, discussing business and current events. Not only did it relieve Charlotte, but the conversation engaged Severt's mind, distracting him from his illness.

On the tenth of November, Joseph carried the newspaper into Severt's room.

"They've declared Wilson the winner of the election."

Severt rolled from his side to his back. "Is it settled?"

Joseph shook his head. "Not until the official count comes in from California, but they expect the state to go Democratic."

"How many votes did it come down to?" Severt adjusted his covers.

Joseph sat down on one of the chairs across the room from the bed. "Wilson is ahead by 3,000 votes, and they say the missing precincts can't change the result."

"Are the Republicans going to ask for a recount?" Severt cleared his throat.

"They aren't conceding yet. The result still depends on a few close states, and they want to wait for the official counts."

"Which states are doubtful?"

"Minnesota, New Mexico, and New Hampshire. Hughes is leading in Minnesota, but they expect the state to go Democratic. It hardly matters. Even if all three states went to Hughes, there wouldn't be enough electoral votes combined to change the result."

"What a disappointment. I had my doubts Hughes could win, but it would have been easier to take if the headlines hadn't declared Hughes the winner on Tuesday."

Joseph nodded. "I agree. I certainly don't look forward to another four years with Wilson and the Democrats in control."

"You don't want another four years of peace and prosperity, as Wilson promised?" Severt grinned. "Ha. We're in for another four years of partisanship and promises that change with the winds of public opinion." His weak chuckle ended in a cough.

"His diplomacy won him votes at home but lost the respect of Europe, Asia, and Latin America. The foreign situation is shifting, and I fear with Wilson in office it's only a matter of time and we'll be in this war."

Severt shook his head. "There will be an uproar if that happens. Wilson won on his neutral position." Wincing, he cleared his throat.

"Whether we go to war or not has nothing to do with public opinion. It depends upon what the Germans and the Allies do. One day they may call Wilson's bluff. The trouble is that we won't be prepared to respond."

"Hughes advocated a program of greater mobilization and preparedness, but you must admit Wilson is strengthening the army and the navy." Severt spit into his pocket spittoon.

"Not enough."

"That's what Roosevelt said. But what is enough? If the appropriations for the army and navy increase, the Democrats will just push through more income tax legislation. You don't want to pay even more in taxes, do you?"

"No, I don't, but I also know you cannot negotiate from a position of weakness. The man we need for the times is Roosevelt."

Severt smiled. "Your man Roosevelt. Unfortunately the majority of the country doesn't love him as much as you do. He withdrew because he knew he couldn't win if he split the Republican vote like he did in the last election. And now it looks like Hughes didn't win even with his endorsement."

"If Wilson hadn't lowered the tariffs and his administration hadn't been so extravagant, there would have been enough revenue to meet the deficits without requiring war taxes. He claims he's given us prosperity, but he's emptied the treasury. Unfortunately, Kitchin and the other Democrats in Congress will continue to use the situation to push their agenda for steeper income taxes, and Wilson will continue to support them."

"Perhaps when Wilson speaks of prosperity he's thinking of the competitive advantage he's given foreigners." Severt turned to his side, coughing.

"Higher income taxes will only dampen investments and savings and threaten managerial prerogatives. It won't be for the good of the country, I can tell you that."

Severt's ravaging cough raged from his lungs, and he began to choke.

Joseph stood. "Mrs. Markwell." His voice broke in panic. He had not seen Severt in this state before. He raised his voice. "Mrs. Markwell. You need to come at once."

Severt sat forward, his pale face contorted and his crumpled body convulsing.

The nurse ran to the bed holding a basin and a syringe. Severt lurched forward, and Mrs. Markley held the basin under his chin to catch the bright red, frothy blood that gushed from his mouth.

Horrified, Joseph feared his son was dying.

"Relax, Severt. I've brought your medicine." She glanced at Joseph. "I know it looks bad, but he'll be all right."

Blood smeared Severt's mouth and chin. He looked up at his father. "I'm sorry."

Mrs. Markley set the basin on the table beside the bed. "Nothing to be sorry about. No more talking. You've had enough excitement this morning." Lifting Severt's sleeve, she injected his arm with the hypodermic and then removed his pillow from the bed. "Lie back now. I'll go get you some ice and get the maid to clean up." She faced Joseph as she walked to the door. "Severt needs to rest now, so it's best you leave. I've given him morphine, which quiets the respiratory movements, checks the cough, and helps him rest. I'll sit with him until the spell passes."

Severt closed his eyes. The corners of his mouth curled up slightly. "I didn't take the news Wilson won very well, did I?"

Severt's generous attempt at humor caught the edge of Joseph's emotion. He blinked and swallowed to clear unwelcome tears. Unable to speak, he turned and stepped out of the room. Alone in the hallway, he stood with one hand against the wall to steady himself. He squeezed his eyes shut to contain the tears that blurred his vision. The weight of his guilt pressed on his chest and roared in his head. He had failed his son. There was no one to blame but himself. If he had not sent him to St. Olaf, Severt would not be ill. Joseph had endangered his son, and nothing he had done since had helped Severt. Not the clean dry air of Colorado or the care at Agnes Phipps. Not the care of his sisters in a private home. Severt had not been cured. Instead, his health was deteriorating.

Muttering and scowling, the maid stomped by Joseph in the hall, a solution of chlorinated lime sloshing in the bucket she carried. The bloody bedclothes would be boiled and the room scrubbed, but there was nothing that could cleanse the grievous wrong he had committed.

The Letter
Joseph

Without notice, the maid disappeared after Thanksgiving. When Charlotte finally contacted her, the woman said she had taken a better position with a less demanding and healthy family. Furious, Charlotte declared the woman's irresponsible behavior did not altogether surprise her, and they would be better off with someone else.

Finding a new maid proved difficult, however, and the added workload of cleaning and washing limited Charlotte's recreational outings and stretched her patience. Her tongue sharpened after Ida made plans to spend Christmas at home in Story City and New Year's with Lula and Ed in Stanley, Wisconsin. Though Charlotte did not complain about assuming total responsibility for the housekeeping and daily care of Severt without any help from her sister or a maid, she admitted to being envious of Ida's plans to be home for the holidays and complained that she would be losing her winning auction bridge partner.

As the day of Ida's departure approached, Joseph felt the pressure rise within the family.

The week before she left, Ida decided she needed a new suit and outfit. Severt and Charlotte accompanied her downtown to pass their opinions on what she should purchase.

Joseph was reading when they returned late in the afternoon.

"Did you find some things you liked?" Joseph set down his papers.

"I did." Ida set several bags on the floor and removed her coat.

"I'm so sick of looking at suits and dresses I don't want to see any for weeks!" Charlotte pulled off her shoes and sat down to rub the ball of her right foot.

"We didn't even have time for the movies." Ida massaged her neck. "I did hope to see *Madame Butterfly*."

"Is there mail?" Dark circles enclosed Severt's eyes.

Concerned Severt was overly tired and irritated the girls had kept him out so long, Joseph nodded. "On the table."

Charlotte looked up. "I hope there is one from Cosette, or he will be unbearable this evening."

Ida sighed. "We should have come home earlier, I suppose. I didn't realize the time."

Severt returned smiling, holding up several letters. "One for me."

"No need to guess who that is from." Charlotte sat up straight with her hands on her knees. "Anything for me?"

Severt handed her a letter. "One for you. From Lydia." Walking away, he abruptly turned back and handed her another. "Oh. Another for you. From Jack."

Charlotte rolled her eyes.

Charlotte heard from Jack at least once each week and regularly received letters from her sisters, cousin Lydia, and various friends from St. Olaf. Severt depended upon hearing from Cosette each day. Ida did not receive mail regularly.

Today, Joseph knew there were three letters addressed to Ida. One of the letters came from Lula. The second, postmarked Boston and addressed with graceful script, was from Sarah Oakes, her friend from the conservatory. The third letter, postmarked in Rochester, Minnesota, was addressed with scrawling, masculine handwriting. Ida had received word from Oscar Locken.

While he waited for his children to return from town, Joseph speculated about the letter from the man Ida had loved. He wondered how the young man obtained the rental address in Denver and whether it was the first correspondence since Ida broke their engagement. They could have been exchanging letters for some time and not informed him, although he thought this improbable. Perhaps Oscar wanted a second chance. Joseph knew he had been right to fear the disease, and could not imagine two children consumed by tuberculosis. Oscar had been exposed. His father had died of the disease, and both his college roommates contracted the disease. The doctors explained it was possible to be infected but disease free for years.

But to be fair, Joseph knew now that tuberculosis in the family was insufficient reason to deny a marriage. Oscar could have been tested to determine whether or not he was actually a threat. The girls had lived with Severt and remained free of the disease. Oscar could be as well. Joseph had denied Ida happiness and broken her heart when her health may not have been in danger. Marriage to Oscar could have been less of a risk than living with her brother. Surely Oscar had been tested in medical school, if not before, and would not ask Ida for a second chance if he were ill or posed a threat to her. And if that were the case, Joseph would not object.

He could atone for his mistake.

Joseph watched Severt approach Ida. "Some mail for you as well."

"How nice." Ida smiled at her brother and reached for the letters. "And not only one, but several."

When Ida saw the third envelope, her face froze. Eyes wide, she gasped.

Charlotte looked up, pausing as she slit the top of an envelope with the letter opener.

Joseph watched Charlotte's eyes move from her sister to her brother, and saw Severt nod. It appeared they had expected the letter, which seemed odd given Ida's reaction.

Ida's eyes, tight with fear and hope, locked with Severt's. Severt pointed to the stairs with his head.

Irritated, Joseph wondered what his children were withholding from him.

Forcing a strained smile, Ida hurried from the room.

"Well!" Charlotte held the letter opener like a sword. "Don't mind us, Papa, but we now must read our letters!"

Joseph picked up his newspaper and resumed reading. It was only a matter of time before he would learn what had transpired.

A few minutes later, the floorboards above moaned with the screech of the box spring mattress and muffled sobs broke the silence.

Joseph tensed.

"Oh, my." The pages of Charlotte's letter crumpled as her hands dropped to her lap. For a moment she stared at Severt, then at her father.

Joseph wondered what Oscar had written that had so upset Ida. Perhaps the young man was ill and dying. If so, Joseph hoped he had not asked her to visit him.

After an awkward silence, Severt finally spoke. "Ida heard from Oscar."

"It must have been terrible news." Charlotte bit her lip.

"I would say that is quite obvious." Severt rolled his eyes.

"Severt, please don't." Charlotte stood, dropping her letter on the seat of her chair. One of the pages fell to the floor, and she bent over to retrieve it. "I believe I'll go start supper, and after a bit I'll go up and check on Ida."

"I think I'll go lie on the porch until supper is ready." Severt winced as he lifted himself out of his chair. Shopping was quite a marathon this afternoon." He attempted a laugh, but his eyes were dull and his voice flat. "It seems I'm not ready for a marathon just yet."

Joseph's frown deepened with disquiet as his son left the room, hunched and hobbling like an old man.

Ida did not come down for supper, but no one mentioned her absence. Charlotte and Severt made occasional comments about the day's expedition but otherwise ate in silence. Absorbed by his concerns for Ida and Severt, Joseph said nothing himself and paid no attention to the intermittent, inconsequential conversation.

Charlotte picked at her meal and ate little. After the others finished eating, she scraped her food to the side of her plate. Leaning back in her chair, she folded her hands in her lap. She tilted her head back, exhaled, and stared at the ceiling. "I am to blame for this."

Joseph leaned forward and focused on his daughter. "And why is that?"

Charlotte shook her head. "It was my idea for her to write to him."

"We all encouraged her." Severt shifted in his chair.

Joseph frowned. "Why would you do such a thing?"

His children stared at each other for a moment before Charlotte faced her father. "She never got over him, Papa."

"What did Oscar say?" Severt asked.

Charlotte winced. "He is engaged to someone new."

"Engaged?" Severt threw his napkin on the table. "The cad!"

Though he had not anticipated the news, Joseph did not find it surprising. Over three years had passed since Ida broke their engagement. Oscar had moved on. The opportunity to right a wrong had passed.

"Do we know who she is? Someone from St. Olaf?" Severt asked.

Charlotte shrugged. "Ida didn't say." Her brows tightened, and she bit her lower lip. "I didn't expect it. He was so in love with her."

"Or so we thought." Severt scowled.

"He said she made her choice when she broke off with him. She had her chance, and it is too late now to change her mind."

"I don't believe it!" Severt shook his head. "How could he be so cruel?"

"She is completely heartbroken." Charlotte squeezed her eyes shut for a moment. "Ida was so proud he was going to be a doctor. He's still in medical school, doing his clinical work at Mayo Clinic. It makes her feel all the worse."

"They should teach physicians how to heal hearts instead of break them." Severt glared. "He sounds as cold and heartless as my doctors. If that is the case, Ida is better off without him."

"It never crossed my mind that Oscar might have found someone else. Not once." Charlotte's shoulders sagged. "I only considered your reaction, Papa. When I urged her to write, I was only thinking what you would say. That you would disapprove. But after all that has happened. . . " She bit her lip. "I thought you would want Ida's happiness." She shook her head and covered her mouth with her hand. "I never dreamed Oscar would have found someone else."

Charlotte should not have encouraged her sister to write to Oscar, but Joseph recognized she had acted with the best of intentions. "I am disappointed Ida has been hurt by this, but what is done is done. I trust she will get over Oscar now and once again find happiness." Ida was a desirable and marriageable woman, but was getting older. Perhaps now she would consider the attention of Cosette's cousin, Walter Henderson. Walter came from a respectable family and had pursued her since high school. He would not be a bad choice for her.

Refusal

Joseph

*B*oth Cosette and Jack came to Denver for the holidays. Cosette had made her plans months earlier, but Jack arrived with only two weeks' notice. Charlotte's sour disposition dissipated and seemed as happy as the day F. Melius Christiansen asked her to teach his freshman theory class.

On Christmas Day, Severt surprised the family by announcing he and Cosette would finally get married and move to San Diego in February when the weather turned cold. A three-year engagement was long enough. Cosette had wanted to marry for some time, but until now Severt resisted, not wanting to commit until he was cured. After reading Benjamin Truman's book *Semi-tropical California*, Severt believed his chronic cough would disappear within months of residing in the remarkable climate, and he could soon pronounce himself cured.

Later that evening, after her brother had gone to bed, Charlotte remarked that he seemed like a little boy who had received permission to do something he had wanted for such a long time.

Joseph did not express his concerns, but feared for Severt's fragile emotional state which depended upon Cosette and would collapse if she were to break with him. He could not imagine Cosette's parents would approve the marriage before Severt recovered completely. He would not. And though Cosette had never given reason for him to doubt her intentions, Joseph could not understand why a healthy young woman would choose to marry a sick man with whom she could not share a bed nor have children. She had stuck with Severt throughout his illness, but she had not been responsible for his daily care and did not share in the workload when she visited. Cosette had never managed a household, and with Severt ill and unable to work, the demands upon her would be greater than she realized.

Joseph was also skeptical of the testimonials about California. Physicians promised a cure in the cool dry air in the Colorado mountains, the warm dry air of Texas and Arizona, and the warm, moist air of southern California. The climate did not seem to be as great a factor in a cure as the quality of the physician, living arrangements, diet, exercise, and state of mind. Joseph kept his opinion to himself, however, and said nothing to dissuade Severt from moving. The lease on the Denver house was up in June, with no option of extension. Severt would have to find another place to live, and if he and Cosette wanted to move to San Diego, and Cosette's parents approved of the marriage, Joseph would not object.

After the holidays, Joseph turned his attention to bank and real estate matters in South Dakota and Iowa. To fund additional real estate investment, he and his brother Andrew executed the sale and assignment of promissory notes and mortgages they had written through the Iowa & Dakota Land & Loan Co. to the Central Life Insurance Company of Illinois. In exchange for the cash, the brothers provided personal guarantees of payment at maturity as required by the insurance company. The risk could be managed; if any of the farmers were to fall behind in their payments with risk of default, they would repurchase the land and resell it. The one man Joseph needed to keep a close eye on was Charles Elwood, a former postmaster from Minnesota with no farming experience who recently purchased 1,080 acres in Musselshell County, Montana, from Joseph. Included in the notes assigned to Central Life was a first mortgage note from Elwood for $13,500.

While Joseph was in Sisseton, the post office received copies of the new income tax provisions from the Internal Revenue Department. He had anticipated significant tax increases, but was perturbed to discover the corporate tax rate increased from one percent to two percent and the individual income tax rates more than doubled. Joseph would have a significant amount of tax due when he filed his returns on the first of March. Representative Kitchin from North Carolina and his allies on the left had also pushed through a new estate tax. The only good to come from the special revenue legislation was a repeal of the collection at the source provisions that had passed in 1913.

Like Joseph, Andrew would also have a significant tax liability. Before Joseph left Sisseton for Story City, his younger brother approached him for a personal loan to cover his taxes. The request did not surprise Joseph. His younger brother had been overextended and unable to make his tax payments the previous year as well, and Joseph had extended him a loan of $2,500 due with interest on March 1, 1918. While he appreciated Andrew's good taste, generosity, and the demands of his public position, Joseph did not approve of his brother's spending habits. Andrew and his family lived in one of the most beautiful, modern residences in Sisseton, entertained often, and donated generously to the church and community. After reproaching his brother for what he considered to be living beyond his means, Joseph agreed to loan him an additional $3,000, to be repaid with interest on the same date as the first loan.

From Sisseton, Joseph traveled to Story City, where he found bank matters well taken care of.

He had not been in the office more than a couple of hours when Jack Donhowe entered his office and asked to speak with him.

Joseph pointed to a chair across from his desk. "Have a seat."

Hands clasped behind his back, Jack shifted his weight from one foot to the other. "I'd prefer to stand, if it's all right with you."

Joseph sat back. "Is there a problem?"

"Well, sir, there's a personal matter I would like to discuss with you."

Joseph rubbed his mustache. It was not like Jack to be nervous.

The young man's chest expanded as he took a deep breath. He lifted his chin and looked intently at Joseph. "I'll get straight to the point. I'd like your permission to marry Charlotte."

Joseph continued to rub his mustache. He had long since considered Jack a fine match for Charlotte, and it was evident at Christmas how taken the two were with each other. "Have you spoken with Charlotte?"

"Oh, yes."

"And she accepted you?"

Jack grinned. "Yes, sir."

"Then you have my approval, Jack." It pleased Joseph that another daughter of his would marry into the Donhowe family.

Grinning, Jack unclasped his hands and brushed his hair back. "Thank you, sir. I'll do right by her, I promise you that. I think the world of Charlotte."

Joseph nodded. He had no doubts about the young man.

Jack stepped to the chair Joseph had offered and sat down. "I asked Charlotte to marry me when I was in Denver, and she agreed but didn't want to say anything to you or the family. She'd prefer we keep our plans quiet until after Severt and Cosette are married and she is free to leave."

"I see."

"I must say, I don't agree with her—I'd prefer to get married as soon as possible, but she doesn't want our plans to interfere with Severt's plans or happiness."

"Your plans will not interfere with Severt's."

Jack smiled. "It might not be my place to say this, but I sure hope not. Besides, I worry about her out there. I know they boil and disinfect everything, but I'd feel better to see her home."

"I assure you she will be home soon." Joseph appreciated Jack's concern for Charlotte's health and considered it strength of character that the young man would broach the matter with him. "However, before you set your date, I would like to mention a business deal I've been considering."

Jack leaned forward.

"In the coming months, I plan to spend some extended time in Montana. I'm evaluating whether it would be profitable to locate there with a land and trust company, or perhaps a bank. The population is multiplying as new homesteaders are filing claims. And with the increasing national and international demand for grain driven by the war in Europe, farmers are expanding. This is creating great demand for land companies and banks. If I determine it would pay to work in the land business there, I want you to join me in Billings, perhaps in April. If you find the situation out west to your liking, you could stay, and after you are married, Charlotte could join you there. If not, you could return to your job at the bank with your current salary and you'll have lost nothing." Joseph paused to allow Jack time to absorb the offer he had extended. "Would you be interested?"

Jack grinned. "You bet I'm interested!"

Joseph nodded. "Good. As no plans are set at this time and possibly may not materialize, I trust you to keep this conversation confidential, other than to discuss it with Charlotte and your Uncle Peter. Peter knows about the deal, as I've already spoken to him about it. He thinks it would be a great opportunity for you. He told me he'd take it himself, if he weren't already settled here."

Jack jumped up, and reached his hand over Joseph's desk. "Thank you, Mr. Marvick."

Joseph stood and shook his future son-in-law's hand. If the deal came to be, it would be a good opportunity for the young man. Jack had a quick mind, good business sense, and great potential. He would be a good husband for Charlotte, and Joseph would be proud to have him as a son-in-law.

Joseph wrote to Charlotte that afternoon, granting his permission to marry Jack, and told her to make plans to return home.

Honoring Charlotte's request to keep the engagement secret, Joseph did not mention anything to Ida when she arrived unexpectedly at the end of the week. Cosette had come home to prepare for her wedding, but Joseph found it peculiar and unnecessary that Ida accompanied her.

Ida did not disclose why she had come to Story City until Saturday, when she approached him after breakfast.

"Papa? Could I have a moment with you?"

Joseph looked up from his papers and nodded.

From her perch on the edge of the divan across the room, Ida smiled. Joseph recognized the beguiling smile she used when she was about to ask for something. It was the same smile her mother had used when she pleaded with him not to cancel their fateful trip to Illinois, the trip he should not have conceded to take. Squinting, he willed the unbidden memory aside.

"I've come to tell you about a change of plans."

"Oh?"

"Severt has decided he cannot marry Cosette."

Joseph frowned. "What brought this about?"

Ida bit her lip and glanced away.

He watched her eyes flit around the room. Evidently she had been sent as the messenger.

Her fingertips fluttered across her lips before her hand dropped to rest lightly around her neck. "Cosette went to see Dr. Tygard Monday evening." She swallowed. "He doesn't advise their marrying, although he said it is a worthy thing for her to do. He said Severt is a pretty sick boy and his chances just hang in the balance. Cosette would be taking a big risk if she married him." Ida took a deep breath.

Joseph leaned back in his chair. The doctor's harsh words troubled him on two accounts. First, the grim assessment of Severt's condition, and second, that the doctor expressed such an assessment to Cosette without informing Joseph.

Ida leaned forward, tilting her head, her brown eyes round and still. "Of course, we know he'll get well." Her voice modulated lower, soft and soothing. "But after talking to the doctor, Severt has decided he won't marry now until his health has improved."

"I see." The doctor's discouragement of the marriage did not surprise Joseph. To avoid inevitable disappointment, Severt should have spoken with his doctor before he made his impulsive decision.

Ida shifted, stretching her shoulders and back. "Cosette was beside herself, as you might imagine. But, of course, she can't force him to marry her. As Charlotte says, you know how obstinate we Marvicks can be." She smiled. "Then Cosette sprung a new plan, which is what I have come to talk to you about."

Joseph leaned back in his chair, troubled by the doctor's prognosis that Severt's chances hung in the balance. "And what might that be?"

"Cosette will stay out in Denver and then in February when the weather gets bad, she and Severt will go to San Diego, and Charlotte will go along as a chaperone. I can't go just now because I would hate to give up my church position, but I can relieve Charlotte from June until August when the church has vacation. Hopefully after three or four months his health will be much improved, and then they can be married as planned." She took a deep breath. "What do you say, Papa? Do you approve?"

He did not approve. "Charlotte agreed to go?" He suspected she had not yet told her sisters of her plan to marry Jack.

"She wants Severt to be happy." Ida leaned toward him, her hands pressed together as though in prayer. "Papa, if only you could have seen him. The morning after he gave up his plans to marry Cosette, he had a headache, felt sick, and had no intention of leaving his bed. But after he heard Cosette's plan, he got up for dinner and proposed a Denham's Theatre party in the afternoon, and went along himself. That night he felt so well he played bridge with us."

To Joseph's disappointment, illness had weakened Severt's character. His son's state of mind affected his ability to function as much as his physical condition. His disposition depended upon whether Cosette was by his side, and he had come to expect his sisters to wait on him without regard for their own best interests. "I would have expected Severt to write. Isn't it his place to put forward this plan?"

Ida looked down as color flushed her cheeks. "We thought it best to talk it through with you, and didn't want to wait for your next trip to Denver. We all agreed I should come to talk to you when Cosette talked to her parents so we could settle the matter."

They had chosen Ida because they knew he favored her. "I won't permit it."

"But Papa."

Joseph's eyes narrowed as he shook his head. "No."

"Please, Papa. Consider how much better Severt feels when Cosette is with him."

"That may be so. But Charlotte will not be going to San Diego."

"This is the only way it could be arranged as long as they're not married."

"Charlotte has done enough." She had been in Denver a year and a half, much longer than Joseph had intended. She had sacrificed more than enough already. He would not ask her to delay her own marriage to accommodate Cosette and Severt. Charlotte would return home and marry Jack. Joseph had to consider the welfare and best interests of the girls, and shared Jack's concern. Despite the hygienic measures, each day the girls lived with Severt they risked contracting the disease. Severt's health had not improved after leaving Agnes Phipps and had perhaps even deteriorated. Joseph could no longer justify the current arrangements. It was time to consider other options. It was time for both Charlotte and Ida to leave Denver and move on with their own lives.

"Severt will be devastated." Ida looked away, her brow furrowed, her fingers pressed against her lips.

"That is unfortunate."

Ida swallowed. "Then I shall have to give up my position and go with them."

"No. Neither of you will go."

"But there is no other solution."

"If Cosette cannot find another chaperone and Severt insists upon going west, he could go alone."

"You can't let him go alone."

"It would not hurt him to be alone for a time. He may be ill, but after his last examination, Dr. Tygard told you girls not to wait on him so much. Severt needs to be encouraged to do more on his own."

"I don't think the doctor meant him to be alone, just that we should encourage him to do more."

"We would hire a nurse. Mrs. Markley could go with him."

"Without Cosette or one of his sisters, I do believe he would die of loneliness."

Joseph clenched his teeth. "Then perhaps he should remain in Denver."

"Papa, he has set his hopes on California. He is so tired of the cold."

"His doctors at Agnes Phipps believe the clean, cold air is good for his lungs."

Ida bowed her head and folded her hands in her lap.

Joseph considered the conversation closed and reached for his papers.

"You have always wanted the best for Severt." Ida's voice had a shrill edge. For a brief moment, she resembled Margretha. "How can you deny him his happiness?"

Joseph could not remember a time when Ida had pushed him to anger. He took a deep, deliberate breath. "Enough." He picked up his papers and began to read.

Both Olive and Peter supported Joseph's decision. When Peter said he had never thought it wise for the girls to be in Denver, Joseph did not remind him that he had been the one to suggest Charlotte care for her brother.

Not realizing she was revealing a secret, Olive said it would be a shame if Charlotte gave up her plans to marry Jack, even if it would only be for a few months. She and Peter thought of Charlotte as a daughter and had offered to have the wedding in their home.

Joseph considered the matter closed, particularly after Olive mentioned Charlotte's plans to marry Jack.

The following afternoon, when Ida and Cosette raised the matter again, he did not conceal his irritation. Cosette's parents had given their permission for her to go to San Diego on the condition they had a chaperone. Joseph gave the same response he had given Ida, and the conversation did not last long. Cosette was proving to be as obstinate as Charlotte claimed the Marvicks to be.

On Monday, Ida and Cosette returned to Denver.

On Tuesday, Jack asked to have another word with Joseph. Charlotte had written, worried her father would object to their plan, and wanted Jack to talk to him. With Cosette prepared to do so much, Charlotte was willing to sacrifice a few months of being with Jack. She had not told Severt of her own engagement and did not for the world want him to find out for fear he would not like it that she hadn't told him, and would give up his plans on account of her. Jack hoped he was not speaking out of turn, but wanted to say he did not agree with Charlotte and strongly objected to her going to San Diego. Joseph assured Jack that she would not go to San Diego under any circumstances and would be coming home soon. He considered the matter settled.

That evening, Joseph wrote to Severt to convey his disappointment and displeasure in the events that had transpired. His son should decide whether he was going to San Diego or remain in Denver. If he chose to go to San Diego, they would make arrangements for a nurse to accompany him. Under no circumstances would either of his sisters go. Severt had selfishly thought only of himself and had not considered the best interests of Charlotte. If he wanted to be with Cosette, he should remain in Denver. His recovery did not depend upon moving to San Diego. Good plain food, exercise, and keeping his spirits up would do more for him than fresh air or climate. The following day, Joseph sent the letter special delivery. He sent a separate letter to Charlotte, telling her to pack her things and make arrangements to return home at once.

Severt decided to remain in Denver where Cosette could be with him, and Charlotte announced she would marry Jack in June. When Joseph passed through on his way west, he found his son as cheerful as ever, and Charlotte was delighted to be returning home.

The family fuss had been an unwelcome distraction, but peaceful relations resumed, just as momentous events in swift succession brought the United States and Germany to the brink of war. A German submarine sunk the American freight steamer Housatonic off the Scilly Islands, prompting President Wilson to sever diplomatic relations with Berlin. The German ambassador received his passports, the United States recalled their ambassador to Germany, and orders were flashed to the country's navy yards and ports to take every precaution against plot or attack.

The Sacrifice
Joseph

*J*oseph was in Billings when the United States declared war on the sixth of April, 1917. The House vote passed 373 to 50.

The following day, President Wilson proclaimed that all men ages twenty-one through thirty were required to register for the selective draft, which would be held on the fifth of June, the same day Charlotte and Jack had chosen to be married.

Joseph penned a letter to Jack Donhowe.

Dear Jack,

With the country now at war, and the possibility you could be drafted, I have decided it is not the right time to open either a bank or land business in Montana. For the time being, I think it best you remain in Story City in your current position at the bank.

The talk here in Billings is all about Miss Jeanette Rankin, the newly elected Republican congresswoman from Montana. Perhaps you read she joined the pacifist minority to vote against the resolution. My business associates here share my opinion that she is an embarrassment to her family, women, the state of Montana, and the Republican Party. I wonder what Charlotte has to say about it. It seems even Miss Rankin's fellow suffragists have openly criticized her behavior as impractical and sentimental.

I trust all is well with you.

Sincerely,

Joseph Marvick

The financial impact of the war on Joseph would be mixed. Prices for corn and wheat had doubled in the past year, driven by increased international demand for the commodities. To restrict speculation, the Chicago Board of Trade fixed the maximum price of corn at $1.65 the day war was declared. Similar action had been taken earlier to control the soaring price of wheat, which was trading over $2.00 per bushel. Healthy farm profits, however, would be offset by higher taxes. In May the House passed a $1.8 billion war revenue bill to defray war expenses, which included a retroactive income tax amendment increasing the top rate to an inconceivable sixty percent. Congress had yet to debate how additional revenue would be raised, but business would bear the burden.

***

Charlotte's wedding was a small affair at Olive and Peter's home, with only intimate friends and family in attendance.

After the ceremony, Joseph shook his new son-in-law's hand. "Welcome to the family, Jack."

Jack beamed. "Thank you, sir."

Joseph bent down to kiss his daughter. "Congratulations, Charlotte."

Charlotte's eyes glistened. "Look at me. I'm so happy I'm crying."

Ida stepped forward and hugged her sister. "Congratulations, dearest Charlotte. I'm so happy for you. I have to kiss you twice—once from me and a second time from Severt. He made me promise I would give you a kiss from him, since he couldn't be here to congratulate you himself."

Joseph stepped aside, knowing how disappointed both Charlotte and Severt were that he could not attend her wedding.

After John Donhowe congratulated the couple, he sought out Joseph. "Well, this makes one more partnership between our families."

Joseph nodded. "They're a good match for each other."

"I agree. Now let's hope Jack doesn't get drafted."

"He registered this morning?" Registration for the draft was between 7:00 a.m. and 9:00 p.m., with no exceptions for the sick and absent.

"First thing. I actually signed his card as registrar. Difficult thing for a father to do, particularly on his wedding day."

"I imagine."

"Did Severt register in Denver?"

"Yes."

"At least he'll be able to claim an exemption for being sick. You won't have to worry about him being drafted."

"True." Joseph would gladly take the risk of his son being drafted in exchange for his health. Severt was fighting his own battle against disease. Joseph did not like to think about his odds of winning.

"Did you hear my nephew Alfred enlisted?"

Joseph nodded. "I heard the news from both Peter and Anna."

"Quite a few local boys have signed up."

"So I heard. That should help Jack's chances."

"That's what I'm hoping. From what I gather, the war department expects to draft about a million men out of ten million registered. He has about a one in ten chance of having his name drawn, as I see it."

"Well, we should know by the end of the month."

***

Walter Henderson did not attend the wedding, but called on Ida regularly while she and Joseph were in Story City that June. One afternoon, Walter paid Joseph an unexpected visit at the bank.

"Mr. Marvick."

Joseph looked up from his desk.

Walter did not wait to be acknowledged, but strode into the office, smiling, his steps hard across the wood floor.

"Is there something I can help you with?"

"There is." Walter approached the desk and held out his hand.

Joseph paused before pushing back his chair to stand. The younger man's skin was rough and his grip crushing.

Joseph nodded to one of the leather chairs opposite his desk. "Have a seat."

As he moved to the chair, Walter scanned the room.

Walter farmed with his father, and though it was mid-afternoon on a weekday, he smelled of soap, his light-brown hair was damp, his face clean shaven, and his nails neatly clipped. He wore a white shirt that had been pressed but was now wrinkled, an outdated brown tie, ordinary brown trousers, a large silver belt buckle, and slightly scuffed brown shoes. His face and hands were bronzed from working outside in the sun.

The leather of the chair groaned as Walter leaned back. He rested his arms casually on the arms of the chair and stretched his legs.

"How is your father?" Joseph inquired.

"Doing fine, other than all this cold and rain we've had."

"Have much damage?" During the past week, temperatures had been below normal, and some areas had received up to seven inches of rain. Flooding had damaged a considerable portion of the belated corn crop. Joseph had surveyed his rental properties and found he had fared better than most. Relatively flat, the land he owned had minimal hillside erosion and bottom ground flooding.

"We'll have to replant most of the corn. It's a good thing prices are as high as they are." Walter shrugged. "Overall, the prospects seem to be good. If it warms up like they say, we should be able to get back out in the fields next week."

"And what is it that you need to speak to me about?" If Walter had come to ask for a loan, he would refer him to John Donhowe.

"I've come on a personal matter." Walter's intense gray eyes aimed at Joseph.

Joseph smoothed his mustache.

"I'd like your help with Ida."

"How so?"

"I'd like to marry her."

"I see." Walter's intentions did not surprise Joseph. His daughter's feelings toward Walter, however, remained reserved. "Have you spoken with Ida?"

"Yes, but she hasn't accepted." Walter scratched his neck, the white skin beneath his collar in stark contrast to the bronzed skin above. "She claims it isn't possible, least not now."

"Why is that?"

"Says she can't leave Severt."

Joseph frowned. Ida, Anna, and Cosette planned to stay with Severt at the cabin in Estes Park for the months of July and August. Where Severt would live at the end of the summer depended upon his condition. If his health improved significantly, Cosette and Severt planned to marry and move to a warmer climate. If not, Severt would find another place to live that provided the appropriate care. Under no circumstances would either Ida or Anna stay to care for their brother. Joseph had made it clear to them all that at the end of the summer he expected Anna to return to St. Olaf and Ida to move on with her own life.

Walter leaned forward. "I understand it might be hard for Severt to be alone out there without his sisters and no chaperone for Cosette, but it seems to me a woman as beautiful as Ida should be married and have a family of her own. I thought I'd talk to you, see if I could persuade you to allow her to leave."

Joseph had expected Ida to be married by now. If she were to turn Walter down, she could remain unmarried like Margretha. "I'll speak to Ida."

Walter smiled. "I appreciate it."

Joseph stood and held out his hand.

"I understand her birthday is tomorrow."

"It is."

"Not to push matters, but I don't want to wait too long. Neither one of us is getting any younger."

After Joseph showed Walter to the door, he watched the younger man stride away. His aggressive competitiveness could be abrasive but could serve him well if used appropriately. Walter did not share Ida's interests in music and the arts, and she had no interest in livestock judging and disliked shooting, but they shared the same heritage. Walter's uncles were business leaders in the community, and Walter and his father farmed, as Joseph and his own father had. It would be useful to have someone in the family who understood agriculture and could eventually assume some of the responsibility for those investments. And Walter was the picture of health.

The following morning, Joseph found Ida rearranging a dozen red roses in a vase. He watched her adjust the height of several flowers, tilting her head as she turned the vase to view them from various angles.

Ida gently extracted a stem and considered the arrangement. As she eased the flower back into the vase, her hand jerked away.

"Ah!' She inspected her finger, put it to her mouth, and then rubbed it gently.

The song of a warbler floated through the open window.

A light breeze carried the perfume of the fresh cut roses across the room, and Joseph sneezed.

Startled, Ida turned. "Papa. I didn't know you were up. I'll pour you a cup of coffee and get you some breakfast." She moved toward the kitchen.

"I see you have flowers."

"Yes." Ida glanced back at the roses. "They're lovely, aren't they?"

"For your birthday." Twenty-four years ago she had been born on the fifteenth of June.

Ida faced him, smiling, blushing. "Yes. Walter had them delivered yesterday afternoon."

"He has been coming around quite a bit lately."

"He has." Ida twisted the hair at her temple.

"He seems to be quite taken with you."

Ida adjusted the position of the vase. "He's been quite attentive."

"He came to see me yesterday."

Ida looked up. "He did?" Ida's brows furrowed. "At the bank?"

"It seems he would like to marry you."

Ida glanced back at the flowers.

"Has he spoken to you?"

Ida nodded without looking up. "Several times."

"He tells me you have not accepted."

Ida looked down as she rubbed her finger. "No."

"Why is that?"

Ida bit her lip.

"Ida?"

She sighed. "I don't feel I can leave Severt."

"There is no reason why you can't."

Ida shook her head. "Oh, but I have looked forward to spending the summer season in Estes Park again this year. We had such a grand time together there last year."

"In any event, you are free to leave."

Ida frowned. "Severt's health may not improve as much as we hope this summer. Anna will be returning to St. Olaf again in the fall. If he and Cosette don't marry, he will need someone with him."

"There are other options."

"I know there are places like the Oakes Home where he would be well taken care of. But he would be so lonely." She took a breath. "I do believe all the good that has been done could be lost if he doesn't have family nearby. It would put his recovery in jeopardy."

Joseph straightened his shirt sleeve. He did not want to argue with Ida. "It is admirable that both you and Charlotte have been so devoted to your brother." He waited to continue speaking until she looked up at him. "That said, I thought I made it clear to all of you, including your brother, that I will not permit any of you girls to sacrifice your own futures on account of him."

"It is only a matter of time until Severt feels better, perhaps a few months more, and I would be free to go."

"It is time for you to get on with your own life, Ida. Walter will not wait forever."

Ida looked to the window.

"You do understand that?"

"Yes."

"Do you find him unacceptable?"

Ida shrugged. "He isn't . . . " She circled the table, adjusting the corners of the table cloth. "He's very attentive." She glanced at the flowers. "It was sweet of him to remember my birthday."

"I would not want you to lose your chance at marriage." Joseph did not want Ida to end up a spinster like Margretha. Ida shared her birthday with his sister, who turned forty-four today. Both were artistic. Margretha's attractive features had stiffened over time, unsoftened by marriage. He did not wish the same for Ida.

Ida turned toward the window. "Any woman would be fortunate to have the attention of such a charming, good-looking man."

"Consider Walter's proposal, Ida. He would not be a bad husband."

Ida nodded, but did not turn from the window, where the lace curtains wavered in the breeze.

IV

October 1917—May 1918

"For the sun rises with its scorching heat
and withers the field;
its flower falls, and its beauty perishes.
It is the same way with the rich;
in the midst of a busy life, they will wither away."

JAMES 1:11

The Drought
Joseph

Ida accepted Walter, and they set a wedding date in early October. The following day, she and Anna left for Colorado with Cosette.

After stopping in Denver to check on Severt, Joseph continued on to Montana. The dusty, gray wheat lands seemed a world apart from the wet, green cornfields of Iowa. The disparity between the fertile humid Midwest and the arid western plains had always struck Joseph, but the summer of 1917 was the driest ever on record, with less than a third of an inch of rain in the month of July. Battalions of grasshoppers and cutworms devoured wheat as it withered in the brutal heat. Rattlesnakes and gophers multiplied. Unrelenting winds stormed from the west, confiscating precious topsoil and burying sun scorched crops beneath drifts of dust. Barbed wire fences bayoneted tumbleweeds as they fled to the east.

Joseph's decision not to open a bank or land and loan company proved wise. Extended in response to the wartime demand and rising prices for grain, few farmers had any cash reserves, and they flooded the banks in search of loans. Those behind on their debt payments or tax bills abandoned their homesteads when their livestock starved, their food ran out, and either the banks foreclosed or the county seized their property. By the end of the summer, the land market dried up, and banks and implement dealers began writing off loans that had seemed so safe during the boom of the past ten years.

Joseph extended personal loans to each of his renters to cover their share of the year's crop farm loss. The risk of losing them in the exodus of dejected and destitute families outweighed the risk of nonpayment. His tenants had conserved the little water available and as a result would have enough food to last the winter. They harvested enough vegetables to can and store in their root cellars, their few head of dairy and beef cattle would provide milk, butter and meat, and, despite the constant threat of coyotes and chicken hawks, they had hens for eggs and stewing.

Joseph also extended a personal loan to Charles Elwood, who had fallen behind on his mortgage payments to the insurance company. Having personally guaranteed the loan and convinced Elwood would fail, Joseph made several offers to buy back the property. When Elwood stubbornly refused the final offer, Joseph loaned him money to cover the mortgage payments, hoping to minimize his losses.

As he walked to his car from the Elwood farmhouse, two men rode up the drive on horseback.

"Didn't know you had company, Charles," one of the men said.

"I'm just leaving." Joseph guessed one of the men was in his early fifties and the other about ten years younger.

Charles adjusted his spectacles. "This here is Joseph Marvick."

"Heard the name." The younger of the two men shifted in the saddle. "You're the real estate man that's bought up a bunch of land."

Charles bobbed his head in agreement. "I bought my land from him myself." He turned to Joseph. "The Newmans own the stock farms to the west of here."

Joseph nodded at the ranchers. "How long have you lived in this part of the country?"

The older man squinted. "Long time."

The younger rancher smirked. "We were herding sheep in this territory long before you city folk came and started buying up land, and I reckon we'll be here when you leave."

Charles' face reddened. "I keep telling you, I have no plans on leaving."

The older man stared down from his horse. "We'll see."

"They don't believe in dryland farming," Charles said to Joseph.

The younger man turned in the saddle to face the fields. "Don't look to me like it worked too good for you, Charles."

Charles wiped his brow. "Wait until next year. We didn't get any rain this year."

"What makes you think it'll rain next year?" Deep lines etched the dark skin of the older rancher's expressionless face.

The younger man shrugged. "We keep telling Charles, this dry spell was long overdue. Could last years."

"Like the Good Book says." The older man paused and turned his head to spit a stream of tobacco. "Seven years of plenty, seven years of famine. We got lucky with these ten wet years. I always said it would never last."

"That's right." The younger man pulled the reins to steady his horse. "If you think it can't get no worse, wait 'til next year. You'll see. There ain't no crops where there ain't no rain. You think them piles of dust are big now. You wait. After another dry year or two, they'll cover up them fences altogether." Squinting, he nodded slowly. "Yep. I've seen dust piles taller'n a man."

"That's no tall tale he's telling you." The older Newman's low bass voice was rough as gravel. "When the rains don't come next spring and nothin' grows in the dust, all these settlers who think they're so smart will hightail it out of here back to where they came from. Good riddance, I say. Most of 'em had no business comin' west in the first place."

"That's right." The younger man lifted his hat and wiped his brow. "This here land wasn't meant for no crop farming. Better suited to grazing livestock."

"Take my advice, Mr. Marvick. If you buy land here, you should think about raising sheep." The older Newman tipped his hat and pulled the reins to turn his horse.

"Appreciate the advice," Joseph said.

The younger man stared down at Charles. "Just came to tell you your cows are out again. Might want to go find them." He kicked his horse, and the two ranchers rode off.

Disquieted, Joseph stood in the shade of the cottonwood tree and watched the choking dust billow behind the horses' hooves. In the branches above, a black and white magpie flitted nervously about, chattering loudly.

***

Severt's health did not improve during the summer in Estes Park as hoped, but instead took a turn for the worse. His weight dropped, his more or less constant cough settled deeper in his lungs, high fevers persistently flushed his cheeks, dark blood came up in gurgling gulps when he hemorrhaged, and he spent more time confined to bed where his sweats soaked the sheets several times each night.

Despite Ida's objections, Joseph insisted she return to Story City in September to prepare for her wedding. Too ill to meet the acceptance criteria at

Agnes Phipps, Severt moved into The Oakes Home, managed by the Episcopal Church in Denver.

Ida and Charlotte begged their father to allow Severt to come home for Ida's wedding. He had been away for three years, and it would mean the world to him. When Joseph expressed his doubts about whether Severt would be well enough to make the trip, the girls argued that his mental attitude greatly affected his physical condition. Surely the prospect of returning to Story City would brighten his mental state, and his health would improve. When Peter and Olive offered to construct a tent house in the field behind their house, and Mrs. Markley said she could accompany him, Joseph agreed Severt could attend the wedding if his health permitted. Privately, Joseph worried about his son's chances for recovery and considered that it would possibly be the last time Severt would ever come home again. He would not deny his son the opportunity.

Severt's hemorrhages abated, and he arrived in Story City the second of October. Charlotte, Ida, Cosette, and Joseph met the train.

"There is Mrs. Markley." Charlotte pointed to the third car. "And Severt is right behind her."

Gripping the stair railing with one hand, Severt waved to them from the train car door. Mrs. Markley assisted him as he hobbled down the stairs to the platform. Severt appeared more skeletal than the last time his father had seen him, and Joseph wondered if he had made a mistake in allowing his son to travel. Seeing the joy on his son's emaciated face, Joseph blinked and swallowed to quell a surge of unfamiliar emotion. Perhaps it was the context of seeing Severt in Story City, but Joseph could no longer ignore his son's deterioration. The next time Severt came home, it would be in a coffin.

On the way from the station to Olive's house, Charlotte drove slowly. Animated, Severt twisted from side to side beside her in the front seat, pointing out familiar town sights to Mrs. Markley and remarking on the changes that had taken place during the past three years.

Expecting them, Peter, Jack, Henry, and John Donhowe stood waiting on Main Street, and when Charlotte stopped at the bank crossing, they rushed into the street.

"Good to have you home, Severt." Peter reached into the car and shook his brother-in-law's hand.

"It's great to be here." Severt grinned and reached for Jack's hand. "Jack, old man. Congratulations in person. I hope Charlotte is treating you better than she did me."

Charlotte smiled. "Watch yourself, Severt, or I'll drive you right back to the station."

"You wouldn't dare."

If Severt's condition shocked the Donhowe men, they gave no indication. Joseph watched as more than a dozen townspeople crowded the car. Only a couple gave Severt the glad hand, and although it did not surprise him, Joseph felt resentment toward them. He hoped his son did not notice others who held back in the doorways and on the sidewalk with expressionless stares and furtive whispers. It occurred to Joseph that perhaps Severt had grown accustomed to the rude behavior toward him and wondered if that was perhaps worse.

That evening, the family celebrated Severt's return home at Olive and Peter's house. Walter could not attend, but joined them for supper the following evening.

"Good to see you, Severt." Tanned and muscular, Walter ignored the hand Severt offered and instead slapped him on the back.

Severt took a step forward to keep his balance. "It sure is good to be home. Quite the welcome I've received."

"Glad you could get out of bed to come. To hear Ida talk, you'd think she was looking forward to your homecoming more than our wedding." Walter looked at Ida.

Ida flinched. "Walter, what a thing to say."

Severt forced an uncomfortable laugh. "I'm sure that's not the case."

"I sure hope not." Walter laid his hand on Ida's shoulder.

"We're all just so pleased that Severt could be home after all this time." Olive smiled at her brother. "And it means so much to Ida to have him home for her wedding."

"That's right," Peter said. "Don't worry, Walter. Next Tuesday, your bride will only have eyes for you."

"How long you home for?" Walter asked.

Severt nodded. "A couple of months. Not long enough if you ask me, but I'm not complaining."

"Seems like a waste building that house out back for such a short visit." Walter said.

Peter's eyes narrowed. "Worth every penny, if you ask me, to have the chance to have Severt home."

Olive smiled. "That's right."

If Joseph did not know better, he would have found Walter's rude behavior threatening.

"You men relax for a bit while Ida and I get supper ready." Olive turned toward the kitchen.

"What do you think of the war revenue bill the Senate passed yesterday?" Peter asked Walter. "Except for Severt's return, it was the talk of the town today."

"Sounds like a lot more people are going to have to pay taxes," Walter said.

"That's the truth," Joseph said. The exemption for income tax dropped from $20,000 to $2,000.

"Unbelievable how much they increased the rates," Severt said. "The top rate went from fifteen percent to sixty-seven percent? I call that excessive taxation."

"That's a fact." Peter nodded.

Joseph had been prepared for his taxes to double, but not increase fourfold. "It seems the Democrats think there's too many people and companies making too much money. Taxing 'excess profits' will restrict industry investment and individual philanthropy, just when the economy needs it."

"Even after four years at war, the income tax in Great Britain isn't more than 42 ½ percent." Severt coughed, and spit into his sputum cup.

"How do you know that?" Walter scoffed.

"It was in the paper." Peter glowered.

"Must have missed it." Walter shrugged.

"Supper's ready," Olive called.

As they walked in silence to the table, unease fed a spark of doubt within Joseph. He had never questioned Walter's character. He knew the family he came from, but he realized he did not know the man he had encouraged his daughter to marry.

✳✳✳

Ida married Walter the following Tuesday on the ninth of October. Joseph had always thought Ida's wedding would be like Olive's, a grand celebration with special music by the choir and a feast for over 200 guests. Instead, like Charlotte's wedding, it was a small gathering of close family and friends at

Olive and Peter's house. And because of wartime flour conservation, there were no dinner rolls or bread served at the wedding reception, but only one small cake.

"I wondered if we'd ever see the day Ida married," Margretha commented to Joseph at the reception. "It was a long time coming."

Across the room, Walter stood smugly beside Ida, his hand possessively pressed against her back. Smiling, Ida held Cosette's hands. Though stunning in her wedding attire, Joseph's favorite daughter did not radiate the joy of a woman in love. He remembered the unreserved love Ida bestowed on Oscar the day Joseph gave them his approval to marry. He hoped she did not still think of him. "She seems tired."

"Severt is the one who seems tired. Although that is an understatement." Margretha pursed her lips.

Hunched in his oversized dark suit, Severt sat at a table with Jack, Peter, and Ed. His dark eye sockets, in the hollows of his prominent brow, nose, and cheekbones contrasted with his otherwise pale skin. He laughed at something Jack said, and then bent over in a coughing spasm.

"I don't think it was wise to bring him home." Margretha's voice had a hard edge.

Joseph took a deep breath. "Yes. You've said as much."

"I'm thinking as much of him as the rest of the family."

"This is not the time or place to discuss this, Margretha." The high-pitched voices of his grandchildren carried from the other room. He knew his sister implied he had put them at risk by bringing Severt home.

"Cosette stills talks as though she wants to marry him." She raised her eyebrows.

"The doctors advised against it."

"I can't imagine what she is thinking." Margretha shook her head. "Surely her parents won't allow it."

"Severt is convinced he will improve in Arizona." Determined not to spend another winter in the cold, Severt had made arrangements to move to the Montezuma Place, a health resort in Phoenix.

"I hope I am wrong." Margretha lowered her voice. "But I don't think the change in climate is going to make much difference."

***

That night, Joseph tossed in bed, unable to sleep. Uncomfortable, he bunched up the flat pillow, his neck and face pricked by feather tips that needled through the pillowcase. Each time he turned, he fought the bedcovers that twisted tight around him. In the darkness that pressed in from confines of the closed room, his sins descended upon him from the shadows like stealthy bats. He had risked his daughters' health when he sent them to care for Severt in Denver, and now he had risked the health of the rest of the family by allowing Severt to return home for a visit. If any of them became ill, he could not forgive himself. Yet he also could not forgive himself for sending Severt to St. Olaf. If he had not imposed his will upon him, Severt would be a healthy, married man like his brothers-in-law. Joseph bore the blame for Severt's suffering, and he would bear the blame if his son were to die. Nothing Joseph had done had reversed the damage done. Severt's health had not improved; it had deteriorated. His children and grandchildren trusted him to do the best for them. He had failed his son. He could not bear it if he had also failed the others. Haunted by Walter's jealous response to Ida's love for her brother and possessive demeanor toward her, Joseph feared he had again erred in his judgment and made the wrong choice. He refused to allow her to marry Oscar and then allowed her to live with a brother ill with the fatal disease he feared. She had never declared her love for Walter, yet Joseph encouraged her to marry him.

Father in heaven, Joseph prayed, forgive me for my grievous sins. I have been a proud man. I deserve to fall. But I beseech thee, Almighty God, save my children and grandchildren. They do not deserve to suffer for my sins. Punish me, not them. Take my fortune. Take my life. But I beg thee, spare my children. If it is not thy will to heal Severt, give him strength and do not take his life, I pray of thee. I cannot bear to see my son suffer. He did no wrong. Keep my daughters and grandchildren safe, and grant them health. Forgive me for placing them at risk. And forgive me, I pray, for the great pain I brought upon Ida, the daughter I love so much. Do not punish her for my sins. I loved her more than the others. That is my sin. She deserves to be happy. I beseech thee, grant her happiness and love, and do not let her suffer more than she has already. My children followed thy commandments. They honored their father. Do not punish them. Thy will be done, Father. Amen.

***

Cosette joined Severt in Phoenix on Christmas Day, and they married on New Year's Eve in a private ceremony with no family in attendance. Though Joseph understood how happy Cosette made Severt, he did not understand why she would marry an invalid who had become too ill to leave his tent bed, could not have marital relations, and whose prospects of recovery had worsened.

Meanwhile, Joseph's other children flourished. In December, Olive delivered her fourth child, Paul Kermit. Lula was pregnant with her third child, and Charlotte announced at Christmas that she would have a baby in July. Although he did not let on, Charlotte's pregnancy particularly pleased Joseph.

To Joseph's disappointment, he did not see much of Ida during the holidays. He assumed practicing with the church choir for the annual cantata scheduled for the Sunday after Christmas occupied her spare time, and he looked forward to hearing her sing again as a soloist.

Ida, however, did not have a solo in the cantata. More surprising, she did not sing with the choir at all, but instead sat near the back of the church in the pew beside Walter.

After the performance, Olive and Peter invited the family for dinner. Ida and Walter declined to attend, and went directly home to their farm in the nearby town of Randall.

"I do love 'The New Born King,'" Anna said during dinner. "We've sung it so many times, but I seem to enjoy it more each year."

"It certainly is a favorite." Olive rocked the baby in her arms, watching her five-year-old son struggling to cut his meat. "Laurentia, could you help Joseph Oliver?"

Joseph's grandson handed his knife and fork to his older sister.

"I was surprised Ida didn't sing," Joseph said.

"That would have been nice, wouldn't it?"

"No one can sing 'Come to My Heart' like she can," Anna said. "If only I could sing like her."

"You have your own gift on the piano, Anna." Charlotte set her fork down and sat back in her chair. "I hope I feel better soon."

"Must be a boy," Olive said. "I was sick the first few months with both Joseph Oliver and Paul Kermit."

Jack nudged Charlotte's elbow. "You should eat more. You're eating for two now."

Charlotte grimaced. "Nothing smells or tastes good to me."

Olive smiled. "It will all be worth it when you hold your new baby in your arms."

Jack put his arm around his wife's shoulders. "I hope it is a little girl just like you."

Peter grinned. "Be careful what you ask for. You just may get it."

Charlotte smiled. "And just what do you mean by that?"

"Jack will have his hands full if he has two strong-willed girls in the house."

Joseph smiled at the banter.

Olive's house girl entered the dining room. "Are you ready for me to clear the table?"

Olive nodded. "Thank you, Brita."

Anna set her silverware across her plate. "I suppose it won't be long before Ida is pregnant."

"I expect not."

"I shall have lots of cousins to baby-sit!" Laurentia announced.

Anna smiled. "That will be fun, won't it? I remember when you were a baby, and I helped take care of you. Such a lovely baby you were!"

"Isn't Ida singing in the choir?" Joseph asked.

"No." Charlotte glanced at Jack.

"Why not?"

"If anyone who should be in the choir it is Ida, with her lovely voice and training," Anna said. "When I asked, she said she has been so busy fixing up her house, she just hasn't had the time."

Olive looked up from the baby. "It is such an old house and in such great need of repair. It is quite a bit of work for Ida."

Anna reached for her water glass. "She has fixed it up so nice—with such a grand kitchen, anyway."

"Surely Ida cannot be too busy to sing." Joseph rubbed his forehead. "She should hire a girl to help her."

"They don't have the means to do that, Papa," Olive said.

Peter raised his eyebrows. "It isn't just a matter of money. Walter doesn't believe in hired help."

"Why do you say that?" Olive asked.

"He told me, last time he was here. Said Ida wouldn't be hiring any girl to help. Said she'll have to learn to handle the household chores on her own like his mother did."

Joseph frowned. "Even without help, it seems she could make the time to sing in the choir."

"I agree with that." Jack patted his wife's shoulder. "Charlotte's not only been taking care of the house without help, but she's been sick, and she found the time to sing."

Charlotte glared at her husband.

Jack shrugged. "Well, it's true, isn't it?"

Joseph shook his head. "I just don't understand why Ida wouldn't want to sing."

"Actually, I think she would like to sing," Jack said.

"Oh?"

Charlotte elbowed Jack.

Peter nodded. "The truth of the matter is that Ida wants to sing, but Walter won't allow it."

Olive frowned. "Peter, you make it sound worse than it is."

"Do I?"

"Perhaps Walter is a bit possessive."

"A bit?"

"But you have to consider he is a newly married man. You can't blame him for not wanting to let her out of his sight."

"Jack doesn't seem to mind."

Jack laughed. "I might mind, but Charlotte does what she wants."

His wife smiled. "I certainly do. I've never been as sweet as Ida."

"Enough of this conversation." Olive lifted her baby to her shoulder, and stood, patting him on the bottom. "I'd best feed this little boy of mine. The rest of you can go relax in the other room. Brita will clean up."

"Have you heard from Alfred this week, Anna?" Charlotte asked as she pushed in her chair.

"I had another letter today. He had such an exciting Christmas in Hawaii."

Joseph did not listen to the details of Alfred's letter and did not pay attention to the conversation between his sons-in-law.

Ida had married a man who would not allow her to sing.

Severt's Will

Joseph

*I*n the middle of April, Joseph received a letter from Severt. Written in Cosette's hand, Severt asked his father to come for a visit. There was a matter he needed to discuss, something he wanted to take care of as soon as possible.

Cosette signed her husband's name and added her own note at the bottom of the page: "Please come quickly - C."

After receiving Severt's letter, Joseph responded in haste and traveled cross-country without stop. As he climbed down the stairs to the station platform in Phoenix, Joseph saw Cosette's white arm wave above the crowd of dark tanned Mexicans and khaki-uniformed soldiers. "Over here." Her rich contralto rose from the cacophony of greetings, farewells, and boarding announcements that battled with the bellowing engines and clanging bells and scraping of metal wheels on the tracks. His daughter-in-law's loose white shirtwaist and skirt and wide-brimmed white hat were better suited for the arid Arizona climate than Joseph's brown, wool summer suit. As he drew closer, he noted the strain of her smile and shadows in her eyes.

"I am so thankful you arrived in time." She reached up and lightly held his shoulders. Her moist lips brushed his cheek, a cool whisper in the heat. She carried the scent of flowers into the grease and coal infused station.

Joseph drew his handkerchief from his pocket. He wiped the sweat from his brow, conscious of his own body odor rising over the scent of his shaving soap. "How is he?"

Cosette wilted as she dropped pretense, and the energy fell from her face and shoulders. She shook her head. Turning so that the wide brim of her hat obscured her face, she lifted a handkerchief to her eyes.

The move to Arizona must have proven too much for Severt. Noting the dark circles beneath his daughter-in-law's eyes, Joseph feared his son had experienced more than a temporary setback. He hoped the doctors here were as qualified as those in Denver. He would have to speak with Cosette about them.

At Montezuma Place, the nurse greeted Cosette and nodded at Joseph. "He is sleeping at the moment. Much of the time you were gone he was fretting and fitful, and I do believe he wore himself out once again."

"I'll look in on him," Cosette said.

Joseph followed her into the tent house, toward the rasp of his son's labored breathing.

Severt's deterioration horrified his father.

Emaciated, his son lay flat on his back in bed. Shoulders, elbows, and wrists protruded sharply from his emaciated body; thin skin stretched across the bones. His dark hair glistened wet and heavy around his pallid, gaunt face, his eyes sunk in black sockets, his lips encrusted with dried blood. A cough racked his body in sleep, propelling his chest forward. Dark, clotted blood gurgled from his throat.

The nurse rushed in. "He's hemorrhaging again." Joseph gripped the cold iron footboard as the nurse administered to his son. After the coughing subsided, Joseph saw the red stain of his son's blood on the cloth and bed sheets.

Severt's eyelids drifted open, and his brown eyes gradually and dully focused on his father. He did not attempt to smile. "Papa." His arid voice was unrecognizable, dust brushing sand and cactus.

"Severt." Joseph's grip on the metal bed tightened. He swallowed to clear his constricted throat. "I came as soon as I received your letter."

Severt's eyelids closed in on the pain.

Agony exploded in Joseph's heart. My son!

Cosette poured a glass of water from the white porcelain pitcher at Severt's bedside and held it to his lips. "Severt, darling. Would you like some water?" He lifted his head from the mattress, and she tilted the glass. The black tissues of his lips clung together, stretching like wet cobwebs as he opened his mouth to drink. His swollen red tongue rolled outward, sticking to the roof of his mouth. Water drooled down his chin. Cosette reached for a cloth and wiped the sides of his mouth.

Joseph swallowed but could not bring himself to speak. He felt as though he were dreaming, powerless to move or call warning.

"Your Papa is here, Severt, just as you wanted." Cosette smiled.

Severt's head remained immobile on the pillow as his eyes slowly rolled from Cosette to Joseph's hands gripping the metal footboard. His eyelids dropped for a moment, as though to rest, then lifted, and his eyes focused on his father. His ribcage rose as he inhaled, falling as he breathed out, "Papa."

Cosette's smile dimmed as she turned toward her father-in-law. "Severt has a matter he would like to discuss with you."

Joseph cleared his throat and smoothed the sides of his mustache with the thumb and forefinger of his right hand. "He seems rather tired. Perhaps tomorrow, Severt, when you have more energy."

Severt jerked forward from the pillow. "No!" He began to cough and sank back as his body struggled with the seizure, his hand clasped over his mouth with the bloodstained white cloth.

"Don't upset yourself, Severt, dear, or the nurse will shoo us away. Your father is here now, just as you wanted." When the coughing subsided, Cosette stood. "I'll leave the two of you now, to talk."

She stepped away from the bed, gesturing to the chair. "Please."

Joseph shook his head. "No need. I am fine standing."

Cosette moved toward him and placed her hand on his arm. "It is better if you sit beside him. It isn't so much effort for him to talk then."

Cosette's eyes betrayed exhaustion and anguish. "I'll leave you. It's better for you to be alone, I think. Severt and I have no secrets, but this is a conversation that should be private."

The scent of flowers drifted over the disinfectant and blood as she left.

Joseph did not move for a moment. Unprepared, he did not wish to be alone with his son.

"Well, Severt." Joseph willed himself to walk to his son's bedside. He gripped the seat of the chair. "You would like to speak to me." He attempted a smile, but abandoned it when his facial muscles would not respond.

"No time," Severt whispered.

"We have time, Severt. I have rearranged my schedule . . ."

Severt frowned and shook his head violently. "No. No time left."

No time left?

Clutching the bed sheets, Severt attempted to pull himself up, lunging toward his father.

"Now, now." Joseph stiffened. "No need to sit up. Lie back and relax."

Severt hovered on his hands, leaning toward his father, the sweat dripping from his forehead.

Joseph patted the edge of the bed. "Whatever you need, Severt. Anything at all. Ask, and I will make arrangements."

Severt lay back. His eyes closed, and he seemed for a brief moment to be asleep.

Joseph sat back in the chair, relieved to see his son relaxed, almost peaceful. He focused on the yet unspoken request and felt his own shoulders loosen. Perhaps Severt wished to go home. Joseph could arrange for the necessary equipment to be installed and for additional nursing staff. Severt clearly required uninterrupted care.

Severt's eyes opened and fixed on his father. "I need to take care of things." He spoke slowly, every word an effort.

Joseph nodded, indicating his support, but unsure what he was agreeing to.

"I need a will, Father."

A will? His son wished to prepare his last will and testament? The pressure of the request grew within Joseph's chest, expanding as he found it impossible to breathe.

"I want to take care of Cosette, want her to have my inheritance." He blinked to clear the tears that had begun to pool. "She has been so good to stick by me." He swallowed. "Married me, an infected lunger." The tears joined to form clear glistening streams. "I wanted to live with her . . . more than I ever wanted anything in all my life." He choked as he gasped for breath. "I thought I could beat this . . . thought I would find the cure here." With effort, he flung his left hand awkwardly across his face to interrupt the tears. "I want to leave her . . . with something."

Joseph pinched the corners of his eyes, pressing hard to prevent his own tears from betraying him. He frowned and ground his teeth together and constricted his throat to contain his cry. He could not utter the words of assurance he wished to offer.

"You do not object, do you, Father?" Severt's eyes pleaded. "Surely not." He swallowed. "You know how much Cosette means to me . . . how much joy she has given . . . me."

Joseph coughed to find his voice. "No, Severt." He swallowed his own unspent pools of tears. "I do not object."

Severt strained forward, the ligaments of his neck extended. "You would arrange . . . for her to receive my . . . inheritance?"

"Yes, Severt."

As Severt sighed, his tension sank and the pillow and sheets seemed to rise around him like the evening tide of the ocean upon the shore. His eyelids drifted down, but did not close. "I have a few other bequests," he whispered. "Not many. I've told Cosette."

Joseph wanted to excuse himself, wished to remove himself from this clouded confusion. An invisible, unassailable, inescapable tide rose, and he struggled to focus as Severt struggled to list his bequests.

"$1,000 each to . . . St. Olaf and St. Petri. . . . Same to Story City . . . for a nurse at the schools. $500 each to foreign mission fields . . . and Agnes Phipps. $250 each . . . to Albuquerque Presbyterian sanatorium . . . and the Lutheran churches in Denver and Phoenix. $250 to Story City for needy lungers." Severt's tongue stuck as he licked his lips. "Income to Cosette . . . until she dies . . . or marries again. After that, split the inheritance between the nephews and nieces."

With each bequest, Severt seemed to grow smaller, lighter, and more remote.

The odors of flesh and blood commingled, and Joseph recognized it as the sweet stench of death.

Broken Wings

Joseph

*J*oseph returned immediately to Story City. Though he attempted to attend to business, he could not concentrate. He shuffled through correspondence without comprehending the contents. He signed documents without reviewing them. The voices of others drowned in the torrent of his own thoughts, and he responded to expectant glances by nodding or responding with "I see" or "Hmm."

He could no longer deny that Severt's health had deteriorated to the irrevocable point of death. After the shock of the initial diagnosis, Joseph had refused to consider a fatal outcome. A realist, Joseph never expected Severt's lungs to clear completely, despite the testimonials of people who claimed to be cured. But while he had not expected a miraculous healing, he hoped his son would be one of the many tuberculars whose condition improved after treatment, were discharged as patients, and returned to civil life. Many of the doctors at the sanatoriums and health spas were infected, yet led productive lives. As the years passed, however, it appeared increasingly improbable that Severt would return to the bank or have much of any future in business. Yet improvements had always followed the downturns. In the worst case, Joseph always held firmly to the conviction that with best available care and doctors, Severt would survive.

Any day now, his son would die.

He found it difficult to go to the bank. The daily interactions between John Donhowe and his son Jack accentuated Severt's absence. Joseph would never work with his son, would never teach him what he knew of business. He would never hear Severt talk eagerly in anticipation of the birth of his first child. He could accept Severt's inability to work or have children, but he could not bear his son's suffering and death.

He welcomed the distractions of the day. The evening hours, when sleep eluded him, seemed endless. In the shadows of night, Joseph replayed the events of the past. He had failed as a father. God had punished him for his sins, and Severt would pay the price.

When sleep finally came, he did not escape his living nightmare. Severt appeared, skeletal, rising from bed, arms outstretched, imploring his father to save him. Joseph tried to explain it was too late, death had already come, but Severt insisted his father could do something, that he trusted in and depended on him. In another dream, Joseph stood before a court, the jury filled with family and business acquaintances, shaking their heads solemnly as the judge proclaimed the guilty verdict of murder and sentenced him to death. He protested, tried to explain he had done his best, had done all he could, imploring his mother and Margretha, who were members of the jury, to testify on his behalf. His mother pointed her finger at him, and Margretha shook her head, silent.

***

More coffee?" Olive held the pot over his cup.

Joseph nodded. "Yes."

"I'm afraid Paul Kermit's crying is keeping you up at night."

Joseph shook his head. "He doesn't bother me." It was not the wail of his grandchild that disturbed his sleep. The cries of the boy broke through the barrage of self-incrimination. Joseph found some peace in the creaking floorboards as Olive crossed the upper floor to the boy's room and rocked him back to sleep.

"His ear is bothering him."

"You should take him to the doctor."

"Don't worry, Papa. The doctor has seen him and says he will be just fine."

"Good. You don't want anything to happen to him." He stared at his eldest daughter. He wished to warn her, to spare her the agony of losing a son and knowing she could have prevented it.

Olive looked away.

Joseph understood. She thought he was overreacting to the earache. She did not know her brother was dying. She did not realize how seemingly small decisions could swing the balance from life to death.

Olive handed him several envelopes. "Here is your mail. You have another letter from Anna."

Joseph had forgotten the earlier letters from Anna that Cosette forwarded from Arizona. "I must write to her."

"I know she is anxious to hear if you will be attending her concert and recital next week." Olive sat down at the table, pencil in hand, a partial grocery list before her. "I hope you will be able to go. You remember how important the junior recital was for Ida."

He would not have missed Ida's concerts or recitals. He could not have been more proud of her performances and had rarely felt as much pleasure. Perhaps he had been too proud and felt too much pleasure. He had never intended to favor her over the others. He never intended her to marry a man too jealous to allow her to sing at church.

Olive scribbled several things on the list. "Brita is going shopping this afternoon, and I must finish this for her." She looked up. "Anna has quite a program planned and is so hoping you can see her perform it."

"I have no doubt she will have a success." He heard his youngest daughter practice the piano during her Christmas break, and her mastery of the difficult music impressed him. It seemed only yesterday she was a little girl taking lessons from Olive, and Severt was a young healthy boy with so much promise and a long life before him.

"Tonight you will be at Ida's for supper, isn't that right?"

"Yes."

"I'll tell the girl not to plan on you being here then."

***

The overcast skies burst open late that afternoon. Joseph held his umbrella against the driving rain as he walked from the car to the old farmhouse. He slipped in the thick mud on the rutted drive, nearly falling as lightning flashed before him with a thunderous explosion. His overcoat protected him from the rain but did not keep out the damp cold.

Walter greeted him at the front door. "Hello, Joseph. Quite a spring storm we're having." The hinges of the screen door squeaked as he opened the door and held it for his father-in-law.

Joseph stepped inside and turned to shake his umbrella before closing it up.

Walter hung Joseph's coat on the tree stand. "Ida's in the kitchen. Supper should be ready soon."

Joseph turned toward the kitchen.

Walter gripped his father-in-law's shoulder. "We can wait in the living room."

"I'd like to greet Ida."

"No need." Walter smiled. "We wouldn't want to distract her as she's getting our meal ready, now would we?"

Joseph stepped back, pulling his shoulder from Walter's grasp.

"We didn't expect you back from the west so soon."

"Change of plans."

While Walter talked about spring plowing and planting, Joseph stared at the unsightly brown siding that covered the interior wall of the living room. As he had when he first visited, he wondered why the original owners had not removed it when adding on to the house and why Walter had left it unchanged.

"It's about time our submarines are finally across the Atlantic. That'll give the Germans in their U-boats something to reckon with," Walter said.

"It will certainly strengthen the allied fight."

"I'd like to be over there myself." Walter shot an imaginary machine gun, his arm recoiling as he added sound effects of the burst of fire. A cruel smile of satisfaction spread across his face and he nodded, "You bet. I'd like to take out a few Huns."

Joseph would not want to face his son-in-law on the battle field. "It's good married men have an exemption."

Walter shrugged. "I just may enlist. I wouldn't sign up for submarine duty, though. You wouldn't get me closed up in a boat underwater. No." He shook his head emphatically. "No, I'd sign up to be an airman. Fly in and drop bombs on the Kaiser land—that's more my style."

"You wouldn't enlist now that you're married."

"I don't know why not. They need more good men over there to help win this war." He grinned. "It would be quite an adventure, wouldn't it? It would sure beat farming."

"There's a shortage of food. The country needs each and every farmer to increase production to feed the troops."

Walter scoffed. "That's what Ida says. Says it's my patriotic duty. I think she doesn't want to be left alone, especially with the baby on the way."

Joseph sat forward. "Ida's expecting?"

Walter snickered. "I reckon I just spoiled the surprise. Ida was going to spring the news today."

Ida appeared at the doorway, dark circles beneath her weary eyes and her face flushed. "Hello, Papa. It's good to see you." She looked at Walter. "Supper is ready. You can sit up to the table now."

Joseph stood. "Walter just informed me you are expecting."

Ida's shoulders sagged. "Oh, Walter, how could you? You knew I wanted to tell Papa myself."

Shrugging, Walter lifted her chin with his finger. "It just slipped out. Can't blame me for being proud I got my wife pregnant, can you?"

Ida blushed and turned her head.

Concerned by Ida's exhausted condition and affronted by Walter's crude remark, Joseph frowned. "In your condition, you need to take care of yourself. Get your rest."

"Yes, Papa." Ida turned toward the door.

"She's doing just fine, aren't you, darlin'?" Walter grabbed her shoulder from behind and twisted her to face him.

Ida winced. She glanced briefly at her husband, then turned to her father. "No need to worry about me, Papa." Her smile did not reach her eyes, which reflected a glint of pain. "We'd best go eat before it gets cold."

"We wouldn't want that," Walter said.

Troubled, Joseph followed them into the dining room.

Ida had painted the walls a soft cream color and added a blue rug and draperies of the same shade. She had set the table with a white cloth and white dishes and contrasting blue napkins.

"Please sit down." Ida pointed to a chair on the side of the table.

Ida had prepared a roast of beef, mashed potatoes, gravy, creamed corn, and bread. He smiled at his daughter. "It looks good."

Walter nodded. "I'll say the grace." His head tipped forward. "We give thee thanks for these thy gifts. Amen." He looked up. "We don't speak Norwegian in this house."

Joseph suppressed the urge to argue with his son-in-law. There was nothing wrong with using the traditional table prayer.

Ida pointed to the platter of sliced beef. "Please, help yourself. I'm sorry I don't have dinner rolls. I'm trying to do my part in conserving flour for the war effort, and so I made corn bread instead."

Joseph selected a slice of beef and passed the platter to Walter.

"How was Severt when you left him?" Ida asked.

"Not so well." Joseph concentrated on the bowl of potatoes Ida passed him.

"Cosette wrote that he has had a bit of a setback and is confined to bed again."

"Yes."

"It seems the weather has been grand. I was so hoping he would get better in Phoenix. Especially now that he and Cosette are married."

"She is very good to him." He took some comfort in knowing how happy Cosette made Severt and that she would be with him during his last days.

"She must be a better cook than my wife." Walter dropped the meat fork onto the platter, metal crashing against china. "I can't eat this. It isn't done." He pushed the platter across the table. Meat juices spilled, a dark stain spreading on the white cloth.

Ida jumped from her chair, nearly tipping it backwards. "I'm sorry."

As she reached for the platter, Walter caught her wrist. "You know I don't like my meat bloody."

"I didn't think it would hurt to have it a little pink in the middle. I didn't want to overcook it for Papa, and I thought the end pieces were done the way you like it."

"You thought wrong. You weren't thinking of me, though, were you?"

Ida tried to pull her hand away. "Walter, please."

Walter's fingers closed tighter. "I hope you are listening. You are my wife and you will cook my meals the way I like them cooked, not the way you had to cook for your invalid brother."

Joseph pushed his chair back. "That's enough."

Fear flickered in Ida's damp eyes.

"Enough?" Walter glowered at his father-in-law. "Enough of what?"

"Let go of her."

"Don't tell me what to do with my own wife. I'm the head of this house, and I'll do as I please."

Joseph stared at his son-in-law, the man he encouraged Ida to marry. He had made a grievous error in judgment.

Ida pleaded silently with her father.

For her sake, Joseph clenched his teeth. If he said more, she would pay the price. Walter was right. As much as Joseph disapproved, as cruel as Walter could be, Joseph could do nothing. He had encouraged his daughter to marry this man, and now she was pregnant with his child.

As the rain pelted the window behind him, Walter recognized Joseph's acquiescence and he relaxed back in his chair.

The confrontation averted, Joseph's eyes met Ida's. As the tension fell, her brow smoothed in relief, her eyes dulled in resignation.

She bent down, her voice yielding. "Walter, dear, this is all my fault. I should have known better. Let me go brown some of this meat on the stove for you."

Walter nodded, and released her wrist. "You do that."

Ida's wrist and hand bore the red mark of her husband's hand.

Joseph stared at the food on his plate. For Ida's sake, he would try to eat it, but he had no appetite. He could not bear to think of how Ida would suffer as Walter's wife. He had failed his beloved daughter, and there was nothing he could do now to rectify it.

***

That night, after tossing in bed for sleepless hours, Joseph dreamed his house was collapsing. The rain saturated the structure, and water began seeping, then pouring from the corners of the walls and ceilings. He stood in the hallway of the second floor and noticed the walls beginning to crumble and the floor start to sag.

Beside him, Severt and Ida did not comprehend the destruction. Joseph ran to the stairs, yelling for his children to follow. At the bottom of the stairs, he turned and looked up to see Severt and Ida motionless at the top of the stairs, water gushing past them. The upper floor began to crack and give way. It was too late to save them. He watched in horror as his two favorite children stared at him as they slid toward the widening gap in the floor.

Anna's Recital

Anna

*L*ook at me and smile, Anna!"

Anna turned to the camera and forced a smile for her cousin Lydia, straining not to squint in the glare of the late afternoon sun.

"That's better! Don't move and keep smiling—I'll take a few so you're certain to have a good one for your scrapbook and some to send to your family!"

Focusing on the lens of the black camera box and her cousin's chatter, Anna held her smile, straightened her back, and lifted her chin. She would not be disappointed. She had been foolish to hope her father would appear in time for her junior recital. Anna had first written to her father in Montana, informing him of the dates of her recital and the St. Olaf Choir concert. When he did not respond, she posted a second letter to Phoenix. Later, when Charlotte wrote that their father had returned to Story City, Anna wrote a third time, telling him how much it thrilled her that he had returned in time for her recital and how she hoped he would stay long enough to attend the choir concert.

Her father did not say specifically in his letter whether or not he planned to attend, but she had chosen to interpret he would. She thought of the letter, which her father had oddly misaddressed.

> 4/9/18
>
> Dear Daughter Ida,
>
> Northfield, Minn.
>
> Your letter at hand, also two returned after being opened at Phoenix. I note what you say about the concert and also about your recital. I hope you have a success of the recital which I feel sure you will. Nothing new—Charlotte was not as well as she

might have been for a while. She is feeling quite well now, but not as strong as she was. We have quite a time about the school house site here as some are opposing the park site which the directors have decided on. Fine weather and good roads.

> Your Loving Father,
>
> Joseph Marvick

She had reread the letter several times. Confused by the address to Ida, she initially thought her father had written to her sister. But that made no sense. Her father would not write to Ida from home when she lived only a few miles north of Story City. He must have had her older sister on his mind when he wrote and inadvertently addressed her instead. Perhaps he thought Ida would attend the recital and concert. If so, he was mistaken. Ida wrote that she would love to come, but Walter didn't like the idea. Anna could not imagine having a husband so perverse. Jack would have encouraged Charlotte to come if she wasn't so far along in her pregnancy and feeling so sick. Walter had always seemed so charming, and he had been so entertaining at New Year's. He had always paid special attention to Anna and amused Olive's children with magic tricks at Christmas. He certainly seemed to have a different side to him. Not allowing Ida to sing in public or even in the church choir was like putting a bird in a cage and shutting it away in a dark room where no one could hear its lovely song.

Her father had attended all of Ida's recitals and nearly all her concerts, including many when the choir and band were on tour. He arranged his schedule to travel with her on the Norway tour. Joseph Marvick had always taken an interest in his children's musical performances from the time they were young, and Anna assumed he would make arrangements to attend her piano recital and the choir concert. He appreciated the significance of a music student's recital, particularly in the junior and senior years, and he knew what an honor it was to sing in the St. Olaf Choir under F. Melius Christiansen.

Anna had planned a program worthy of a Marvick and had practiced the demanding pieces to perfection. She would begin the program with the first movement of Beethoven's Piano Concerto in C minor, scored for two pianos, a strong powerful composition which would be quite impressive. Morton Luvaas would then play three pieces, after which she would perform Chopin's famous Nocturne in E-flat major, Chopin's "Minute" Waltz in D-flat major, Grondahl's Liszt-inspired Etude No. 6 in A major, and Schumann's "Papillons." Morton would then complete the program.

"There." Lydia joined Anna beside the steps of the chapel. "You looked so glum a moment ago. And you're so quiet. Do you have a case of nerves? It isn't like you."

Anna turned from the exposure of the sun, forcing Lydia to squint as she faced her. Focusing on her cousin, she cleared her thoughts and smiled. "Thanks for taking the pictures, Lydia. I do have a bit of nerves, I suppose. But isn't that the case of all great performers?"

"You laugh, Anna, but you truly are a great pianist. I've heard people say you are the best pianist that's ever been to St. Olaf. Your side of the family certainly got the musical talent."

"Dear Lydia, I hope my recital lives up to your high expectations."

"I have no doubt about it." Lydia looked around. "Say, I haven't seen your father. I suppose he's paying a visit to President Vigness like my father does whenever he's here."

It was nearly six o'clock, and the recital would begin at seven. If her father was coming, he would have been here before now. She smiled brightly. "I'm afraid Papa wasn't able to make the trip, so I'm depending upon you to write up a review for the family. I hope you'll be kind."

"Oh, Anna. What a great disappointment for you!"

Determined not to show her true feelings, Anna held her smile and shrugged, "Naturally, I hoped he would be here, but you know how difficult his schedule is."

"I'm so sorry. You won't have any of your family here."

Anna leaned down and patted the shorter girl's arm. "Oh, but you are here, dear cousin." She tossed her head and stepped back. "And there is always next year."

Lydia smiled. "That's the way to look at it. I would be moping around, but not you."

"I'd better go in now and warm up my fingers." Anna turned toward the chapel. "Thanks again for taking the pictures, Lydia."

"Good luck."

Anna found Morton Luvaas at the concert grand Steinway in the front of the chapel, working on a difficult passage of his Schumann Concerto. Anna sat down in the first pew, reserved for the performers and their teachers, and waited for her turn to warm up. Relieved to have the awkward conversation with Lydia over, she winced as Morton hit a wrong note.

Anna played the opening piece of the program, which had been her preference. She never liked the impatient tension of sitting in the audience waiting for others to perform. Happily, when she gave Morton the choice, he elected to close the program.

After being introduced by her teacher, Anna stood and strode up the aisle to the piano. She did not glance toward or acknowledge the hushed, expectant audience that filled Hoyme Memorial Chapel. She approached the Steinway, her heels rhythmically striking the wood floor to the rustle of her skirt. She sat on the edge of the bench and rested her fingers on the keyboard with her right foot on the pedal. Rising forward, she pushed the bench back a bit and then a little to the side. She sat down, and, satisfied with the position, adjusted her skirt. She straightened, lifted her head, and, after taking a deep breath, nodded at her music teacher, Esther Woll, who would accompany her on the second piano. As Esther began the introduction, Anna let her hands fall loosely to her sides and closed her eyes, swaying as the music rose and fell. When her fingers met the keys, nothing existed but the intensity of the music.

The enthusiastic applause from the audience amplified as she took her bows at the end of the recital. Her performance had been technically clean as well as lyrical, and she achieved what she had intended. She played the Beethoven Concerto with a mixture of passionate strength and profound serenity. When she returned to the stage, she evoked a suave and glamorous mood with the Chopin Nocturne, then raced through the fast and exciting Chopin Waltz, flowed freely through the expressive, rich Grondahl Etude, and ended by dancing the colorful and imaginative Schumann's "Papillons."

Her teacher rushed forward. "Well done, Anna. I've never heard you play as well as you did today."

F. Melius Christiansen stepped forward, extending his hand. "Bravo, Anna." He grasped her hand with both of his. "You are to be commended for a fine program. The pieces you selected made use of the whole piano, and your technique was immaculate and richly musical." The choir director's eyes sparkled, his smile warm and wide.

"Thank you, Professor Christiansen." Anna had never felt so exhilarated.

Her teacher's husband, Carsten, and Adelaide Hjertaas, both members of the faculty of music, joined the circle.

"High praise, indeed, but well deserved." Carsten took Anna's hand. "Excellent recital, Anna."

Adelaide nodded. "A very polished and poetic performance, Anna."

Esther raised her eyebrows, smiling at her student.

"I expected to see your father and sisters here," F. Melius glanced around. "I didn't miss them, did I?"

In a flash, the painful absence of her father surged to collide with the elation from the accolades. Anna blinked, suppressing the sadness with a wide smile and shook her head. "No. I'm afraid they were unable to be here today."

"What a shame. I always enjoy speaking with your father. He has been a most important financial supporter of the school and the choir, and I will forever be grateful to him for sponsoring the Norway tour the year your sister Ida was the soloist."

"Will we see Ida at the choir concert?" Adelaide asked.

Anna shook her head. "I'm afraid not. She recently married, and it isn't possible for her to get away."

"Ah! I hadn't heard that news. Congratulate her for me." Professor Christensen smiled. "Ida has a great talent, and I wish her the very best."

"I will."

"Hopefully we'll see her next year." F. Melius glanced over at Morton. "I must go congratulate your fellow performer on his recital." He offered his hands and held Anna's hand warmly. "Please greet your father for me and tell him I said he missed a brilliant performance."

"Thank you. I'll do that."

"Give my warmest greetings to both Ida and also to Charlotte. Is Charlotte still in Denver with your brother?"

"No. She's also married and due to have a baby in a couple of months."

"How wonderful for her."

The choir director nodded and walked toward Morton.

The recital was indeed a great success. Papa would be proud.

V

May 10, 1918

"Before each person are life and death,
and whichever one chooses will be given.
For great is the wisdom of the Lord;
he is mighty in power and sees everything;
His eyes are on those who fear him,
and he knows every human action.
He has not commanded anyone to be wicked,
and he has not given anyone permission to sin."

SIRACH 15: 17 - 20

Thy Father's Will

Joseph

The crows circled, black against the clear sky, their unsettling caws breaking through Joseph's thoughts. A few birds shifted in their watch from atop the grove of trees, while others dove to the field below. Joseph halted on his way from the parked Ford to the house, speculating what they fed upon. With a deep breath, he straightened his shoulders, habitually adjusted the Hart Schaffner & Marx vest and suit jacket, and solemnly continued to the screened kitchen door.

Joseph noted the broken glass of the attic window, peeled white paint on the siding, splintered window frames, ripped screen sagging on the misaligned kitchen door. Walter had made no repairs before the wedding and had made none since.

Inhaling deeply, he rapped firmly and announced himself. "Hello."

Ida appeared in the hall doorway at the other side of the kitchen. "Papa." Her fingers flew to her flushed face, nervously brushing back the fallen tendrils. "You're early." She pulled at the high lace collar of her white blouse, hands coming to rest together at her throat.

Joseph faced his daughter's discomfort. "May I come in?" This daughter he favored, once so pleased in his presence.

"Yes. Certainly." Ida smoothed her apron and rushed forward, her skirt whipping around her legs.

The door creaked as he entered the house.

"I wasn't expecting you. Supper won't be ready for several hours."

Joseph smoothed the sides of his thick gray mustache with the thumb and forefinger of his left hand. He offered no explanation.

Turning to the stove, Ida lifted the lid of the white enameled coffee pot. "Would you like some coffee, Papa?"

"That would be good." He watched her fill the pot from the water pitcher and measure the coffee.

"Any news from Severt?" Ida struck a match and lit the burner.

"Yes." Joseph stared up at the cracked plastered ceiling. "A letter from Cosette yesterday." He swallowed and frowned. "Severt is too weak to write."

He pulled a chair out from the table and sat down. He would not see his son again. Ida did not know the end had come. Joseph had tried to save him. First Agnes Phipps, then the furnished house with his sisters risking their health to care for him, the summers in Estes Park, and finally Phoenix. He had sinned, and his son would die. No hope remained.

"It's good Cosette is with him," Ida remarked.

"Yes." Joseph studied his large, square hands with the clean, trimmed nails. Cosette. Engaged to Severt just after he graduated from St. Olaf and came on as cashier at the bank. The year the new bank was built and the year his son became ill. She stuck with Severt throughout his illness, married him at the end. She would never live with him as man and wife, but would be a widow soon, within weeks or perhaps days. She would receive income from his inheritance.

"Papa?" Ida held the back of a chair.

Joseph focused on his daughter, vaguely aware she had asked him a question and waited for a response. He cleared his throat, uncertain how to respond and unwilling to admit he had not been listening.

Ida repeated, "Would you like some rusks with your coffee?"

Although he had no appetite, Joseph nodded. "I wrote to Ida. Asked her to write Severt to raise his spirits. He always enjoyed her sense of humor."

Ida stood still, staring at the tin on the counter, her back to her father.

Joseph wondered if she felt ill suddenly.

Picking up the tin, she turned. "Ida, Papa? I am Ida. Do you mean Anna?"

"Ah. Anna. Yes, Anna." Joseph examined his knees and brushed his pant legs for possible lint.

Ida set the tin on the kitchen table. "How was Anna's recital?"

He watched Ida open the tin and begin to arrange some rusks on a flowered china plate. "She wrote it was a success."

Ida stilled again, looking up at her father, her brown eyes hard. "You didn't go to Northfield for her junior piano recital?"

"No." Joseph grimaced at the disrespect but did not admonish his daughter.

"Anna must have been so disappointed." Ida straightened and held the small of her back.

Joseph looked down. This daughter so like his wife Annie, the woman he had loved, buried so many years now. The large round eyes, full mouth, thick wavy hair braided and wrapped around her head. A voice like an angel. The daughter he was so proud of. The daughter he favored, although he had denied it, even to himself.

The coffee came to a boil, and Ida turned to stir it with a wooden spoon. As she bent her head, he noticed a dark bruise above the lace of her collar.

Joseph closed his eyes. He encouraged this marriage, despite Ida's hesitation. He wanted her happiness, did not want her to be a spinster like Margretha. He could still see her desperate eyes when he demanded she break off her engagement to Oscar. Her pleading. Her sobs. He wanted to save her from tuberculosis, had thought he was doing the right thing, protecting her. He could not bear to lose her, as he was now losing his son. But in the end, he lost her, first when she broke with Oscar and now in her marriage to a cruel man.

He had grievously sinned. He bore responsibility for the destructive death of his only son and the breaking bondage of his beautiful daughter.

Ida poured coffee into a cup and set it before her father. "I have wet clothes that must get on the line to dry." She brushed her hands on her apron.

Joseph noted how red her once tender hands were. The Marvick house always had household help and sent out the laundry.

"Don't mind me." He had a task of his own to attend to. "I would like some writing paper if you have it." A message to be written.

Ida returned from the other room with a sheet of letter paper and a lead pencil.

Bruises on his daughter. How many hidden beneath the skirt, long sleeves, and high-necked blouse?

Ida. His favorite daughter, unhappy, bruised, silenced. Isolated on this run-down farm by a husband who refused to allow her to sing. He had not judged Walter to be the jealous and cruel man he now showed himself to be. Joseph had been so sure in his judgment of character.

And now a baby on the way.

Joseph had desired the best for his children and believed he had known best. Ida had pled and Severt had argued, but both had obeyed their father's will. Ida broke off with Oscar and instead married a man he had recently overheard his other daughters call a sadist. Severt left Cornell and contracted tuberculosis from a roommate at St. Olaf.

His favorite children suffered for his sins.

Leaving most of his coffee and an untouched rusk on the saucer, Joseph carried the writing paper and pencil to the sitting room. Using a magazine resting on his knee for a desk, he wrote his letter with a steady hand. Finished, he reread the letter and signed it. Nodding, he folded the paper in thirds, lifted his jacket, and placed it in the inside pocket.

Standing, Joseph glanced around the room. Relieved to have the letter written, he walked to the secretary to put away the pencil.

In the right drawer lay Walter's pistol. Joseph picked the small gun up and studied it, the metal cold against his large, sweating palm. The weapon had killed so many song birds. Sport, Walter called it.

Joseph pushed the gun drawer closed and pulled the left drawer out, setting the pencil in the desk's compartment.

The floorboards creaked as he moved deliberately through the house.

Once outside, he found Ida behind the house, pinning one of Walter's work shirts to the clothesline.

He watched her pin another two shirts to the line, relieved for once that she did not acknowledge him immediately.

After hanging the sheets, his daughter turned to face him. "Do you need something?" She lifted a white embroidered handkerchief from the pocket of her apron and dabbed the moisture from her forehead.

"I thought I'd walk over to the old picnic grounds." It was not unusual for them to spend afternoons visiting the nearby grounds, a mile or so from the farm, just this side of the gravel pit.

Ida shaded her eyes against the sun. "Shall I pack you something to eat or drink?"

"No. Continue with your housework. Don't worry about me." Joseph approached his daughter and reached out his hands.

Ida awkwardly held out her own hands, and her father grasped them.

"Goodbye," he said.

Ida pulled her dry rough hands from his and stepped back. "I'll see you for supper, then."

Above her a crow swooped, loudly cawing.

Looking up, Joseph thought aloud, "How many crows Walter has killed."

Ida frowned at the remark, and bent to pick up some of her husband's socks from the basket of clothes.

***

Joseph did not stop at the picnic grounds, but continued on to the gravel pit. The sun shone high in the sky as he stepped down the worn path to the bottom of the deserted pit. He wiped his wet palms on his pant legs and reached into his pocket for the small mirror he had taken from Ida's dresser. Holding it up, he observed his solemn face. The accusing gray eyes stared back. His pride had been his downfall. His son would not live to have children or gray hair. His daughter had a life of hardship before her.

He faced himself in the mirror. The high forehead, receding hairline. Metal glinted in the sunlight at the edge of the mirror.

The farewell letter had been written. He had begged the forgiveness of his children and his mother. Bid goodbye to his associates. The time had come. He had sinned greatly and must be punished.

Joseph Marvick pressed the small revolver to his temple and pulled the trigger.

High above, at the edge of the gravel pit, the large black crow settled in the tree, silent.

Author's Note

*I*nspired by a letter written by my great-aunt Charlotte to her cousin, *Thy Father's Will* is a work of fiction based on the final years of my great-grandfather's life. Using family letters, newspapers, probate files, and other historical records, I unearthed real people and pieced together real events, and from that skeleton of history, imagined personalities, conversations, and interactions.

All characters existed in real life, although I changed the spelling of my great-grandfather's name from Marwick to Marvick to be consistent with the spelling used by his children. Reverend Markus Olaus Böckman was a Lutheran seminary president at the time; however, the sermon he preaches in the book is entirely my invention.

The excerpts from the *Story City Herald* article reporting Joseph's death came from an actual newspaper clipping from 1918. Severt's letter to his father and Joseph's letter to Anna are extracts from actual letters written in 1913 and 1918; Charlotte's letter to her father includes excerpts from actual letters written to Jack in 1916; all other letters in the book are largely invented.

Principal sources for historical facts included the following: family letters and newspaper clippings from the historical period; probate court files; Katherine Munsen's *Dear Ones: Jacobson–Donhowe Family History; The Marvick Family History: 1400s–1993*, co-authored by David Cross, Marie Cross, Katherine Munsen, and Gretchen Quie; Ancestry online database collections; historical information on the Mayo Clinic, Evangelical Lutheran Church in America, U.S. Treasury, National Oceanic and Atmospheric Administration, Library of Congress, Stanley Hotel, Billings and Montana State websites; *Triglot Concordia: The Symbolical Books of the Evangelical Lutheran Church* (Concordia Publishing House, 1921); *America Past and Present: An Interpretation with Readings* by Vincent P. De Santis et al (Allyn and Bacon, Inc., 1968); Sheila M. Rothman's *Living in the Shadow of Death: Tuberculosis and the Social Experience of Illness in American History* (The John Hopkins University Press, 1995); *Tuberculosis: A Treatise by American Authors on its Etiology, Pathology, Frequency, Semeiology, Diagnosis, Prognosis, Prevention, and Treatment,* edited by Arnold C. Klebs, M.D. (D. Appleton and Company, 1909) and *A Tuberculosis Directory*, compiled by The National Association for the Study and Prevention of Tuberculosis (The National Association for the Study and Prevention of Tuberculosis, 1916) both found online at Google; *The Electic Practice of Medicine* by Rolla L. Thomas, M.S., M.D. (The Scudder Brothers Company, 1907); Paul G. Schmidt's *My Years at St. Olaf* and Joseph M. Shaw's *The St. Olaf Choir: A Narrative* (St. Olaf College, 1997); Katherine Garetson's *Homesteading Big Owl,* 2nd ed.(Allenspark Wind, 2001); and Dave Walter's "Weaving the Current: Montana's Watershed Events of Two Centuries: Part III: 1903-1921," *Montana Magazine* (May/June 2000).

Acknowledgments

*M*y deepest gratitude to Leonard Flachman and Karen Walhof at Kirk House Publishers for publishing and bringing this book to an audience.

Thanks to my writer friends, Beryl Singleton Bissell, Mary Alice Hansen, and Virginia Reiner, who offered early advice and support.

I am grateful to Helen Roe Warren for compiling her mother Lula's letters from 1912 to 1913, and indebted to Elisabeth "Lis" Donhowe Christenson for generously entrusting me with boxes of original letters written by her grandparents, Charlotte and Jack, between 1915 and 1917.

Heartfelt thanks to my father's sisters for encouraging me to tell this story and for their insights and advice as writers and authors. My aunt, Marjorie Hart Cuthbert, who has the portrait of Joseph pictured on the cover, cheered me forward from the beginning. My aunt, Katherine Munsen, family historian, generously shared her albums of original family photographs and letters, reviewed my drafts, and offered valuable suggestions.

Special thanks to my sister and friend, Cyndi Meldahl, who enthusiastically followed the progress of this book and eagerly read numerous manuscript drafts. I am especially thankful for my parents, Phil and Diane Jacobson, who have loved and believed in me always, and who were the first to read and comment as I wrote and revised each chapter. My deepest thanks and love to my husband, Joe, who encouraged me to follow my heart, endured the time I disappeared from the present into the scenes of the past, and toasted my progress from completion of the first draft to publication.

Finally, enormous gratitude to my amazing writing friend and soul-sister, Cynthia Ekren, whose perceptive readings, insightful questions, and deft editing made me a better writer and this a better book.